The Kaleidoscope

Don D'Ammassa

This book is a work of fiction. Names, places, and events are not based on real people or places. Any resemblance is purely coincidental.

Managansett Press First Edition 2015

Some people just don't learn from their mistakes.

On Ted Croner's tenth birthday, his parents bought him an expensive battery powered toy truck big enough that he could ride seated above the cab and travel with moderate speed across the neatly mowed grass in the yard behind their house. Ted thought it was almost the best thing ever, but there were a couple of features in the design that he thought needed to be improved. For one thing, there was a corny Road Runner logo on the side that he considered too childish for someone of his maturity. For another, the seat was set at an angle that ensured his center of gravity was toward the rear, a safety feature which thwarted his desire for excitement. And finally, it didn't really go fast enough to suit him.

He borrowed some of his father's painting equipment to cover over the logo, and he might have done a good job of it had he taken his time, but even then Ted was fond of shortcuts and he did such a hasty job that he was forced to admit that the new look was even worse than the old. His father shook just shook his head and told him to clean up the mess.

Ted considered himself something of a mechanical prodigy, an effort pardonable because both of his parents encouraged him in this delusion. He borrowed some of his mother's tools – she was the handy one in the family – and set about adjusting the seat to his preference. The result did accomplish much of what he intended; he now rode tilted sharply forward with his head hovering over the front end of the vehicle. Unfortunately, the seat wasn't intended to be placed in this position. It was no longer firmly attached to the body of the vehicle and swayed precariously. Even more frustrating, the smooth plastic seat was inclined so sharply that Ted found himself sliding off unless he tensed his thighs hard enough to hold himself in place, which made extended trips very wearing.

Finally, he addressed the problem of speed. There wasn't much he could do about the batteries, but he thought he could improve their efficiency by tightening the wheels and making other small adjustments. The result, of course, was that they would no longer move at all, and when he tried to return them to their original position, they were too loose and turned at different rates. When he tried to find a happy medium, he was careless and broke one of the connections. His toy truck was now functionally inert and Ted abandoned it in frustration.

A wise parent might have used this incident to illustrate a point, that nothing is completely perfect in the world and that we need to make compromises if we're going to be happy. Unfortunately, Ted's parents were not wise and they doted on their only child and promptly bought him a replacement. But by then he'd grown disenchanted and after the first week, it stood parked in the rear of their garage until the batteries were exhausted. They sold it for ten dollars at a yard sale when Ted was fourteen.

It didn't set the pattern for Ted's life, but it reflected it.

Ted Croner's six year old station wagon threaded its way through the back streets of the town of Managansett. It was a bright, sunny Saturday morning and the established neighborhoods on the north side of Main Street were bright with early summer flowers. Lawnmowers buzzed and chewed up neatly tended lawns while robins flocked to harvest the insects disturbed by their passage. Ted was in no hurry and had taken a circuitous route home, his eyes on the alert for yard sales or, even better, abandoned furniture or appliances left out on the curb in anticipation of Monday's trash pickup. Technically none of this should have been placed on the sidewalks until Sunday afternoon, but scavengers prowled the area looking for abandoned bargains – Ted among them – and most people figured that was better than sending more junk to the landfill.

This was prime yard sale weather, hot and clear. The town square had been turned into a small but chaotic flea market, and he'd spent almost an hour there. Not everyone was willing to carry their wares that far, however, and he'd passed at least a dozen yard sales during the short trip home. No, that wasn't true. He hadn't passed any of them; he'd stopped every time. The cargo area behind him was packed solid with carton boxes full of assorted items he'd accumulated during what was supposed to have been just a quick trip to the nearest convenience store. Ted believed in spontaneity and luck. Opportunity lay concealed on every side, according to his personal mythology. It was just a matter of time until success ceased to elude him.

The last stop had been particularly rewarding. Someone had finally begun renovating the old Sheffield place. The property had been locked up and abandoned for at least twenty years, ever since its last resident – Paul Alan Sheffield – had died intestate and with no known relatives. The lawyers had finally tracked down some ninth cousin twelve times removed or something like that. Whoever was responsible had made no effort to sort things out. They were asking twenty dollars per mixed box of debris, but Ted had argued them down to half that for an assortment he'd chosen from multiple boxes. No one else had stopped while he was there; the locals had some simmering, long standing prejudice against the Sheffield property. He'd have made a second pass, but the car was full, his wallet was nearly empty, and he realized that Beth would be wondering what had happened to him.

He turned into Bailey's Court, a dead end street that terminated in a wider, circular stretch of pavement where, if you strayed in inadvertently, it was possible to complete a tight U-turn and exit. Three two-story houses were arranged in a semi-circle facing the turnaround. They were isolated from their neighbors by several empty lots to either side and behind them. Originally they were all to have been developed simultaneously, but the property management firm had run into financial difficulties and only three of the proposed twelve houses had ever been built, although there was a collapsed foundation concealed by weeds just behind Ted's house.

Ted drove directly to the middle of the three houses, slowing as he pulled into the driveway. He tapped the control clipped to his visor and the garage door slowly began to open as Ted killed the engine and stepped out. He was twenty eight and looked fit, even handsome, although his weight was starting to creep up bit by bit and sometimes there was more loose hair in his brush than he cared to see. Like most men his age, he had started making mental notes to exercise more, watch his diet, schedule a physical with his doctor. Like most men his age, these mental notes had no actual effect on his behavior. They were the mystical equivalent of the rabbit's foot that dangled from his rear view mirror. Ted's mind was so completely stuffed with grandiose dreams, career plans, and wishful thinking that there was little room left to accommodate more practical concepts.

Ted's garage bore considerable resemblance to his mind. There were two stalls, although it would have been a tight fit for the station wagon, which hadn't actually been parked inside since the previous winter. The second stall was filled to a point well above eye level with carton boxes, paper bags, and other containers filled with items Ted had purchased at yard sales, flea markets, and auctions, or picked up from the neighbors' curbs on trash day. There were pieces of furniture, small kitchen appliances, fake antiques, genuine but flawed antiques, rusted tools, toys of every description, electronics, old books and vinyl records, glassware, picture frames with and without pictures, mirrors, old video games, pots and pans, jars of buttons, belt buckles, and countless other items. A few of these were in reasonable condition but the vast majority were broken, rusted, stained, torn, scratched, bruised, dented, expired, or otherwise dysfunctional. Ted figured that if he repaired them all and managed to sell them for a reasonable price, the return would be many times greater than his investment. The fact that he'd managed to repair less than a dozen items during the previous year, and had sold only two of these, did not discourage him in the slightest. He interpreted it as meaning that he was on the right track and only needed to increase his commitment to the project to guarantee success. Ted always believed that committing oneself to a goal was half the journey to reach it. "It's all downhill from here," he'd tell himself, and then decide that completing the trip was superfluous since he'd already demonstrated in principle that he could accomplish it.

The rest of the garage was unremarkable. Gardening tools were arranged against the exposed side wall and a work bench was set flush at the rear. Cabinets and pegboards held a few tools, but Ted kept most of his equipment in what he liked to think of as his basement workshop. A large axe was mounted on the wall. When he and Beth had bought the house, they had decided to remove a large tree stump in the backyard. Ted had announced that he needed the exercise and would do the job personally, but the blade of the axe was as sharp as on the day he'd bought it, five years earlier. The stump was still there.

Ted opened the back of the wagon and began carrying boxes into the garage. The first one he set on the workbench, but he started adding the others to the towering accumulation that now threatened to spread into the open stall. The pile had acquired a slight tilt over the course of the last few months. Some of the lowermost boxes must have buckled under the growing weight, throwing off the center of gravity. Ted made a mental note to rearrange them before a collapse damaged his potentially valuable stock. The mental note came to rest on a pile of similar ones.

He had unloaded about half of the boxes when the connecting door to the house opened and Beth Croner stepped into the garage. Beth was a year or two younger than her husband, but at the moment she looked a few years older. An impartial observer might have described her as dowdy, plain, or even drab. Her hair was lifeless, she wore no makeup, and she was dressed in a rose patterned blouse that was noticeably faded and grey jeans that were shiny with wear. A closer look suggested that she'd been much prettier in the past, and might again be so if she found sufficient reason. The Croners were childless, but she had the weary look of a mother forced to deal with several unmanageable, obstreperous children, or a single unmanageable, obstreperous adult. Although her face betrayed obvious irritation at the moment, it was a subdued, almost resigned strain of anger that seemed exhausted and devoid of any strong feeling.

"Where have you been, Ted?" Her tone was a complex mix of anger, weariness, and frustration. "I sent you out for milk over an hour ago. You know I need the car to go shopping this morning."

"I have it. It's right here." Ted reached into the box sitting on the bench and pulled out a plastic carton of milk. It had long since lost its chill. He handed it to her. "I stopped by the flea market in town, and someone told me they were practically giving stuff away from the old Sheffield place so I went over to take a look. They obviously didn't know, or more likely didn't care, what things were worth. I got some real bargains."

Beth sighed. "I can imagine. You've found us so many bargains lately that we're a month behind on the bills." Strong emotion rippled across her face, tried to break through, compromised with a token appearance. "Ted, you have to stop doing this. On my salary and your unemployment, we can barely make ends meet as it is. And your benefits run out at the end of the month. I don't know what we'll do after that."

Ted refused to let her anxiety spoil his morning. He stepped closer and put his hands on her upper arms. Beth turned her head slightly, unwilling to meet his eyes. "You worry too much. Things will pick up soon, Beth. People get caught between jobs all the time. It's just a temporary low. Once I'm working again, everything will be fine."

Beth set her lips and her voice became more animated. "And when exactly will that happen, Ted? If you keep turning down job offers, the agency will stop sending you for interviews. There are too many people who actually want to work for them to waste their time on someone as," she paused, searching for the right word, "for someone as fussy as you."

"I'm not fussy." There was a hint of anger in Ted's voice and he shook his head slightly. "I'm particular about what I want is all. When they find a decent placement for me, I'll take it. You know I'm not happy unless I'm working."

Beth had heard this all before, in one variation or another. She was no longer moved by Ted's argument, although she recognized that he believed what he was saying. "And what was wrong with that last one? A job at Eblis Manufacturing would have been ideal. You could have walked to work from here. You're always saying you need to get more exercise. And they were offering almost as much as you were making before."

Ted took a deep breath. "We've been over this already. The job was a dead end. I'd have been stuck in the same office forever, building production schedules that no one followed and generating reports that no one read. There would never be an opportunity to show anyone what I'm capable of. I don't want to be a glorified clerk for the rest of my life, Beth." He caught his breath. "And their health plan wasn't great either." He didn't tell her that he'd also been put off as well by the tiny, cluttered cubicle where he'd have been working. Ted valued what he thought of as "aesthetics" and had long since decided that Beth had no sensitivity to the appearance of things. From time to time he'd made what he considered constructive comments about the choices she'd made in furniture, colors, and the physical arrangement in their home, and she'd always reacted angrily, defensively. It had never occurred to him that she'd done the best she could with the money available. After all, their credit cards weren't maxed out yet. Why didn't she

9

just go out and buy something better if that was the problem? That's what credit was for.

Beth shook her head and moved a step away from him. "So it wasn't perfect. I hate to be the one to tell you this, Ted, but that's just the way it is. Sometimes you have to be satisfied with the least disagreeable among several unattractive choices. And there's nothing to prevent you from looking for another, a better job while you're making do with what's available. At least there'd be a check to deposit. We can't get by on my salary, let alone save anything for the future." She glanced at the station wagon. "What happens if we need major car repairs? We couldn't pay for them and there isn't decent bus service out here. How would I get to work?"

They stood only a short distance apart. Either of them could have reached out and touched the other without effort. Nevertheless, the chasm between them stretched like a great canyon across which they threw strings of words that arrived in misshapen form, misunderstood and resented. Ted's smile dropped away and he turned to look out toward the street. "We've been through all of this before. I hear what you're saying but things aren't so desperate that we need to settle for something that I know isn't suitable."

Beth bit her lip, afraid that anything she said now would just make matters worse. Ted's last few words had been tinged with anger. She had never expected to win this argument, or any of their arguments, but she felt a compulsion to make at least a token effort. Ted had seemed so enthusiastic, ambitious, and excited about building a career when they'd first met, and she knew he was smart enough to have succeeded if he'd set a course and stuck to it. Some essential element was missing from his personality, some binding force that would direct his various assets toward a credible goal. For a while she had thought she might provide some of that impetus, but it had quickly become obvious that while Ted's boat might be adrift, he would still repel all boarders, however benevolent their intentions.

Resigned, she half turned to go back into the house, but Ted spoke up again. "You enjoy your job at the bank, don't you?"

Beth felt drained of energy, wasn't sure where this new feint was going, and she was instinctively wary. Ted was visibly irritated and that was never a good sign. "I guess so. Mr. Ross is nice enough for a boss and the work isn't that hard. I do like dealing with the customers, most of them anyway." Beth worked in customer service, a "temporary" situation while they were saving up for a down payment on the house, and then some new furniture, and now seemed likely to be permanent.

Ted's face lit up as though he'd won the lottery and Beth knew he felt he'd scored a major point. "You like it there because that's the right job for you. Well, I would have been miserable at Eblis, stuck in a routine, shuffling paper around, pretending that I didn't know more than my boss about scheduling. I'm a manager, not a clerk. It just wouldn't have worked out."

He waited for her to admit she was wrong. Beth often made a token surrender just to bring a dispute to an end, but this time she disappointed him, kept her face half turned away, her shoulders slumping even further, if that was possible. Ted felt a twinge of regret. He knew he was right, of course, but he'd long since decided that Beth was by nature inclined to see gloom and doom hovering on the horizon. She seemed to derive a perverse joy from being depressed. He decided to be magnanimous. "Look, I'll fix up some of these things." He gestured broadly at the mountain of boxes even though she was looking out toward the street. "Then I'll sell them through the thrift store or something. Make a few bucks. That should help with the bills."

"Sure," Beth answered in a voice so low it was almost inaudible. "Every little bit helps, I suppose." There was a subtle emphasis on "little" which Ted chose to ignore. "I have to put this in the fridge before it goes bad." She held up the carton of milk. "I made a fresh pot of coffee if you want some." Without waiting for a response, she went into the house, closing the door behind her. There was no hint of animation in her face, not even anger.

Ted stared at the door for a few seconds, then shook his head and turned back to the box. One look inside and a smile crept onto his face again. The old radio had a bad dent in one side and was missing one of its dials, but it had only cost him a dollar. There was a nice piece of Fenton glassware, a vase, although there was a chip out of the lip that might be hard to disguise. The three hardcover books had titles and authors he'd never heard of, but they had been published in the 1890s and the pages weren't too brittle, although they were quite yellow and smelled a bit musty. The socket wrench set was complete and still in its original case, and he was pretty sure he could fix the latch so that it closed securely again.

But the prize of the lot was the kaleidoscope from the Sheffield sale. He lifted it out carefully, examining it in much more detail now than he had earlier. It was about eighteen inches long and made of brass, heavier than it looked. The shaft and head were all decorated with finely inscribed symbols, some of which reminded him of hex signs he'd seen painted on barns when he and Beth had driven through rural Pennsylvania on their honeymoon. They covered its entire surface except, of course the eyepiece and the face of the drum, where light entered and passed through the colored crystals and mirrors. He made no effort to look through it, more interested now in the exterior which seemed to be completely undamaged. He had the impression that it was quite old, possibly handmade. There was no manufacturer's name anywhere, unless one of the odd symbols was some kind of trademark.

Ted jumped slightly as Roscoe, the family cat, jumped up onto the workbench to find out if Ted had brought home anything edible. Roscoe was supposed to be Beth's cat. She'd brought it home before taking the job at the bank, back when Ted had been making a decent salary at Sheridan Silver, before the firm went through several rapid changes of ownership in a short period of time and then finally went out of business. Roscoe tolerated Beth, but it had been obvious almost from the first day that he was Ted's cat. Ted didn't even particularly like cats, or any animals for that matter, and he'd been mildly annoyed when Roscoe had first appeared, but he had to admit that the attention had flattered him. Unlike Beth, Roscoe didn't demand much, made no real demands on his time, and never attempted to make him feel guilty when he was too busy to scratch an ear.

"Hi there, Roscoe. At least you still love me. Catch any more mice today?"

Roscoe was a first rate mouser and had brought home proof of his hunting prowess on several occasions, much to Beth's dismay. It had become Ted's job to remove the tiny corpses whenever they turned up. Ted felt a touch of pride on these occasions, as though he was somehow participating in Roscoe's success.

But there were no furry little prizes in evidence today. Always curious, Roscoe peered into the cardboard box and sniffed his disappointment that it contained nothing edible or chaseable, then sat down on the bench and scratched one side of his lower jaw with one foot. "Your enthusiasm overwhelms me," said Ted. He lifted the kaleidoscope to his eye and turned toward the front of the garage. The fractured image was clear and bright and unflawed and he smiled in satisfaction. He'd clean this up and take it to the antique store out on Route 13. He was sure they'd give him a reasonable price for it. Maybe he could even take Beth out for dinner one night this week. She'd want to use the money more practically, of course, but he'd insist. They needed to get out once in a while. It would give her some perspective, show her that they weren't poor, just momentarily underfunded.

He tried turning the drum and found resistance, increased the pressure but with no discernible effect. The drum seemed immovably fixed in place and the kaleidoscope image hadn't changed in the slightest. Ted adjusted his grip and applied more pressure, slowly increasing it until his hand began to ache. He eased off then, lowered the kaleidoscope and regarded it dourly.

"Well, Roscoe, this one might not have been such a bargain after all. I don't see anything obviously wrong. Maybe it just needs a good cleaning." He turned back to the bench and dropped the kaleidoscope back into the box.

The back of the station wagon was still half filled with boxes and Ted reluctantly returned to the job of unloading them, blaming the downturn in his enthusiasm on Beth. She was always concerned with the present, never the future, and he'd decided some time ago that she was somehow holding him back even as she urged him forward. The stack of boxes shifted when he brushed against it and he waited for equilibrium to return before continuing. It finally swayed toward the wall of the garage and came to rest against it, settling into a new configuration. Ted resumed his unloading and was trying to decide where to put an extraordinarily ugly umbrella stand when Samantha Rogers walked into the garage.

Samantha was not quite sixteen years old and like most of her peers was half convinced that the world revolved around her wants and needs, or if it didn't then it ought to. She might have been pretty if she'd made some effort, but she wore her dark hair in a handy but unattractive bun, her glasses were too big for her face, and even on this relatively hot morning she wore a lightweight but bulky, mismatched shirt and slacks that made her look heavier than she actually was. This particular top was dark blue and decorated with large white letters that spelled "THINK!" Ted had tolerated Samantha and her older sister while Beth treated the girls like the family that the Croners said they intended to have, some day, although Ted thought of children as some future test of maturity which could be deferred indefinitely. We'll have kids eventually, he told himself. When it makes sense. When we're ready for the responsibility. When we can afford them on his salary alone and Beth can quit her job and become a full time mother like she wanted to be.

He had known the sisters ever since they'd moved in but he had never stopped confusing their names.

Samantha looked around, appraising the situation. "Hi, Mr. Croner. Do you need any help?" It was a duty offer, with no hint of enthusiasm.

That was just as well because Ted was jealous of his treasures and rarely let anyone else handle them. "No thanks. I'm all set, Heather. I know just where everything is going."

Samantha rolled her eyes. "I'm Samantha, Mr. Croner. Heather is my sister, remember?" It had become a joke between them, but there was still a hint of resentment in her voice. Ted had a good memory for the things that really mattered to him, but he had trouble with data which he considered inconsequential and the names of the two inquisitive and occasionally intrusive teenagers from next door were definitely on his list of inconsequentials.

"Oh right. Sorry Samantha. My mind is somewhere else. How's your mother doing with that arm of hers?" Beth had mentioned the accident and Ted was mildly proud of himself for having remembered it and for being thoughtful enough to inquire.

"It's still in a sling." Samantha stuck her head in the back of the station wagon and looked into one of the boxes. "I think she fell down the basement steps just so I'd have to do the housework for a few weeks."

"Your mother can be very devious when she wants to be." One summer Mary Rogers had maneuvered Ted into volunteering his time at a school bazaar so cleverly that he'd never been able to mount any resistance and he'd been wary of her ever since. After all, he didn't even have kids so why did she think it was appropriate for him to help out with a school function? It was rather presumptuous, at the very least, and certainly a waste of his time.

"Tell me about it. She says I'd better get used to it because that's the way the world operates and there's no use complaining."

"There's truth in that. The trick is to be one of the operators and not one of the subjects. The world isn't locked in a fixed position. If you can find the right leverage, you can move anything."

"Archimedes," said Samantha nodding.

"What's that?"

"It's a who, not a what. Archimedes and his lever. You know, move the world."

"Oh, that." Ted had no idea what she was talking about. "I didn't hear what you said."

Having found a spot for the umbrella stand, Ted returned to the rear of the station wagon and Samantha backed away to give him room.

"Another yard sale, Mr. Croner?"

"That's right." He eased the next box out, tested the weight and balance before lifting it.

"Does Mrs. Croner know yet?"

Ted felt a flash of irritation. "Yes, she does." Beth had made no secret about her opinion regarding Ted's frequent treasure hunts and the growing accumulation in the garage. "Don't you have homework to do?"

"It's summer. No school. No homework. And I'm too young to have a summer job, at least for another month." She sounded like the last was something she regretted.

"There's always an excuse. You could sell lemonade in your front yard."

"This is a dead end street, Mr. Croner."

"You could advertise." Ted carried the box, somewhat awkwardly, to its new home, placing it carefully so as not to affect the stability of the pillar of cartons just beyond. He took a step back and waited to make sure there would be no delayed displacement of its center of gravity. He'd broken an entire box of chipped and scratched dinnerware once when he'd been careless and he still mourned its loss.

Samantha leaned against the side of the station wagon, her eyes running up and down and back and forth across Ted's accumulated hoard of outworn, outmoded, broken, battered, and abandoned junk. "You ought to have your own yard sale, Mr. Croner. You're running out of space." Beth had made similar comments, more than once, before she'd given it up as a lost cause.

Ignoring her, Ted removed the last box from the station wagon and carried it to the workbench. Samantha followed him, obviously bored. She looked into the other box and lifted out the kaleidoscope. Ted opened his mouth to say something, thought better of it, and began unpacking a variety of toy trucks and action figures. Samantha turned away and lifted the kaleidoscope to her eye, then attempted to turn the drum. It refused to budge.

"This is broken, Mr. Croner. It won't turn." She tightened her grip and tried to move it by brute force. Ted impatiently reached over and took the kaleidoscope away from her.

"You'll just make it worse if you're not careful. It needs to be repaired. Don't you have anything better to do than annoy me." He spoke lightly and smiled, but there was a hint of genuine irritation in his voice. "There must be something else you can do. Chores? Drugs?"

Samantha twisted her face into an exaggerated caricature. "Very funny, Mr. Croner."

Ted was about to say something else when they were interrupted by the arrival of Samantha's older sister, Heather. Heather was nineteen, had just finished her first year at college, and had returned for the summer with an affected air of sophistication that was alternately comical and annoying. She had always dressed stylishly and had been very popular in high school, but while away she'd bleached her hair and adopted a style of clothing which Beth referred to, privately, as "sophisticated slut." This morning she wore jeans so tight that it is unlikely she could have bent over successfully, and a filmy blouse that was rapidly turning translucent thanks to sweat and humidity. She had also begun smoking, to the dismay of her parents, and she carried a cigarette in one hand.

16

"Hello, Mr. Croner. " She barely looked at him. "Dad wants you, Sam. I've been looking for you everywhere."

Samantha crossed her arms in front of her and regarded her sister calmly. "I just left the house a minute ago, Heather. Don't make such a production out of everything."

Heather looked away, her face impassive. "Whatever. He's on the back porch and he's waiting for you. Did you throw away some old papers of his?"

"No, but I put his old lesson plans up in the attic. I told him that's where they were."

"Well I'm sure I don't know what the problem is, but you'd better go before he gets really mad."

Ted meanwhile had been clandestinely admiring Heather, whom he'd hardly seen since her return from college. She did not look at all like the girl he remembered, and he found himself calculating the difference in their respective ages. It wasn't that much of a gap, he thought to himself, not even ten years. "Good morning, Heather. So how was your first year at college?"

Heather turned her head, as though seeing Ted for the first time. Her effort to act sophisticatedly indifferent amused him. He even found it vaguely attractive, verging on sexy. "It was okay, I guess, Mr. Croner."

Samantha made a disgusted noise. "It was so okay that she's on academic probation." Heather's face twisted briefly into malevolence, then reverted to a warier version of her previously assumed ennui. It was obvious that she was trying to think of a cutting reply but Samantha stalked off before her thought processes had produced anything suitable.

Ted took a step closer, trying to strike a compromise between avuncular friend and dashing older man. "Freshman year is always rough. I almost flunked out myself. I'm sure you'll do much better as a sophomore, once you've adjusted to things."

Heather blinked, growing aware of Ted's sudden interest in her but unsure whether or not she should play up to it. On the one hand, she was flattered. On the other, he was so old. "Whatever. I'd rather go to secretarial school anyway. You know, learn something practical. But Dad says I need to have a degree and Mom always goes along with whatever he says."

Ted hesitated, trying to chart a course between openly

contradicting Heather's father, which might have repercussions later, and echoing his position, which was closer to what Ted actually believed but which would almost certainly not be something Heather wanted to hear. He might be almost ten years older than she was, but he thought of himself as younger in spirit if not in body, and still something of a chick magnet. "I'm sure he's only saying what he thinks is best for you. That's actually good advice, for most people, but I've always believed that in the end, everyone has to decide for themselves what their goals are in life and the best way to get there. If we all walked the same road, we'd be stumbling over one another."

Heather answered with a theatrical shrug. "Tell it to my Dad. He keeps lecturing me about the value of a formal education in today's marketplace. Like I was trying to sell myself." She suddenly seemed to realize that she might be talking out of turn and took a step back, mentally as well as physically. "I really have to go. Mom wants me to help her sort linens or something useless like that. It was nice talking to you, Mr. Croner. Say hello to Mrs. Croner for me."

Ted watched as she walked away, admiring the way the tight jeans outlined her body. He couldn't see it, but Heather smiled, feeling the metaphorical touch of his gaze until she was out of his line of sight, enjoying the effect she knew she was having on him. When she was gone, Ted shook himself as though waking from a trance, looked around the garage, mildly disoriented. He was surprised to find the kaleidoscope in his hand, but he didn't put it down, instead carried it into the house.

The kitchen was very much Beth's territory. It was furnished with an inexpensive stove and refrigerator and a cheap Korean microwave with cracked enamel sat on one counter. A collapsible table stood against the opposite wall with four uncomfortable looking chairs tucked beneath. They ate most of their meals either there or more casually in the living room while watching television, but they'd done that a lot less since they'd been forced to give up their cable connection. Temporarily, of course. The house had a tiny alcove that was supposed to be a dining room, but they couldn't afford even an inexpensive dining set and Beth used it for her sewing. They did have a hutch that they'd inherited from one of Beth's aunts, but it was almost empty. The drawers were currently filled with thread, buttons, patterns, and other paraphernalia, but except for repairing buttons, Beth hadn't used the room in months.

There were a few pictures on the walls throughout the house, mostly cheap prints of flowers and sea shells, and a crack in the kitchen wall was currently covered with a boring landscape of snow covered trees. An elaborate kitchen witch stood on top of the refrigerator, wearing a patchwork dress and a conical hat and holding a straw broom. Ted had won it for her at a carnival sideshow when they were still dating. In one corner stood a litter box and just beyond that, two dishes, one full of water, both labeled "ROSCOE". The kitchen was neat and orderly but there was a hint of shabbiness. The curtains on the window were frayed around the edges, the tablecloth had a small tear and the edges were unraveling, and one burner on the stove had stopped working several months earlier.

When Ted entered the room, he thought at first that he was alone, but Beth had just bent down to refill Roscoe's food dish. She straightened up, wincing slightly because she'd just started exercising a week earlier and her body had yet to adjust to the new set of strains. She insisted that she was gaining too much weight, although Ted hadn't noticed any change. He was suddenly conscious of her figure, which was what had attracted him to her when they'd first met, and felt a rush of arousal. To his credit, he also felt guilt and regret about the way they'd drifted apart, although it was a passing mood. Beth had apparently lost her enthusiasm for sex and made no effort to conceal her feelings when Ted was persistent, although she had never actually objected when he pressed her. He could tell the difference, however, and resented it.

Beth gave a slight start when she saw Ted standing there, perhaps reading something in his face, and quickly defused the moment with a banality. "You do remember that we're having the neighbors over tomorrow?"

Ted nodded. "I don't suppose there's any way we could call it off. I'd really like to get a start on fixing up some of this stuff." He waved the kaleidoscope to illustrate his point, then set it down on the table.

Her eyes flashed with anger. "No, there isn't. They're just

about our only friends, Ted, and we haven't done anything together since early spring. Heather has been home for two weeks and I've barely spoken to her, and I'm tired of making excuses about why we won't come over for a drink in the evening."

Ted raised his hands in surrender. "All right, I'll be good, even if I have to sit through another of Carl's tedious lectures about the state of the economy."

"That is his field, you know. You might learn something if you paid attention." She went to the sink and washed her hands briskly.

"He teaches basic economics at the high school, Beth. He's not an adviser to the White House, for Christ's sake."

"You don't have to swear."

"Sometimes I do," he muttered under his breath. "Okay, I'm sorry. I didn't sleep so good last night and I'm a little grouchy."

Beth started to turn away, stopped abruptly. "Oh, I almost forgot. Jennifer is going to be able to come after all."

Ted was suddenly interested though he pretended, not entirely successfully, that he didn't really care either way. "Oh? I thought she was going out of town, some conference in California."

"Her trip got cancelled. Something about a case being moved forward so that she needed to be in court next week."

"Well, it'll be nice to have her over." He wanted to sound enthusiastic without being too enthusiastic. Beth had caught him staring at their unmarried next door neighbor once or twice in the past, but even the tension of jealousy seemed to have drained out of their marriage. If anything, she'd seemed amused. Ted felt no guilt. He hadn't actually done anything, not even a mild flirtation. Looking couldn't do any harm though, and he was only human. Guys need to look at other women, he told himself. It helps keep them on edge.

"Before I forget, she offered to let me use her roasting pan. Ours has a broken handle. When you have a minute, would you go next door and get it from her?" There may have been a hint of sarcasm there, but if so, it was so subtle that Ted couldn't be sure. And he didn't much care.

"Sure. I'd better run over now before I forget about it."

Ted made a quick stop in the bathroom first, fussed with his hair, straightened the collar on his shirt. He didn't consider himself vain, but it didn't hurt to make sure you were presentable. Jennifer had never encouraged his attentions, may not even have picked up on his interest, but he had fantasized about her many times and had half convinced himself that she felt something for him, something she was perhaps hiding even from herself. If only he had the freedom to show her how he really felt, he was certain she'd reciprocate.

He went out the back way, letting the screen door slam shut before he remembered that the spring was broken. Beth had asked him to fix it at least a half dozen times and he had to admit that he'd been at fault, although that was no reason for her to keep nagging at him. It's not as though it was some kind of emergency. There was still the smell of fresh cut grass in the air. Beth had insisted that he mow the grass in anticipation of the Sunday cookout, otherwise he'd have let it go for another few days. Jennifer had a yard service come in once a week to do her lawn, trim the shrubs, and weed the small flower garden she'd started during the spring of the previous year, shortly after moving in. Lawyers could afford to pamper themselves, obviously. Ted thought he'd have made a good lawyer if he'd chosen that profession. He had a good mind for detail.

He crossed the lawn to the small patio behind her house. There was a glass and wicker patio set, a circular table with an umbrella in the center, four upright chairs, a matching chaise lounge, and a pair of smaller tables. He glanced down at a magazine lying on the lounge. Some kind of law review. He wouldn't have been surprised if she kept a Victoria's Secret catalog hidden inside it. His hand hovered over the buzzer but instead he knocked lightly on the door.

Jennifer didn't answer right away and he was poised to knock again when the door suddenly swung open. "Well good morning!" She was wearing some kind of sarong and had her hair up. "Come on in and enjoy the air conditioning."

"Finally got it fixed, I gather." Jennifer had installed central air conditioning, but the system had failed the first week of summer and it had been unseasonably cool at the time and she had been so busy that she hadn't gotten around to calling the service people until the heat had become unbearable. "Beth told me you'd been having problems." He hadn't been in Jennifer's house often and not once for the past few months. He'd only seen her a few times since the warm weather started, although he kept a watchful eye on the patio.

"Yes, it's working at last. At least for the moment. I can't say the service people left me with a warm, fuzzy feeling about how long it will last. Or even a cool, fuzzy feeling. Can I offer you some coffee? I can do iced or hot."

"Not for me, thanks." Ted shifted his eyes away from her by force of will. Jennifer was approximately his age, but looked much younger. She was so petite she seemed almost childlike, and Ted still couldn't imagine her standing in a court room and addressing a jury or grilling a witness. She was also one of the most attractive women he'd ever known personally, and the sarong clung to her body like a second skin. Unlike Heather, she seemed completely unconscious of the effect she was having. Ted assumed that was a pose. "I'm on a mission for the boss, actually. Something about a roasting pan."

"Oh, right. I'd completely forgotten about that. Follow me and we'll see if I can still remember where I put it."

They walked through a small foyer into Jennifer's living room, which was tastefully furnished and immaculately maintained. The paintings on the walls weren't originals, but they were signed prints. A very elaborate aquarium stood in one corner, filled with tropical fish which Jennifer casually referred to as her "fellow sharks." It was the only room Ted had seen previously. They'd gone over for drinks a couple of times during the first couple of months that she'd lived there, but Jennifer had never offered to show them the house. Her schedule had since become so busy that they rarely saw her after that, and she hadn't spoken to Carl and Mary Rogers more than casually until she dropped in at their New Year's Party. Jennifer left for work at the crack of dawn and often worked into the evening hours. Ted had once calculated that she worked an average of sixty hours a week. Someone had told him that lawyers charged a hundred dollars per hour so he did the math and shook his head. He had definitely gone into the wrong line of work.

He followed Jennifer into the kitchen, which was not at all what he'd expected, although he would not have been able to describe just what it was that he had expected. She'd installed a central island with a marble counter top, obviously very expensive, and the various appliances ranged around the room looked like they were state of the art. Some of them he couldn't even identify. Spatulas, strainers, long tined forks, ladles, serving spoons, egg whippers, colanders, and scores of other implements hung from overhead hooks or were arranged in wall racks. There looked to be more cabinet space in this one room than the Croners had in their entire house. Everything was spotless and orderly, of course, and he sensed that much of it – like the tools he had accumulated in his basement workshop - had never even been used.

"I hadn't realized you were a gourmet chef. This looks like something you'd see on the Food Channel." Beth used to watch the Food Channel a lot, when they'd had cable.

"I'm not quite on that level, but I do know my way around a kitchen. My dad was the head chef at the Loft for almost twenty years, and he used to let me come in and watch some times. Mom used to joke that she only married him for his cooking. But I don't get much time for that nowadays. We're short handed at the firm and my case load keeps growing."

She crossed the room to a row of cabinets, paused thoughtfully, then bent down and opened one of the lower doors. Ted moved a step to one side so that he had a better view.

"You should always reserve a little time for yourself." His mouth was dry and he wet his lips. "It's not healthy to let your job become an obsession." He'd never had that problem. They called it "work" for a reason, he figured. If it had been pleasant, they'd have called it "play."

Jennifer had started shifting items inside the cabinet. "I hear what you're saying. I keep telling myself the rush will only last another few weeks, but the end never seems to get any closer. Would you believe I haven't even completely unpacked yet? The spare bedroom is half full of cardboard boxes and it's been weeks since I've even gone in there."

"Perry Mason would have found a way." It was a lame joke and she didn't laugh.

"Television lawyers aren't much like the real world. They just stand around and look wise until it's time to outwit the other lawyer with some clever trickery and save the day. Most people have no idea how much preparation, even rehearsal, goes into a successful presentation in a real case. The way you lay out your arguments in the courtroom is just as important as the actual facts. If your presentation looks sloppy, you could lose even if the preponderance of evidence is in your favor. And vice versa."

Abruptly she plunged deeper into the cabinet. "Here it is!"

With some difficulty, she maneuvered an oversized roasting pan out of the cabinet. Ted partially averted his eyes and she stood up smoothly and turned to hand it to him. "I hope this is big enough. And please tell Beth that I'm going to make raspberry tarts for dessert. It was my dad's specialty and I haven't had an excuse to make them in years."

"Torts at work and tarts at home." Ted's second attempt at humor was even worse than the first and he was angry at himself the moment the words escaped him.

Jennifer sketched a polite smile. "Not my field. I'm just a glorified public defender. Tell Beth I'm not in any hurry to get the pan back. I haven't used it in months." She made a vague gesture toward the crowded cabinet. "Obviously."

Ted couldn't think of anything to say and the silence became awkward. "Well, I'd better get back. Thanks for the loan. We're looking forward to seeing you tomorrow."

"It should be fun. I haven't been to a cookout in ages. Not since my college days."

"Then we'll try extra hard not to disappoint you."

Ted allowed himself to be showed out and walked slowly back across the lawn to his own house, running through the encounter in his mind, trying to find something he could interpret as more than just an impersonal conversation. He had to admit that she'd betrayed nothing suggesting more than a very casual friendship, although she had revealed a good deal of leg while crouching at the cabinet, and certainly that could not have been completely accidental.

Beth wasn't in the kitchen when he arrived and he set the pan down beside the sink. "I'm back! Mission accomplished!"

There was no response. Ted glanced around, picked the kaleidoscope up from where he'd left it on the table, and walked to the tiny room where they spent much of their time at home. Like the rest of the house, it was cheaply furnished. A drab and not very realistic still life depicting a bowl of fruit was set above a couch which was in dire need of reupholstering or at least a slip cover. A threadbare arm chair stood opposite, next to an end table barely large enough to support a second hand Victorian lamp. Their telephone sat on a shelf built into the table. At the far end of the room, an elderly television stood on a rickety and barely presentable platform made of particle board stained to look like real wood. Beth was sitting in the chair, reading a magazine, and she didn't look up when he entered the room.

"Didn't you hear me? I said I left the pan in the kitchen."

"Okay, thanks." Beth didn't even look up from the magazine. For a moment Ted thought she was mad at him again, but there'd been no animosity in her voice. She just didn't care. That bothered him even more than hostility and he turned away, annoyed. It wasn't his fault that she was in a bad mood.

"I'll be down in the workshop if you need me."

Her failure to respond was an eloquent statement that this was an extremely unlikely scenario.

In sharp contrast to the rest of the house, the corner of the basement which Ted thought of as his workshop was not furnished with castoffs and flea market items. He had a modern work bench which he'd bought the first year they were married, and a bright red rolling toolbox that was as high as his chin and whose drawers were filled with top quality, well maintained tools, many of which had never been used. Most of these had also been purchased during the first few years they'd lived here in Managansett; a few more recent additions had been acquired without Beth's knowledge. They both had credit cards but she scrutinized each statement diligently and he resorted to cash payment when he thought she might question an expenditure. Even that had become risky because she had reduced their personal allowances to the bare minimum; fortunately, she had no way of knowing when he managed to siphon off a few dollars when taking a cash advance. Not that he cared if she did know, he told himself. It was his decision to make, not hers. But it was easier to avoid uncomfortable conversations if she didn't know everything he did. He thought of it as a kindness he did her, sparing her an argument in which she'd inevitably take the wrong side.

Pegboard on the wall held at least a score of screwdrivers, both Phillips and regular, of various sizes, lengths, and grip styles.

Next to them was an elaborate array of specialized wrenches to complement the even greater assortment stored elsewhere. There were claw head hammers, mallets, chisels, pliers, and portable vices and other grippers. Paint supplies were housed on another bench, a smaller wooden one with built in cabinets. Ted had installed two banks of fluorescent lights over his work area and the floor was covered with a piece of indoor/outdoor carpeting.

He crossed to the bench and set the kaleidoscope down, then pulled out a low backed stool and sat down to think about the problem. He opened a drawer and found his magnifying glass, then bent low to peer at the kaleidoscope in more detail. Unable to see clearly, he returned to the drawer and found a penlight, then carefully examined the narrow space between the drum and the shaft, looking for distortions, rust, or other impediments.

"Now let's see what's going on in here." He found a small screwdriver, designed for use in watch repair, and began probing inside the gap, slowly rotating the kaleidoscope in a complete circle. Halfway through the process, Roscoe descended the stairs and jumped up on the counter to find out whether or not whatever Ted was doing involved anything edible.

"Hey, Roscoe. Coming to help?" His probing met some resistance but it was relatively soft. "We've got some grease and grime gumming up the works, but I can't find anything actually broken." He used the tip of the probe to cut through the obstruction, then raised the kaleidoscope and blew into the gap, displacing small particles of unidentifiable dirt. He alternated between probing and blowing out the residue several times. Roscoe lost interest and curled up to nap in the middle of the bench, one eye half open to keep watch for any late arriving consumables.

Ted worked patiently and methodically, finishing one complete circuit, then a second, which went more quickly. Finally he was satisfied and set down the probe. "There. Let's see if that did the trick."

He raised the kaleidoscope to his eye and bent his head back so that it was aimed at one of the fluorescents. With his other hand he attempted to turn the drum. It resisted at first and he had almost decided to try something else when there was a very slight movement, followed by another. The mosaic display slowly shifted and fell into a new pattern. The drum had completed a full quarter turn, but then it became stuck again, refusing to budge even when he increased the pressure. Ted tried twice more before lowering it from his eye and glaring at it resentfully.

"Damn! What's the problem? If it moved once, it should move again."

He had just picked up his probe preparatory to another exploratory mission when Beth shouted down to him from the top of the stairs. "Ted! Can you come up here please!"

He sighed, set down the probe and kaleidoscope with exaggerated care. "What now?" he said, too softly to be heard upstairs. "I'll be right there," he shouted back, then slowly climbed down off the stool.

Beth was in the den, standing next to the telephone and looking preoccupied. The kitchen witch was propped up on top of the television and Ted wondered why she had moved it from its usual spot on the refrigerator. He stopped in the doorway, waiting to be noticed, and did a slight double take when he noticed that the painting over the couch had been replaced with a landscape he didn't remember ever having seen before. If he hadn't been concentrating so completely on Jennifer Hastings's figure earlier in the day, he might have recognized it as the same one which had been hanging in her living room during his brief visit.

"Where did that come from?"

Beth – who had changed into a sleeveless plaid blouse - gave a start, blinked her eyes, and followed his gaze to the wall. "A yard sale, remember? Where else? Listen, I just got off the phone with Mary next door. Carl wants to move a bench in their garage and he can't manage with that bum arm of his. I told her that you'd go over and give him a hand with it."

Ted was immediately offended that his services had been offered without his having been consulted in the matter, but he wasn't in the mood for a renewal of their fight just now so he satisfied himself by acting put upon rather than protesting that he was too busy. "What's wrong with Carl's arm anyway? It was Mary who fell down the damned staircase."

Beth gave him a strange look, impatience and contempt and puzzlement all mixed together. "Just skip the jokes and go help him, would you please? It should only take a couple of minutes out of your busy schedule. I'm sure you can spare the time."

Ted considered the situation and decided against making an issue of it, at least for the moment. It might provide ammunition in some later battle if he chalked up some martyr points. They had both gotten into the habit of storing up resentments, inflating them into injustices, and flinging them at each other at convenient moments. So instead of arguing, he threw up his hands in mock surrender. "All right. I'm going. Get off my back."

It was hot outside. Ted usually didn't mind the heat but it was humid as well and the normal breeze from the nearby reservoir had yet to make an appearance that morning. Three sparrows were using the birdbath on the Rogers' front lawn and a stray cat was watching them intently from the street. The Rogers' garage door was open. The contents were neatly arranged, bicycles, garden tools, lawn mower, recycling bins, a few tools and automotive supplies on shelves. Carl had built a small loft at the rear where they stored their artificial Christmas tree and ornaments and other seasonal and infrequently needed items including the tent and camping gear they hadn't used since the girls were in their early teens. There was a wide bench set against the side wall that Mary often employed for potting and repotting plants for the house and yard. It had been cleared off now and stood naked. Their SUV had been backed out into the driveway, beyond which Ted could see what he privately thought was the ugliest rose bush in the world, set directly in front of the big bay window, surrounded by lesser plants. Mary had threatened to tear it out on several occasions; it was mostly stem and thorn, with patches of leaves here and there and only a very few blossoms even in its best year. She insisted that there was something in the soil that the roses didn't like. Privately, Ted thought she just had a bad aura of some kind. Her house plants frequently died as well, so he might even have been right.

Carl Rogers was standing at the rear of the garage, tall and thin in his late forties, with a hairline that was just starting to recede, his glasses perched characteristically near the end of his nose overlooking a pencil thin moustache. His right arm was in a sling. Beside him stood Heather, who had apparently changed clothes since she was now dressed in jeans and a THINK shirt identical to the one Samantha had been wearing earlier, except that the colors were reversed, blue letters on a white background. Ted could not help noticing that Heather filled the shirt out much better than her sister had. Heather was standing with her arms folded, holding a leash connected to Toby, the family dog, a wire haired terrier who constantly barked when Roscoe was around, and frequently when he was not. Ted had hated the dog since the day Mary had brought it home. As far as he could see, no one in the family felt any actual affection for the animal, and it served no useful purpose. At least Roscoe kept mice out of the house, and had the good sense to remain silent and out of the way. Toby was constantly demanding attention, although Ted had swatted him a few times and was now safe from Toby's importunities.

Ted sensed that he was walking into a private and not entirely amicable conversation. He could tell by Heather's posture that she was angry about something even before he was close enough to make out what they were saying.

"I don't see why we can't just put Toby in his pen. Or why can't Sam take him for his walk? I just got home from vacation and you're already putting me to work. It's not fair." She stamped her foot. Ted had never actually seen anyone do that before, stamp their foot in anger. It made her seem much younger than she was.

Carl appeared to be unimpressed and his voice was his usual calm drone. "You've been home the better part of a month and Sam is busy helping your mother. All you have to do is take him around the block and let him do his business in that vacant lot on Pine Street. He needs to get some exercise or he'll be jumping up and down all day. It should only take you a few minutes and it's not as if you were doing anything important."

"I was reading," she said petulantly.

Carl sighed. "A fashion magazine. Now if it had been a text book, I might have conceded you the point, but I really think that you can wait awhile to find out what Britney Sears is wearing this week."

"Spears. Her name is Spears."

"Whatever. And it'll do you good to get out of the house for a while."

Heather was clearly prepared to present further arguments but Ted's arrival distracted her, or perhaps she still had enough residual good manners to avoid quarreling in front of outsiders.

She tugged on the leash irritably. "Come on, Toby. Let's get this over with." She raised her chin and walked down the driveway, as if to suggest that she wasn't actually taking the dog for a walk. She just happened to be holding the leash while she was about her own business, and Toby just happened to be attached to the opposite end. Ted nodded to her as she passed, but she ignored him. Maybe she thought that if she didn't see him, metaphorically, he wouldn't see her in this moment of indignity.

"Good morning, Ted." Carl raised his good hand in greeting.

"Morning, Carl. I guess you're looking forward to having Heather back for the summer. Isn't this the first time she's been away from home?"

"Just about. And it might be longer than just the summer if she doesn't do something to get her grades up."

Ted felt the urge to come to Heather's defense for reasons he didn't completely understand. "Well, you know how freshmen are. They need to goof off a little to get things out of their system. Living away from home is a pretty big adjustment. I'm sure she'll settle down next year." If for no other reason, he thought to himself, because her only alternative might well be to come back and live under Carl's reproachful gaze. He remembered his own enthusiasm about escaping parental authority.

Carl, however, did not seem either cheered or convinced by Ted's argument. "I hope you're right, but Heather's always been a lot more interested in the supply side of life rather than the demand side. She thinks she knows what she wants, but she hasn't given much thought about what it will take to achieve her goals. The job market is very competitive and she needs to add value to her resume if she wants to do something more than waiting tables or running a cash register at Foodworld."

Ted turned his head away so that Carl couldn't see him roll his eyes. For as long as he'd known Carl, the man had been stuck in lecture mode, as though he viewed the whole world as an extension of his classroom. Maybe he did. Everything he said was a pronouncement, every point illustrated by examples and cast in terms of economics. Ted wondered if his pillow talk was structured in terms of production and consumption.

"Beth tells me you need some help here. Just what exactly is it that needs to be done?"

Carl waved toward the work table as he approached. "I want to move this bench over to the back wall so that we can put some shelves up along here. We're finally going to do something about putting a finished family room in the basement and that means redistributing a few things. Mary's sorting things out and I have to figure out where they all go." Ted waited for Carl to use the familiar term "division of labor" but he missed the opportunity this time. "I could probably manage by myself, but it would go a lot easier if there's two of us."

Ted glanced around. "That shouldn't be too much of a problem." He moved to one end of the bench and tested the weight with both hands. Carl moved to the opposite end, bent slightly forward, and placed his uninjured hand awkwardly.

"Let me just ease this out a little way first." Ted slid the bench to his right so that he could get a better grip on the left hand corner. As he did so, a long legged spider raced up the wall and disappeared. Ted retreated hastily.

Carl raised his head. "Is something wrong?"

"Just a spider," said Ted, but there was a very faint tremor in his voice. "I hate spiders. Always have. They give me the creeps."

Carl was clearly amused although he attempted to hide it. "Never minded them myself. They eat the smaller bugs, and the birds eat them, I suppose. It's all a balanced system."

Ted was in no mood for a lecture on the benefits of an integrated ecology. He edged closer to the wall and looked things over. "I think it's gone now."

"We can switch sides if you want."

"No, that's all right. Let's get this done."

Carl did the best he could, but with only one hand that wasn't much and Ted ended up doing most of the work. The bench was heavier than it looked and he had to slide it across the floor rather than lift it, but the job still only required a few minutes before the bench was neatly set flush against the back wall. By the time they were done, Ted's face was red and he was breathing heavily. His shirt was sticky with sweat. Why couldn't Carl have picked a cool day for heavy lifting?

"Thanks a lot," said Carl. "I know it's not quite noon yet but I'd offer you a cold beer if we hadn't run out. Mary's going to pick some up while she's running errands this afternoon so you'll have to take a rain check."

Ted knew that Carl loved his beer in the hot weather, and that Mary didn't entirely approve, that they "ran out" by design more often than not. "Beth already laid in stock for the cookout tomorrow. There's a cold case in the basement refrigerator. If you get really desperate before this afternoon, you're welcome to come over and have one." He regretted making the offer as soon as the words were out of his mouth, but it was too late then.

"I might just do that. Everyone should be allowed one vice, don't you think?"

"Absolutely. At least one." For a change, Ted felt the hint of an actual bond of friendship between the two of them. He leaned back against the bench, remembered the spider, and stepped away from it, just in case it had hitched a ride somewhere out of sight. "What did you do to your arm anyway?"

Carl looked acutely embarrassed. "I fell down the goddamned basement stairs in the dark. I thought you'd heard about it. Mary has been trumpeting my stupidity to all and sundry. She gets a perverse joy out of telling people how clumsy I am."

"Two of you in the same week? I think I'd do something about those steps if I was you, before something worse happens."

Carl's brow creased with confusion. "Two of us? I don't understand."

"You know, you and Mary having the same accident."

Before Carl could answer, the door to the house opened and Mary Rogers appeared. She was prematurely grey, almost as tall as her husband and every bit as thin. Her face wore its usual expression, severe, although she had a particularly acute sense of humor that sometimes made people uneasy in her presence. She wore a housedress with a rose pattern and held a cigarette in one hand. Neither of her arms was in a sling.

"I came out to see how you boys were doing."

Carl spoke up immediately. "All done, thanks mostly to Ted."

Ted felt a sudden disorientation, kept looking back and forth between Carl and Mary. "I must have misunderstood Beth. I thought it was Mary who had fallen down the stairs." But he hadn't misunderstood. She must have misspoken.

Mary laughed. "No, Carl is the clumsy one in the family. I've

32

told him more than once that he needs to fix those steps, but he kept putting it off. Then he decided to go down to the basement with his arms full and nature took its course."

Still running through his memories, Ted had another thought. "But your daughter said…" He shook his head. "Forget it. It doesn't matter. She was probably just teasing me. Is there anything else I can do for you while I'm here?" He willed her to say no so that he could make his escape.

Both heads shook in unison. "No, we're fine," said Mary. "Thanks for coming over."

"Any time." Still slightly disturbed, Ted walked out of the garage and angled down to the mailbox in front of his house. It was too early for the mailman to have come, but he was still trying to rearrange the pieces of memory in his mind. As he reached the curb, Jennifer Hastings backed her bright red sports car out of her driveway, then drove past, waving casually as she did so. Ted answered her wave enthusiastically, but there was no sign that she even noticed. She went directly to the end of Bailey's Court and turned right, toward downtown Managansett rather than left toward the small strip mall.

The mailbox was empty, of course. Jennifer's brief appearance had put other matters out of his mind and Ted turned back to the house. He'd make one more attempt to fix the kaleidoscope, and if that didn't work, he'd put it out in the garage and deal with it in the future.

When he closed the front door behind him, he heard the television set and poked his head into the living room. Beth was back in the chair, watching the screen without enthusiasm. She'd turned on the fan but they only ran the air conditioner when they were desperate in order to keep the electric bill manageable. "Mission accomplished." He tried to keep his voice neutral, not wanting to risk drifting toward another battle, but sarcasm leaked through. "Is it all right if I go back to what I was doing now?"

If Beth detected anything in his tone, she ignored it. Or maybe she was just as tired of their thinly veiled conflict as he was. She didn't even turn to look at him when she answered. "I'll get lunch ready in a little bit. I may have to go to the store first. Did you put the keys back?"

Ted patted his pockets, then turned and glanced back toward

the key hook he'd mounted beside the door to the garage. Yes, he'd put them there automatically at some point. But they looked odd. "Yes, they're where they're supposed to be." He walked back through the kitchen and peered at the keys. They looked perfectly ordinary except that the key chain had a rabbit's foot attached to it, just like the one that dangled from the rear view mirror. His puzzlement gave way to surprise. Beth must have done this as a surprise and then asked him about the keys to direct his attention to it. Perhaps it was meant as a peace offering. He went back the way he'd come and stuck his head around the door.

"Thanks. That was a nice touch."

She didn't look in his direction. "What are you talking about?"

So he wasn't supposed to acknowledge it for some reason. Ted shrugged. "Nothing I guess."

Ted retreated to his workshop and sat on the stool, lost in thought but not about the rabbit's foot. It was relatively cool in the basement. Roscoe had run off somewhere but the kaleidoscope was still sitting right where he had left it. He picked it up, but his mind was elsewhere. He was wondering what it would be like to be married to an energetic, successful, bright young woman like Jennifer Hastings. Admittedly, she wasn't very domestic and probably worked long hours, but then again, Ted enjoyed having lots of time to himself, and he speculated that she'd probably need an outlet for all that pent up energy when she finally did come home. As far as he knew, she'd never entertained a man in her house, at least not overnight, but that didn't mean she wouldn't be good in bed. Was she as sophisticated about sex as she seemed to be about other things, or completely naïve? Ted tried to decide which he'd prefer and found pros and cons to both situations. He decided that he preferred her to be experienced, or at least enthusiastic and imaginative. Naïve was cute in its way, but after a while it was just annoying.

Beth had been quite sophisticated when they'd first met, although even then she had shown a certain degree of reserve. She'd never refused to have sex with him, and had eventually gone along when he'd suggested variations, some of them pushing the edge a bit, but he had sensed more than once that she felt this was an obligation that she'd incurred through marriage, that she didn't really enjoy it. Ted concluded that this was the result of the way she'd been brought up rather than through any fault on his part. He considered himself a competent, thoughtful lover and would have been shocked to discover that Beth had faked more orgasms than she'd experienced and considered him far less skillful than either of her two previous lovers, about whose existence she'd never spoken.

Ted had long since decided that marrying Beth was most likely a mistake. Knowing what he did now, would he marry Beth if he had it all to do over again? He considered the question dispassionately, or as much so as was possible, and decided probably not. Although his complaints were individually rather minor, the tally had risen rapidly over the years. She didn't understand him, of course, and while that was a cliché, there was a certain degree of truth in clichés, right? And she contributed very little of substance to their life together. True, she had worked steadily since their second year of marriage, but it wasn't a very high paying job, and there was no real future for her in banking unless she went back to school first and got herself a degree. She might get promoted to customer service manager for the branch or something, but it wasn't like they were going to elevate her to an executive position, after all. She was a fair cook, though nothing special, and her housekeeping he pegged as barely adequate. The fact that she worked a full time job while he was at home all day never figured into his calculations, nor did the fact that the drabness in their house was largely due to the necessary cheapness and worn state of their furniture.

He shook his head, telling himself that nothing could be done about it, that he'd just have to learn to live with the situation and console himself with the occasional casual flirtation. He had never been unfaithful, wouldn't have dreamed of it, except that he did dream of it, and if an opportunity arose where there was absolutely no chance that word would ever get back to Beth, then he might cheat just a little. It would probably help their marriage, after all. It would take some of the tension out of their lives if he wasn't so frustrated all the time. And what she didn't know wouldn't hurt her, not even her feelings. The possibility of divorce never occurred to him. It would be an admission that he had made a fundamental mistake in the shaping of his life, and that would damage the image he believed that he projected.

He sighed and turned his attention back to the kaleidoscope, made a perfunctory effort to turn the drum. It still seemed immovably jammed. Another close examination turned up nothing that he'd missed earlier. The interface seemed to be clear and mostly clean; he couldn't find any obvious flaw that would prevent it from turning. His mind wandered and he compared the kaleidoscope to his marriage. There weren't any obvious flaws there either, he thought wryly, but we don't seem to be functioning the way we're supposed to. Feeling vaguely guilty, he shook off his mood and told himself to concentrate on the matter at hand.

He put the kaleidoscope back down on the bench and stared at it for a moment. "Ve haff vays of making you vork," he said with a fake German accent.

Ted turned to the large vice set attached to the edge of the workbench and cranked the jaws open. From one of the cabinet drawers, he took a reasonably clean rag and wrapped it around the shaft of the kaleidoscope, then placed it between the jaws and closed them until they bit into the cloth and held the shaft firmly without scratching or denting. He tested it again, trying to rotate the shaft, but it still wouldn't budge.

Next he found a wide mouthed wrench, opening it far enough that he could fit the jaws around the drum. He hesitated, then wound a second, smaller rag around the drum before using the wrench to try to force it to turn while the shaft was held immobile by the vice. His first, tentative effort was a complete failure, in part because he was afraid to exert too much force. If he broke it now, he would have lost all the time he had invested.

"Carl would not consider that a sound use of capital resources," he said aloud, then addressed the kaleidoscope. "Now don't make me have to hurt you."

He gradually applied more pressure, straining so much that he began to feel the effort tightening the muscles in his arm. The rag slipped a bit, then caught, but the drum still didn't turn. Ted eased off, took a deep breath, and tried again. He was about to abandon this effort as well when he heard a faint, metallic sound and the drum began to rotate again. He was able to complete a full quarter turn and felt a surge of elation that died quickly when the mechanism jammed again.

Ted sat back and put the wrench down. He opened the vice and unwound the rags, examining the rim of the drum carefully. He was happy to see that the wrench had left no marks, not even a scuff. A quick look through the eyepiece showed a typical kaleidoscope display, but he was unable to tell how much it had changed since his last view. When he tried to turn it with his bare hand, he had no luck, but he felt less discouraged now that he'd at least managed to turn it a bit further than his first modest effort. The most likely explanation is that there was still grit of some kind caught between drum and shaft. Every time he managed to move it, however slightly, some of the obstructing material would become dislodged. It was probably just a matter of time before it was turning freely, and then he could take it to the local antique shops and find out how much it was actually worth.

The possibility that he'd found something really valuable overcame his normal aversion to fussy work. He repeated the entire process again, wrapping both shaft and drum, securing it in the vice, and applying gradually increased pressure, but this time he could make no headway at all. After several attempts, he was red in the face and actively annoyed, all thoughts of profit driven from his mind. Enraged, he threw down the wrench so hard that it skidded across the surface of the bench, released the vice, and furiously unwrapped the kaleidoscope. "Damned piece of junk!" He stood up, weighed it in his hand, then threw it into the cardboard box that served as a wastebasket at one end of the bench.

Ted waited until he felt calm again, or at least relatively so, then went upstairs.

He thought about bringing down some of the other items from the stockpile in the garage, but his lack of success with the kaleidoscope had sapped his enthusiasm. This was a familiar pattern, one he even recognized; he would work at a project diligently as long as things were going well. At the first suggestion of failure, he'd throw over an entire project. His employers had not considered this particularly character trait an asset and more than one of his job performance reviews had alluded to his lack of focus and ease of discouragement. Ted's failure to complete two major projects in a timely fashion had cost him his job at Fuller and Ashton. He'd had less responsibility at

Talmadge Assembly, but his inability to carry through difficult assignments when faced with unexpected problems had contributed to his termination there as well. Ted felt that this was an unfair characterization. When situations arose outside the parameters of his assigned work, it wasn't fair to hold him responsible. If the job had been properly described to him so that he could plan properly, he would have finished it without complaint.

Ted busied himself rearranging his work area slightly, feeling at loose ends, then went back upstairs. He peeked into the den, wondering if Beth would let him take the car for an hour or so before she went shopping. He hadn't been to the flea market out near Foodworld for a couple of weeks and he was convinced that most of the dealers there didn't know their business and that there was always a chance that he might make a profitable deal. He'd heard that someone over in Swansea had bought a framed picture just for the frame, and found a second and valuable painting mounted behind the big-eyed puppy picture that had been on display. Surely that couldn't be the only lost treasure. He didn't have much cash left, but most of the dealers knew him well enough that they'd probably extend credit if necessary, or at least hold an item until he had a chance to stop at an ATM.

But the den was empty and the television was off. The fan was blowing but had been turned so that it was facing a wall. The kitchen witch had gone away as well, presumably having returned to its home on the refrigerator. The landscape painting was also missing, replaced now by an ornately framed mirror which looked a lot like the one the Rogers had hanging in their dining room. "I wish you'd make up your mind," he said under his breath. Beth had a habit of moving furniture around, her endless quest for the perfect configuration as she called it, but they both knew that no amount of rearranging could ever make their collection of mismatched styles and colors into anything resembling an appealing gestalt.

His stomach rumbled and he realized that he was hungry. A glance at his watch told him it was nearly noon already. Lunch wouldn't be as good as a trip to the flea market, but it would satisfy a more immediate need.

Still looking for Beth, Ted walked into the kitchen, but he had no better luck there and felt a flash of irritation. It was bad enough that he had to fend for himself while Beth was at work. She could at least prepare meals on time during the weekend when she was home. "Beth? Where are you? It's time for lunch!" He waited for her to reply but there was no sound except the ticking of the kitchen clock and the hum of the refrigerator. Ted knew instinctively that he was alone in the house. She might have gone over to talk to one of the neighbors about the cookout. Or could she have gone shopping without telling him? It was entirely possible; she had planned to go in the morning until his delay getting back from his own errand had made that impossible. He walked into the front room, opened the door, and stepped outside to see if the station wagon was still parked in the driveway.

The wagon was gone and the garage door had been closed. Ted swore under his breath. No wheels and no lunch, unless he decided to fix something for himself or wait for her to get back. He felt another, stronger twinge of resentment. It's not as if I don't do my share around the house, he told himself. He had cut the grass the day before without complaint, despite the disruption to the plans he'd made, and he hadn't seriously resisted when she'd suggested inviting the neighbors over. The least she could do is show a little appreciation for his efforts.

He was about to go back inside when he noticed the anomaly. The ornate birdbath which normally stood in front of the Rogers house had been moved and was now sitting right in front of the forsythia Beth had planted in front of the house. For a few seconds, he thought it might be some kind of optical illusion, an after image, but it didn't blur out or go away, even when he walked toward it. Someone had moved the birdbath. "Damned kids." There had been some recent trouble with two of the boys from the next street over. Flowerbeds had been torn up, trash cans overturned, a couple of windows had been broken, and eggs were found smashed on the windshields of parked cars. Ted thought it had all been cleared up after Chief Dowdell sent a couple of troopers out to talk to the parents, but obviously that had only provided a respite.

From up close, the birdbath looked even uglier than from a distance. Ted shook his head in disgust. Well, he'd just have to carry it back. He wrapped both arms around the base just under the lip and tried to lift it. He quickly reconsidered. Not only was it heavier than he expected but the weight was unbalanced. He staggered and let it fall back in place. "Okay, let's try this again."

He adjusted his feet, flexed his arms a bit to loosen them up, and tried a second time, this time braced for the imbalance. Although he was able to lift the birdbath into the air, even take a step toward the Rogers house, the strain was more than he had expected. He felt his grip loosening, had visions of dropping the birdbath onto his foot and perhaps breaking some toes, and carefully set it back down. He stepped back, shaking from the exertion. Obviously more than one kid had to have been involved in the prank, and equally obviously Ted wasn't going to be able to put it back where it belonged without some help. And Carl had a bad arm. And Ted was still hungry.

"Need some help, Mr. Croner?"

Ted turned and saw Samantha Rogers crossing the driveway toward him. It was the first time he had seen her without her glasses, and she was wearing her hair differently. He suddenly realized that she looked a lot more like her sister Heather than he had realized, and dressed as she was now, in a halter top and shorts, her figure wasn't bad either. He felt a momentary flash of guilt; after all, she was only a kid. Then he told himself that she was almost grown up and it wasn't as if he'd ever actually get involved with someone that young. Her sister was right at the limit for him. Any younger was jail bait. On the other hand, there were parts of the world where she'd have been married and given birth by now. It was only natural that his body reacted to her presence. That was how males were designed. He couldn't be blamed if his hormones responded the way they were supposed to.

Ted found his voice. "I just wanted to move this back to where it's supposed to be. It's heavier than I thought it was and I don't want to drop it."

Samantha came closer and leaned forward, examining the birdbath critically. "I could help if you want." She didn't sound entirely sure that this was a good idea. Ted was skeptical as well. There was just no safe way to get a grip on the birdbath bare handed, even with a second pair of hands to help. He wondered if he could borrow a hand truck some place.

Samantha provided a brief glimpse inside the halter top by

bending down to examine the birdbath and Ted averted his eyes, but only after sneaking a quick look. She wasn't wearing anything beneath it. He felt suddenly flustered and uncomfortable. "Thanks, Samantha. Maybe later."

She straightened up. "It's Heather, Mr. Croner. Samantha is my sister, remember?"

It was true that Ted had confused their names more than once in the past, but that was only because he had never exactly thought of them as people, or at least as individual people. Even though they'd been almost teenagers when the Croners had moved in next door, he'd always thought of them as kids, and he didn't really have time for kids, was always uncertain what they expected of him and what he could expect from them. But he was quite sure that he had the two girls straight in his mind at the moment and it was Heather who had gone off to college, so this had to be Samantha. Obviously they were having a joke at his expense. He had to hand it to her; there wasn't the faintest hint of trickery in her face, but he wasn't patient enough to play along.

"And your mother doesn't smoke and your father didn't break his arm, I suppose."

Samantha/Heather looked genuinely puzzled. "Mom smokes all right. The house reeks. But Daddy's arm is fine. Is this some kind of joke, Mr. Croner?"

Ted shook his head, not wanting to play her game. He wondered if the sisters had moved the birdbath. It was pretty heavy, but they might be stronger than they looked. If they had tilted it up on one side, they might have rolled it across the lawn if they were very careful, although that should have left marks on the grass. "Have it your way, kid. I don't have time for games. You didn't happen to see my wife, did you?"

Samantha/Heather looked as though she thought she had just been insulted, but she nodded. "She drove away just before you came outside. I think she was going up to Foodworld. She said something about buying a big ham for the cookout tomorrow."

"Well then, I guess I'm on my own for lunch." He was talking to himself rather than his companion.

"Peanut butter sandwiches again?" With the air conditioner off, Ted had frequently lunched at the picnic table outside and Samantha had waved to him from time to time. It wasn't true that he always settled for peanut butter sandwiches, but they were easy, filling, had positive food value, and they were convenient to take outdoors.

"I can probably manage something a little better than that." But the thought of actually cooking something felt like an unnecessary complication. "Take my advice and stay single, Samantha. It's a lot easier in the long run."

"I'm Heather, Mr. Croner," she answered wearily.

"Whatever."

His lunch, however, was to be delayed again. Ted had just started to turn back toward the house when a red sports car turned into Bailey's Court. Jennifer Hastings was driving at her usual sedate pace. He paused to watch as she drove by, pulling up into her driveway and killing the engine. She waved in their direction and called out. "Hi, Ted! Hi, Heather! Would one of you mind giving me a hand?"

Samantha/Heather took one step in her direction but Ted stepped in front of her. "I've got it covered, kid." He started to walk across the grass without looking back to see whether she was following. The teenager watched him for a few seconds, then shook her head irritably and turned back toward her own house.

Jennifer was halfway out of the car when Ted reached the driveway. He could see that the back seat was filled with bags of groceries. As he drew closer, she stood up, poised slightly awkwardly, and retrieved her shoulder bag from the passenger's side seat.

"What can I do for you, young lady?"

Jennifer stepped back from the car and turned around so that she could use her hip to nudge the door shut. As she did so, she rotated her body and Ted realized that her left arm was in a sling. He froze, feeling the pulse beat in his forehead. What was going on here?

"If you could help me carry in these groceries, that would be great."

His mouth was dry and he had to try three times before he could speak. "What happened to your arm?"

"Would you believe I was reading a brief and not watching where I was going? I fell down the courthouse steps. It's just a hairline fracture. Nothing serious, according to the doctor, but I won't be playing tennis or swimming the English Channel for a while. It itches like crazy and I feel like a complete idiot."

She started for the door, jingling her keys in her good hand. Ted felt a tingling in his body that wasn't at all sexual, and distinctly unpleasant. This couldn't all be part of some elaborate practical joke, could it? It had to be just a string of coincidences coupled with a lapse of memory. He took a deep breath, told himself to calm down and go with the flow. Maybe things would become clearer if he played along for the time being. With exaggerated care, he lifted two of the grocery bags out of the back seat and carried them to the front door.

Jennifer had unlocked it and pushed it open, leading the way inside. Ted followed her into the kitchen, where he noticed that Beth's kitchen witch, or one just like it, was sitting on the microwave. "Where should I put these?"

"Just set them down on the table or the counter, would you please? Whichever is easier. I actually only went out to pick up some cat food but I got carried away."

Ted carefully set down one bag, then the other. "I didn't know that you had a cat."

"Oh yes. I discovered long ago that a cat is a lot easier to live with than a boyfriend."

"Or a wife," he muttered under his breath.

"Pardon?"

"Nothing. Just talking to myself. Hang on and I'll get the rest." He walked back through the house, failing to notice the picture of a fruit bowl mounted in the front room. It took two more trips to bring in the rest of the groceries, and when he put down the last two bags, Jennifer was busily, if somewhat awkwardly, storing the contents away in a row of cupboards.

"This is the last of them. Is there anything else I can do for you while I'm here?"

Jennifer seemed to have momentarily forgotten his existence. She stared at him for a beat or two as though he was a stranger, then shook her head. "No, I think I'm all set. Thanks again for the help, Ted. I really appreciate it."

Ted let himself out and was walking home just as the mail truck turned into Bailey's Court. He waited at the mailbox until Fred, the mailman, shuffled through a stack and sorted out a small selection of envelopes. "Mostly junk mail, Mr. Croner."

"Better that than bills, Fred."

"Can't argue with that."

Fred headed toward the Hastings house while Ted sorted through his mail. There was a magazine for Beth, a selection of circulars from local stores, a begging letter from some charity he'd never heard from, and a catalog of aquarium supplies. He thought the last must have been meant for Jennifer, but the label indicated it was for Mary Rogers. The Rogers family had a dog, but maybe they were thinking of adding tropical fish. He thought about bringing it over to them, but decided that later would be soon enough.

The renewed rumbling in his stomach demanded more immediate attention, however, so once inside he went immediately to the kitchen and opened the refrigerator. Beth had obviously been making room in anticipation of the next day's party and had thrown away most of the leftovers. He poked around and finally found one Tupperware container that she had missed, but when he opened it and looked inside, he made a face and closed it immediately. "I'd rather starve." He put it back where he'd found it and swung the door shut.

He crossed to the large cabinet that Beth referred to as her pantry. A variety of canned and packaged pre-cooked meals were scattered among the various soups, beans, condiments, oils, and spices that she stored there. Ted knew he didn't have the patience to cook something on the stove, or even make up a flavored rice package in the microwave, and he closed the cabinet door with a little more force than was actually necessary after extracting an almost empty box of crackers which he devoured absentmindedly while he continued his search. They were out of peanut butter again! There were other food items in some of the overhead cabinets and he began poking through these, hoping for inspiration. "Cookies. I know she keeps cookies around." Although now that he thought about it, he hadn't seen any for a while. Probably another "luxury" she'd decided to eliminate until they were on steadier financial ground.

He stopped abruptly when he opened the next to the last cabinet in the row. His face changed, displaying confusion. Stacked against the right side of the cubbyhole were several brightly labeled cans. He reached up and took one out, holding it daintily as though it might bite him. "Dog food? Why do we have dog food?" Beth was mildly afraid of dogs, even Toby. Ted suspected that she distrusted all animals and that Roscoe had instinctively sensed this and that was why he avoided her company.

He shook his head and put the can back where he'd found it, then swung the door shut. Thoughtfully, he turned and walked over to the corner where Roscoe's food dish and litter box were kept. The litter box was gone although the food and water dishes were both in their usual places, but both were marked "TOBY". A small rawhide bone, thoroughly chewed, lay a few inches beyond.

Ted narrowed his eyes, looked around suspiciously, his voice unsteady. "What the hell is going on here?" His hunger forgotten for the moment, he wandered aimlessly into the den and dropped into the padded chair, staring at the opposite wall for a few seconds. He closed his eyes and massaged his temple with both hands, then shook his head as though clearing away cobwebs of confusion. He glanced down at the phone and a memory came back to him – Beth, having just gotten off the phone, telling him that Carl Rogers needed help moving a bench because his arm was injured, except that his arm hadn't been injured just a few minutes before. It was Mary who had broken her arm. He was sure that he'd heard that correctly. What had happened to change things during those few minutes?

He tried to retrace everything he'd done or seen or heard that morning. He'd returned from the yard sale and had unloaded the car. Samantha had been there and, yes, he remembered her confirming that her mother was the one with the broken arm. She'd complained because she was stuck doing most of the housework. So whatever had happened had occurred later.

Beth had sent him next door to get the roasting pan, which he had done. Everything had still been all right, as far as he could tell, when he got back. He'd taken the kaleidoscope down to the workshop and tried to fix it, but with limited success. Then Beth had called him back upstairs and told him that Carl was the one with his arm in a sling. So whatever had caused the change must have happened while he was in the basement, or shortly before that.

Narrowing things down made him feel a little better, but not much. And he remembered that it was now Jennifer whose arm was in a sling. Was Carl similarly afflicted or had he miraculously recovered? Ted suspected that if he walked over and rang the bell on the Rogers house, Carl would be in perfect health. So whatever had happened earlier, while he was in the basement, had happened again after he'd returned from the Rogers house. And when he'd returned, he'd almost immediately gone downstairs again to give the kaleidoscope another try. And while he was there, things had changed again. He remembered the picture on the wall that had been replaced, then become a mirror, and glanced up. It was still a mirror. So not everything changed, even those things that had changed the first time. Or had Beth actually replaced the picture with a mirror and the only variable element was the broken arm? But then he remembered the kitchen witch, which was now in Jennifer's house. She might have borrowed it, but why consider the possibility of a string of coincidences when the central fact was so fantastic? It all had to be part of the same puzzle.

His head ached. "Ridiculous. This has to be some kind of elaborate practical joke they're all playing. It can't be real." If he ignored them, refused to react, they'd lose interest.

But what if it was real? An image from the kaleidoscope suddenly filled his mind, the separate elements constantly shifting and falling into new patterns, each pattern containing all of the original elements, but now arranged in a new configuration. "It can't be." Ted liked to believe that he had left his childhood behind him, but in most ways he had never really grown up. He was egocentric, spoiled, and wanted to world to function as it ought to rather than as it was. And although he would have denied it vehemently, on some fundamental level he stilled believed in magic.

What if he'd actually stumbled across a piece of genuine magic this time?

Ted stood up, drawn almost against his will to cross the room and go to the door leading to the basement. It was closed and he hesitated, almost afraid to open it. A calendar hung from a pin on the door, the picture showing an elaborate rose garden. Ted didn't think he'd ever seen the calendar before and was almost afraid to touch it. Finally he reached out and swung the door open, and almost immediately a small body rushed past his legs. It was Toby, who had apparently been trapped downstairs. He barked once, then scuttled off toward the kitchen.

Ted flicked on the light switch and descended slowly, almost warily, as though expecting some horrible creature to be lying in wait for him. His eyes darted around the cellar, which seemed darker and more cluttered than usual, although that was probably just his imagination. The possibilities he was considering had changed his entire perception of the world and even the most familiar things suddenly had new attributes, shades of color, altered shapes. He hesitated again on the bottom step, inclining his head as though listening for some barely audible hint of the supernatural. The water heater hummed slightly but that was the only sound.

He shook off the feeling of unreality, or convinced himself that he had, and walked briskly over to the bench. At first he was puzzled by the absence of the kaleidoscope, then remembered that he'd become so frustrated that he'd pitched it into the trash. When he looked into the waste bin, it was on top and he lifted it out carefully, as though it were some delicate antique, or perhaps a volatile explosive. He set it down on the bench, lying on one side, and regarded it thoughtfully.

The possibilities chasing one another through Ted's mind threshed and sorted themselves into one pattern after another. It was his imagination, a practical joke, a miracle, a curse, a trick, an hallucination, a dream, a mental breakdown. Each conclusion formed, then broke up into component parts, shifted and realigned itself with other possibilities, fell into new patterns which were considered and rejected. Ted didn't know what was going on, inside his mind or in the world around him, and he didn't like the uncertainty. It frightened him.

"All right," he said aloud, momentarily startled by the sound of his own voice. "It's crazy. But what if it's somehow true?"

Moving very deliberately, Ted slowly raised the kaleidoscope so that he could examine the symbols inscribed all over its surface. They didn't convey any additional meaning to him. Some looked vaguely familiar, others he'd never seen before. At first he had thought that they were painted on, but he realized now they were inscribed into the metal. They formed no recognizable pattern but

47

when he slowly turned the kaleidoscope they gave the impression of concerted movement, although he could not have described just how that was accomplished.

"Well, here goes nothing." He peered into the eyepiece and gave the drum a tentative turn, or tried to. It was still stuck and wouldn't budge. Ted clamped his jaw shut, shifted his grip, and slowly began to increase the pressure until his muscles ached with the strain and the cold metal seemed to burn the skin of his hand where he touched it. His breathing grew more rapid and he could feel his heart beat. The ache spread up his arm and through his shoulders into the muscles of his back and still he kept trying.

Finally, when he was close to admitting defeat, Ted was rewarded with a slight movement, so faint he almost didn't recognize what had happened. The display changed a little and then the kaleidoscope was jammed tight once again. Sweating profusely, his breath suddenly uneven and heavy, Ted slowly lowered the kaleidoscope and set it down on the bench in front of him. It was done, whatever it was, at least in some small fashion, and all he had to do now was go back upstairs and see if things had changed again. He flexed his arms, which ached more than slightly, and for a moment wondered if he would end up wearing the sling.

Toby came bouncing down the stairs and ran past him, chasing some phantom prey of his own. Ted watched him disappear behind a pile of boxes. "Well, you're still here, Toby, so maybe it's just me losing my mind."

Ted started up the stairs.

At first it appeared that nothing had changed. The mirror was still on the wall in the den, and Beth was still gone. He thought some of the appliances in the kitchen might have moved, but he couldn't really be sure. Beth had been doing a lot of rearranging in preparation for the cookout, and he wasn't really that observant of things that didn't directly concern him. Except for the presence of Toby, who followed him for a while, then lost interest and disappeared somewhere on a mission of his own, things looked very much like they had before this had all started. Whatever "this" was. Ted began to wonder if there wasn't some logical explanation that he'd just overlooked. Maybe they were supposed to babysit the dog for some reason. Maybe Carl was having the house fumigated. He wouldn't be surprised if the dog had attracted fleas.

Satisfied – and rather disappointed - that the house was not concealing some appalling or exciting secret, Ted walked to the front door and stepped outside. He was relieved to see that the birdbath was no longer standing on his lawn, but it wasn't in front of the Rogers house either. It was now standing next to Jennifer Hastings's driveway. Okay, that was explainable. The kids who had moved it the first time had come back to elaborate on their prank. It seemed to Ted that it was an awful lot of work for a not particularly funny joke, but kids were like that. He remembered when he was a kid someone had left a complete, porcelain toilet bowl in a neighbor's yard one Halloween.

Jennifer's flashy sports car was not in sight, but her garage door was closed so he didn't know if she'd gone out again or just put it inside to protect the paint job from the glaring sun. He glanced back at the Rogers house, but their SUV was not visible either, and their garage door was also closed.

The normality of it all made him feel a lot better in one way, although also disappointed. He walked out into the front yard, the hot sun beating down on his body as though it was burning all the uncertainty away. It had to be stress. The difficulties he'd been experiencing trying to find a new job, the pressure from Beth about taking some position inappropriate to his worth, and perhaps a bit too much hot, humid weather had lulled him into a half dreaming, half waking state. He had probably taken a mid-morning nap, dreamed bits and pieces, and his mind hadn't quite sorted those bits back to the right places. Everything had a logical explanation if you took the time to look for it.

He felt better despite the disappointment, but there was still a flicker of uneasiness that refused to be extinguished. "All right," Ted told himself. "Let's find out just how crazy I really am." He walked directly to the Rogers' front door and, after a brief hesitation, pressed the doorbell. There was a brief pause, then the door opened. It was Samantha, wearing blouse and slacks, no glasses. It was the third outfit he'd seen her wear during the course of the morning, but maybe she was having trouble getting comfortable. Or maybe teenaged girls just changed clothing a lot. She sketched a smile when she saw him, but it was polite rather than warm.

"Oh, hi, Mr. Croner. Did you want to see my dad?"

"Hi, yourself, Samantha." He paused, waiting for her to correct him, but she seemed to accept the name. Well, if it had been a practical joke earlier, she'd dropped it. "Yeah, is your father in?"

She shook her head. "No, I'm sorry. He and my mom both just went out. They should be back any minute though; they just had to pick up a few things at the drugstore."

Ted felt a wave of uncertainty. Everything seemed perfectly ordinary. But he had wanted some confirmation that things were normal, or back to normal, and the little flicker of doubt wasn't completely extinguished. On the other hand, how could he ever prove that nothing had changed? There were so many details that he didn't know. Was the furniture he could see through the door in the same place as usual? He couldn't remember. Ted groped for something to say that would extend the conversation. "Actually, I just wanted to borrow something." He hesitated. Having committed himself this far, he had to go forward. But what could he borrow? "A plunger. You know, for the toilet. Mine is all clogged up and I can't figure out what I did with ours, and my wife is off with the car so I can't pick up a new one."

Samantha looked uncertain. "Okay, I think we have one. Come in for a sec while I look." She stepped back and opened the door wider so that Ted could enter.

Ted glanced around the Rogers' living room. Nothing leaped out at him as strange or out of place, at least not right away, but he had to admit to himself that he'd never paid much attention in the past. The picture over the fireplace was familiar, and he remembered the dreadful couch, but one of the lamps looked unfamiliar and he thought the rug might have been a darker color before. He had always considered a visit to the Rogers house as a chore rather than a pleasure. Carl was dull and stodgy, Mary always seemed slightly wary of him and he considered her a prude, and the girls were no more interested in him than he was in them. He did notice that there was an aquarium in one corner that looked a lot like the one he had seen in Jennifer's house. He was quite sure that hadn't been there the last time he'd been in this room, but weeks had passed since then and he did remember the catalog mixed in with his mail. They might well have bought one since his last visit and he wouldn't have been any the wiser unless he happened to notice it when it was delivered, which he hadn't.

"I'll go look for it." Samantha vanished in the direction of the bathroom.

At first he thought he'd been left alone, but then he noticed that Heather was sitting curled up at the far end of the couch, watching television, wearing a lightweight sun dress with her hair tied up in an unattractive bun. She was also wearing glasses, the first time he'd ever seen her with a pair, but maybe she only wore them for television and reading. Heather was obviously watching some kind of horror movie – the scene was dark, the outside of what appeared to be a typical suburban house, though he could only see part of it. A young woman was running from left to right, pursued by a shadowy figure brandishing an axe. There seemed to be no soundtrack, or Heather had the sound turned down so low that it was inaudible. The young woman stumbled, fell on her face, struggled to get up, and the darker figure caught up to her, raised the axe, swung it down.

Ted averted his face. He'd never been a fan of horror movies. As a child he'd refused to watch even the relatively tame versions that showed up on television. In one of his rare critical moments, Ted's father had told him that he was being childish, that it was all make believe and he shouldn't allow it to bother him. But for Ted, make believe and reality were not mutually exclusive states of existence. They overlapped at times. And his imagination always extrapolated far more horrible things than were actually shown and unlike his peers, he wasn't able to laugh or cheer when the psychotic killer began slashing semi-nude victims. He became noticeably upset watching even the most unrealistic depiction of blood and gore. It wasn't that he had a weak stomach, he told himself. But why did they always have to resort to such explicit detail? It was disgusting.

"I'll just be a second, Mr. Croner," Samantha called from somewhere out of sight. "I think it's in the other bathroom."

"Okay, thanks." Ted called back, then looked over at Heather who raised her head and half turned in his direction. There was a book in her lap and Ted realized she wasn't actually watching the television. A faint ghost of a welcoming smile flitted across her face so quickly that Ted wasn't sure that he hadn't imagined it. She turned back to her book without saying a word.

"So what are you planning to do with your summer, Heather?" He moved to the near end of the couch. "Got a job lined up for yourself?"

Heather raised her head and half turned to face him and Ted noticed for the first time that her right arm was in a sling. He felt as though the floor had suddenly shifted beneath his feet and he almost reached out to grab something for support. A second or two passed before he realized that Heather was speaking and forced himself to concentrate on the words.

"Kind of. Dad had arranged for me to do some office work for Flynn, Keller, and Anderson, but I can't start for another week thanks to this." She flapped her wounded arm. "It itches like crazy but the doctor said I can take the sling off on Monday. Dad says that if I'm really serious about switching to pre-law, that I should at least have some first hand exposure. I'm not sure how much exposure I'll get by copying, filing, and running errands, but at least it's a start."

Ted cleared his throat, relieved to find that he still had a voice. "So you want to be a lawyer. What happened to secretarial school?"

Heather made a face at him. "Come on, Mr. Croner. I'm a little more ambitious than that. Do you know what secretaries get paid?"

"Yeah, sure. Have you talked to Jennifer about it? She might be able to give you some good advice."

Heather frowned. "You mean Miss Hastings? Why would I talk to her about being a lawyer? She's just a high school economics teacher."

Ted was able to mask his reaction only because Samantha returned at that moment, brandishing a wooden handled plunger. "Is this what you're looking for, Mr. Croner?" She held it out toward him and Ted took it automatically. He noticed that Samantha was wearing a pendant on a chain around her neck. No, it wasn't a pendant. It was a rabbit's foot.

"Yes. Yes it is. Thanks." His mouth was dry and his hands were trembling. "This should do the trick. I'll bring it right back, I promise."

There must have been something odd in his voice because Samantha looked mildly uncertain, even nervous. "That's okay. We're clog free at the moment."

Ted told himself to leave but it felt as though his shoes were filled with lead, and his head stuffed with cotton. He might have been dreaming earlier, but there was no doubt at all that he was wide awake now. Whatever was happening was real, not an illusion, unless he was in a coma somewhere and this was all happening in some weirdly realistic dream state.

His paralysis was broken by the sound of an automobile pulling into the driveway. Samantha, looking suddenly relieved, started toward the window. "That must be Mom and Dad."

Ted followed Samantha and stood behind her as she drew the curtains back to look outside. He was expecting to see the SUV but instead it was the station wagon parked there, although it was Carl Rogers who climbed out of the driver's seat. He walked around to the rear and opened the tailgate door, joined there by another figure. His wife. His wife Beth. Ted's jaw dropped as he saw the two of them begin to unload plastic bags.

He gasped, turned it into a cough. There was no way that he could pretend not to be shaken if he waited to speak to them. "Listen girls, I don't want to bother your parents while they're busy. Just say hello for me, will you?" He turned and headed for the back door.

Heather ignored him but Samantha turned away from the window. "Okay, Mr. Croner. I'll tell them you stopped by. Good luck with your toilet."

On his way out, Ted nearly stumbled over a food dish lying on the kitchen floor. It bore the name ROSCOE, but he didn't notice.

Outside, Ted paused to take several deep breaths. He had suddenly begun to feel claustrophobic and his head was spinning. He looked at the plunger as though he had never seen one before and when he started toward his own backyard, his knees felt weak. He passed the barbecue grill and paused at the picnic table, still feeling disoriented. The earlier changes had been inconsequential, things moved about, nothing that would actually alter his world. But this? If Beth was married to Carl, where was Mary? And was Ted still single? The possibility that they'd swapped made him sick to his stomach.

He knew that he should return to the house, search for evidence that would clear things up in his mind, but then he noticed that Jennifer Hastings was sitting on her patio wearing a tight shirt and shorts. Her unconscious sexuality cut through the fog of his thoughts like a knife. He set the plunger down on the picnic table, straightened his shoulders, and walked directly toward her. Might as well find out what else has changed, he told himself. Or just how crazy I really am.

She didn't notice him until he was almost close enough to touch her, half turning in the seat to face him with a friendly smile. As she turned, he could see the word "THINK" emblazoned across the front of her blouse. Beside her stood a small wicker table with a pitcher of lemonade, a glass, and a bowl of fruit. She was reading a Stephen King novel, the same one Beth had started earlier in the week. The cover showed a dark figure chasing a young girl past the front of a typical suburban home. The dark figure carried a large ax, just like the one hanging in his garage.

Ted stepped up onto the patio and found his voice. "Working on your tan?"

Jennifer shrugged her shoulders, much to Ted's delight. Other parts of her anatomy moved sympathetically. "Just a token effort, I'm afraid. My skin's so sensitive I go straight to third degree burn unless I'm very careful. It does feel good to be able to sit outside and relax and know that there's nothing stopping you from spending every day for the next month goofing off. I'm so glad I didn't take a summer job this year. This is the first time I've been able to afford that luxury since I started teaching."

"It must be nice to have three whole months to yourself." Ted squatted down so that their heads were on more or less the same level.

Jennifer carefully folded the flap of the dustjacket into her book to mark her place and let it fall into her lap. "Only seven weeks, actually. I let myself get talked into volunteering for the curriculum committee this year. And I have to write some lesson plans and come up with some new test questions with answers that the kids haven't passed around to each other already. If they spent as much time studying as they do trying to figure out how to cheat, they wouldn't need to."

"How long have you been teaching now?"

"Five long years." She didn't look entirely pleased.

"You sound as though you don't enjoy it. I'd have thought you'd like working with kids." Actually, he had never understood why anyone would go into teaching. The hours weren't bad, he supposed, but the pay wasn't great, there weren't many chances for advancement, and who would want to have to deal with undisciplined, insolent, pimple faced adolescents all day every day from June until September, year after year after year? And the younger kids were even worse.

"Sometimes I do. A lot of the time, I suppose. But every once in a while it feels like I've made a mistake. It's as if I missed a turn somewhere along the way and failed to become whatever it is that I was supposed to be."

"Like what? A lawyer?"

She nodded. "Yeah, something like that. I started out in pre-law as a matter of fact, but I changed my mind and switched. It's funny, but I don't even remember why. I guess I was just tired, or bored, or impulsive. I suppose everyone wonders from time to time whether or not they've made the best decisions. You know, the right shoes, the right job, the right husband. It's not as if we could reset the clock and start over, and accepting the cards you've been dealt is part of the game. But sometimes I try to guess what I'd be doing now if I'd decided things differently when I was younger." She laughed. "Do I sound like I'm miserable and hate my life? I don't mean to. I'm really pretty content with things as they are. I just feel sometimes that life could have been even better if I'd had more control over things, if I'd been able to look at all the facts and consequences and make informed decisions."

"Yeah, I know what you mean." And Ted might just have found a way to beat the system, if he could only figure out how to use it. Decisions didn't have to be final, if you had a way to change them retroactively. He felt a rush of excitement so powerful that it made him feel giddy and he almost lost his balance. "Maybe it's not too late."

Their eyes met and there was an awkward moment before she averted her eyes. Then she raised her head and looked around. "That sounds like your car. Your wife must be home."

Ted had by now managed to forget that Beth was apparently Mrs. Carl Rogers. He stood up and glanced back toward his house.

"I guess I'd better go and see if she needs any help. It was nice talking to you. Are we still on for tomorrow?"

"Wouldn't miss it." The awkward moment appeared to have passed. "Remember, I'm bringing dessert."

"Right. Raspberry tarts."

Jennifer blinked. "No," she said quietly, drawing the word out. "That would be a little out of my league, I'm afraid. I'm almost hopeless in the kitchen. But I can manage peanut butter cookies and ice cream."

Ted took it in stride. "Sounds great. Catch you later."

Ted trudged toward the house, hoping that any necessary lifting and carrying would be finished before he arrived. He reached the kitchen through the back door, arriving just as the connecting door to the garage swung open. Mary Rogers appeared, one arm wrapped around a bag of groceries. Or more accurately, Mary Croner appeared. Logically, Ted should have expected this development, but his mind still had not adjusted to the fluid state of reality. He was taken completely by surprise and stopped dead in his tracks.

"No way!" His voice, fortunately, was barely a whisper and Mary wasn't paying attention.

She noticed him without actually seeing him, which was equally fortunate since the expression on his face did not conceal his distaste. "There you are, Ted. Give me a hand with this, will you please? And there are four more bags in the car. Wait until you see the beautiful ham I bought. It was even on sale."

Automatically, Ted took the bag from Mary and set it down on the counter. She dropped the car keys on the table – no rabbit foot this time – and began opening cupboards.

"Just bring in the rest for me, would you? And there's ice cream in one of them, so hurry up before it melts."

Still in shock, Ted walked out through the door to the garage and moved to the side of the SUV. The sliding door was open and four more bags were neatly lined up inside. He took one in each arm, reflected that he'd been spending a lot of time carrying groceries lately without doing anything to satisfy the growling in his stomach, and cut short a quiet laugh because it didn't sound right. He carried the bags into the house. Beth had already emptied the first and she took one from him impatiently. He set the other down on the table.

"The ice cream is still out there, Ted. Melting."

"Right. I'm on it."

His mind started working again on the way back to the SUV. He needed to go back downstairs, to his workshop, and think this through. Something was clearly happening here, obviously, something more than just confused memories or a practical joke, something that he might be able to use to his advantage. He was certain now that the kaleidoscope was changing elements in the real world whenever he managed to turn the drum. The changes seemed to be random but maybe there must be some kind of a pattern. He needed to concentrate, to think things through. He would just bring in the last two bags to keep Mary out of his hair, then go down where he could be alone and consider the possibilities. His heart was racing. This could be the solution to all of his problems.

The last two bags were heavier than he expected, and one of them was wet and soggy because the ice cream was sweating. He managed to get them both securely cradled in his arms and tried to close the sliding door, first with his knee, then his shoulder, in neither case with any success.

"Let me give you a hand with that, Mr. Croner." Heather walked into the garage, her wounded arm gently bumping against her ribs.

"Can you manage it like that?"

She answered by using her good hand to slide the door shut with a satisfying metallic thud. "Sure. I'm not completely disabled, you know." She raised her uninjured arm and made a muscle, though not much of one.

"Thanks." Curiosity got the best of him. "What did you do to yourself anyway?"

"I fell down the damned dormitory steps while I was moving out. I'm such a klutz sometimes. Hey, I just came over to see if you wanted me to take Toby for a walk. I'm sorry that I haven't come by for a couple of days but I just forgot about it."

"Yeah, sure, if you want to. I think he's down in the basement somewhere."

Heather opened the connecting door for Ted and followed him into the house. Mary didn't notice Heather at first and, as she took one of the bags from Ted, her face suggested that she was about to make an angry comment about his tardiness. She changed course in mid sentence to take some of the sting out of the words. "It took you long enough…but thank you anyway. Hello, Heather. I hope you're looking forward to tomorrow."

"Oh, for sure. After nine months of cafeteria food, your cooking sounds better than ever." She dropped her voice slightly. "Mom's okay in the kitchen, but she cooks, you know, really bland. Dad's ulcer has been bothering him again."

Ted put the last bag down on the small table. "Heather has volunteered to take Toby for a walk."

"That's nice." Mary's voice rose to room temperature but still lacked warmth. "He missed you while you were away, Heather. Ted's not very good about taking him out."

Ted shifted his weight from one foot to the other, wanting to escape this conversation as quickly as possible. "I think he's downstairs someplace. Where's his leash?"

Mary rolled her eyes. "See what I mean? He doesn't even know where we keep poor Toby's leash." She walked over to the connecting door and reached behind it to take the leash down from the nail where it was hanging. She handed it to Heather, then turned back to the groceries. "I need to get some of these things into the refrigerator before they defrost."

That seemed like a good exit line. "Follow me, young lady." Ted gestured toward the basement door.

He led the way downstairs, calling Toby's name. There was no response initially, but Toby finally appeared, regarded Ted dubiously, then ran happily to Heather, who clipped the leash to his collar. She crouched and patted his head, used some baby talk that Ted found embarrassing and faintly annoying, then stood up. He had expected Heather to leave immediately but she had glanced toward the workbench. "What's that thing, Mr. Croner?"

He followed her eyes with his own. "That's a kaleidoscope, Heather. You know, you look through it and turn the drum and it makes a series of pretty patterns."

She walked over to the bench and raised her free arm as though to pick it up, but Ted hastily intercepted her. "It's broken, I'm afraid. The drum won't turn. I'm going to try to fix it when I have some time. I could show it to you then if you'd like."

Heather was clearly surprised, if not quite alarmed, by Ted's nervous intervention. "Oh, sorry."

Ted forced himself to speak more normally. "There's nothing to be sorry about. The drum is loose, so I have to be very careful with it." He realized, too late, that he was contradicting himself. The need to be alone with his thoughts was so intense that he shivered with tension and it was difficult to speak normally. "Toby hasn't been out for a good walk in quite a while so keep him as long as you want."

Heather seemed to relax slightly. "I thought we'd go down to the Sheffield Library and back. I'm used to hiking to classes all over the campus and it feels funny to be cooped up in the house so much. A long walk will probably be good for both of us."

Aware that she was still eyeing him warily, Ted made an effort to act normally, even though he felt the urge to take her by the arm and rush her up the stairs. "I always had trouble readjusting when I was home from college for the summer. My parents still thought of me as a kid, and I guess I wasn't quite an adult yet."

"Yeah, some of it's like that. I mean, I know it's home but it feels different now. Smaller, kind of. And right now Samantha has one of her boyfriends over and they're watching some stupid horror movie about an ax murderer. I can't stand that stuff. It gives me bad dreams."

Ted moved his feet restlessly. "Well, like I said, keep Toby as long as you want."

"Okay, but we won't be gone too long." And finally, mercifully, she led Toby up the stairs.

Ted didn't follow Heather, but he stood at the foot of the staircase until she was out of sight. Then he turned and walked directly back to the workbench, stared down at the kaleidoscope without touching it. He dismissed the possibility that he had gone completely insane. This was real. He had in his possession a device with which he could reshape his life. All he had to do was find the combination that best suited him. If he couldn't figure out the underlying system, then he might have to rely on trial and error.

First he needed to have a goal. If he could rebuild his life to order, what would he choose? He wanted to be rich, of course, so that he would no longer have to subject himself to working for people with inferior abilities. A few million would be enough, probably. And a sexy wife. He ran through a list of actresses and super models in his mind. There were several that fit the bill. But what if they had terrible personalities in their private lives? No, he'd be better off with someone he knew. Someone like Jennifer Hastings, for example, but a version of her that wouldn't be too upset if he strayed from time to time. But first he had to figure out how the damned thing worked.

He found a yellow lined pad and began jotting down notes, lists of things that had changed, arranged into groups before and after each time he had turned the drum. That turned out to be more difficult than he had expected. Had the picture in the den changed during the first transition or the second? He couldn't remember. And there were almost certainly many changes that he hadn't noticed. And were all the changes caused by the kaleidoscope? The Rogers might have bought themselves an aquarium. He didn't know that Jennifer's was missing because he hadn't been inside her house since the last change.

The list was shorter than he had expected, and there were question marks next to half the items. He made a perfunctory attempt to grade the degree of change. Did switching wives require more of a turn than moving a birdbath, for example? The birdbath had moved twice, but he'd only switched wives once, so not everything moved every time. Could he somehow decide which elements to move and which to leave alone? Ted tried to recall his state of mind at the different times he had used the kaleidoscope. Maybe only things he had thought about recently were affected. If he concentrated, could he direct the change? What good was this power to him if he couldn't control it? He could try over and over again until he reached a combination he liked, but that seemed terribly inefficient. For that matter, was there a limit to the number of times the magic would work? And was there a limit in scale? Could he change the results of the last Presidential election? Alter the balance of power in the Mideast? Make the Chicago Cubs win the World Series?

He couldn't begin to answer any of these questions without experimenting further, if even that would help. The results might indeed be completely random. He was trying to decide whether or not to try concentrating on a single element and tracking it through several changes, had even picked up the kaleidoscope speculatively when he heard Mary calling from upstairs.

"Come up and make yourself a sandwich, Ted. I have a list of things for you to get done this afternoon. You'd better stop fooling around down there and get going or you won't have time to finish." Pause. "Did you hear me, Ted?"

He sighed. "Anything's better than this." If he'd been fond of either books or movies, he would have known better to suggest that the situation couldn't possibly get worse.

Although he intended to concentrate on switching wives again, he wasn't sure just how to go about it, so he made a picture of Jennifer in his mind and closed his eyes, trying to imagine her lying in the bed upstairs. Then he turned the drum. It resisted at first, but after a few seconds Ted was able to rotate it almost a full half turn. He didn't look through the eye piece when he was done, just set it carefully back down onto the desk. His first impulse was to rush upstairs and find out what had changed, but now that he'd committed himself, he felt strangely reluctant to investigate. What if Mary was still there? He wasn't sure that he could face another confrontation without revealing his anxiety and confusion.

He straightened up the bench and cabinets, neither of which required his attention. Then he gave the symbols on the drum and shaft of the kaleidoscope another thorough examination, even though they meant no more to him now than they had before. He considered copying them onto a sheet of paper and taking them to…where? Ask a librarian for help? Consult books on occultism and witchcraft looking for matches? Even if he could find a correlation, how would that help?

Should he take the kaleidoscope with him or leave it here? Caution told him that it would not be wise to let other people know of its existence. They couldn't know about its power, he supposed, but something might happen to it. The risk was unnecessary. He put it inside one of the cabinets where it would be out of sight. Ted dithered a while longer, untying and retying his shoelaces, then pulled himself together, took a deep breath, and started up the stairs.

He moved as quietly as possible and reached the den without incident. The house felt empty. The landscape was back on the wall and Roscoe was curled up on the couch, asleep, which told him that there had been changes, and not things he'd been thinking about. The television was off. Two cut roses sat on top of it in a narrow necked vase.

"Roscoe! Welcome home, again." He kept his voice low, reached down and stroked the cat, which opened one eye, stretched languorously, then settled back to sleep some more. "I guess you don't even know you were gone, do you?"

A door opened, then closed. Ted froze, identified it as the door connecting the kitchen and garage. His mouth was dry and he was afraid to call out. After a few seconds, he heard a rattle from the kitchen, someone moving pots or pans. He took a deep breath, turned and walked through the small connecting passage and entered the kitchen. At first he thought the room was empty after all, but then he realized that someone was crouched on the opposite side of the table, rummaging in one of the lower cabinets.

He wanted to know who it was, but the strength seemed to have leeched out of his legs and he was momentarily unable to move forward to discover the truth. Sooner or later, whoever it was would stand up and he'd know. That was good enough, he decided. No sense in rushing into things. Let them come to him naturally and he would be able to accept everything calmly. After all, he could always go back down into the basement and change things again if they didn't suit him. What could happen?

The crouched figure abruptly stood up, brandishing a frying pan. Her face was turned away and for a second, he thought it was a stranger because the only blonde he knew of was Heather, and this person was much too short to be Heather. But then the figure turned and he saw that it was Samantha. And her hair wasn't the only thing that had changed. She had lost her glasses a couple of turns back, but she was dressed differently as well, her clothes tighter. Ted thought her figure had improved, although that might just be an illusion conveyed by her new style sense.

But Samantha? "No way," he whispered under his breath. She wasn't even sixteen yet. But what was she doing in his kitchen?

She saw him, of course, but her eyes displayed no flicker of alarm or even interest. He might just as well have been a piece of furniture. The door to the garage suddenly opened and Samantha turned in that direction. "I found the frying pan, but the barbecue tools aren't here."

Ted felt a rush of relief as Beth stepped into the kitchen, one arm in a sling. She was back, obviously. It was the first time in a long while that he was actually glad to know that she was his wife, at least temporarily. She would have to go, of course, but better her than Mary. He found his voice. "What's up, Samantha? Did Beth recruit you into helping get ready for the big event tomorrow?"

Samantha's eyes registered his existence for the first time since he'd entered the room. "Yeah, she says that's what kid sisters are for. To be ordered around, I mean." She seemed indifferent to his reaction and turned away before he could respond. Beth gave him a neutral glance and carried a small grocery bag over to the refrigerator.

"Sisters? Well, that's different." He spoke aloud without meaning to.

"What's different?" It was an automatic response. Samantha clearly didn't have much regard for Ted's opinion. She started opening cupboards at random, apparently still seeking the barbecue tools which, he remembered, were actually out in the garage. Or that's where they'd been originally. They might be in the bathroom now for all he knew.

"Oh, nothing. Just thinking out loud."

Beth finished emptying her bag and closed the refrigerator door. She took a pack of cigarettes out of her pocket, placed it in her bad hand, and extracted one. Beth had always hated cigarettes and the image of her smoking was jarring. Ted was quite proud of himself for managing not to react. On some level, he had almost expected it. He smiled to himself when he noticed that she was wearing a tight tee-shirt with the word THINK blanketing her breasts. It had been quite a while since had noticed Beth's figure and he had to admit that she had kept herself in good shape, better than he had in fact. He was perceptive enough to realize that the events of the last few hours were changing his perceptions of the people around him. Of course, that only made sense since they were changing as well, at least in subtle ways.

Beth glanced in his direction with eyes that betrayed no more interest than had Samantha's, and Ted felt a momentary sense of loss. There had been a time when she had looked at him differently, just as he had seen in her a sexy, interesting person with whom he thought he might be able to spend his life. Had they changed so completely in just these few short years, or had they just gotten so used to one another that there were no longer any surprises? I can make things better, he told himself. All I have to do is turn the kaleidoscope until I find the right combination. That's all life was, after all. Everyone searched for the secret combination that would open the safe and reveal the goodies that lay within. It was a long, tedious, and uncertain process, and Ted acknowledged that it was hard work to maintain a viable relationship. Maybe he and Beth had just been too lazy these last couple of years. Lazy and predictable.

The kaleidoscope might not be predictable, but it could certainly shake things up in a hurry. There had been times when he had told himself his marriage could be exciting again, if both of them put some work into it. Sometimes he had even tried. But in the long run, Ted couldn't stick with it; he always fell back into his old way of doing things. What they had needed was a shortcut. Ted just might have found one.

"Are you going to light this for me or not?" Ted automatically patted his pockets, even though he hadn't smoked since high school. Beth gave him a weary look and nodded toward the table. "The lighter is in the fruit bowl, right where it always is."

He found it and lit her cigarette, trying to disguise the fact that his hands were shaking badly. She didn't seem to notice or, if she did, obviously didn't care.

Beth took a long draw and exhaled a plume of smoke. "We're going to need the galvanized tub for beer and soft drinks tomorrow, and you'll have to go out and get some ice first thing in the morning. And you were going to check and see if we have enough charcoal. I didn't pick any up while I was shopping because you said you thought you had plenty, but you need to double check or we'll be rushing around trying to find some tomorrow."

Ted had been feeling more than slightly divorced from reality but the nagging tone in her voice broke the spell. Newfound sister or not, this was the Beth he knew, and her worst side. His voice became defensive. "The galvanized tub is down in the basement where it's supposed to be. All I have to do is hose it off to get rid of the dust. And there are three full bags of charcoal in the garage, plus what's left in the hopper outside."

Beth made a skeptical sound. "If the charcoal is buried under all of that yard sale junk, we might never find it. Or the weight of the boxes on top of them might have compressed them into diamonds."

"Very funny. No sweat, I know exactly where they are." Or at least, he knew where they had been. The down side of his situation was becoming more evident. He couldn't trust his memories, even about little things. Particularly about little things, because the big things were obvious and he could adjust to them.

"Well, just don't wait until the last minute again." She flapped her injured arm. "Obviously I can't pitch in and help lug things around like I usually end up doing."

Samantha made a sound that was somewhere between amusement and contempt. Her smug expression suddenly irritated him and Ted turned toward the more vulnerable target. "I'm sure your sister would be more than happy to fill in for you and help, wouldn't you, Samantha?"

She faced him squarely and made no effort to disguise her dislike. "Whatever. It's not as if anything I say matters."

Beth either didn't notice the byplay or, more likely, just didn't care. "I've already given Sam a long list of things to do, Ted. I would feel a lot better if you confirmed that the charcoal was really there. We can improvise for a lot of other things, but if there's no charcoal, there's no cookout. It won't take that long to check."

"All right!" His briefly revived affection for Beth had already dissipated and he felt familiar anger, resentment, and frustration. "I'll take care of it right after lunch."

"You might as well do it now," said Beth. "We won't be eating for a while yet. I forgot to defrost the chicken last night. I suppose we could heat up the stew from the other night."

Samantha made a disapproving sound, pulled out a chair and sat down. "Speaking of disgusting stuff, Roscoe left a dead mouse on the front steps again."

Ted smirked. "What did you do with it? I assume you're not suggesting that for lunch."

She made a face. "You don't expect me to touch something that's dead, do you? That's your job. He's your cat."

"Afraid of a dead mouse." He decided to gloat. "I thought only little girls were bothered by things like that."

"I'm not afraid. It's just not my job," she said huffily.

"Man's work, huh?"

"Whatever."

Ted transferred the dead mouse to the garbage can and automatically shifted some of the other trash so that neither Beth nor Samantha would open the can and find the thoroughly chewed and almost unrecognizable corpse. Beth had taken some garbage out once when he'd failed to cover Roscoe's victim and her theatrics had not amused him. For the moment, he put all thought of the kaleidoscope out of his mind.

Although things had returned to something like normal – if having a new and previously non-existent sister-in-law could be called normal – he still had the feeling that he was rushing heedlessly down a slippery slope with no idea of what might lie at the end of the path. His thoughts raced so frantically that he had trouble arranging them in an orderly fashion and decided to escape into familiar routine for long enough to gather his wits. It occurred to him now that he was taking a considerable risk each time he turned the kaleidoscope. What if the magic ran out and he became trapped in some version of reality even worse than the one where he'd started?

He went out into the garage and began shifting boxes. He knew where the charcoal was, almost exactly, if it hadn't moved, but he had to admit that there was quite a bit of stuff blocking the way. He didn't recognize all of the items he moved, but some of them had been here for months and he couldn't honestly claim that he remembered just what he had bought or scavenged. He did find a box of aquarium supplies which he was sure he'd never seen previously, but otherwise he found the physical exertion soothing for a change.

After a few minutes of lifting and carrying, he spotted the corner of one of the bags of charcoal and breathed a sigh of relief. It was still where he had left it, or so close that he couldn't tell the difference. Now it was just a matter of clearing enough away boxes that he could pull the bags out without toppling everything over. That proved to be more difficult than he'd expected because he'd interwoven the stacks to provide greater stability for the whole structure, and he ended up moving fully a third of the cartons and bags before he could safely retrieve the first bag of charcoal.

When he pulled it away from the other two, something scuttled across the back of his hand and he retreated quickly, cursing under his breath. Spiders! God how he hated the damned things. His hands were shaking and his heart was pounding. More than anything else just now, he wanted to leave the garage, forget about the charcoal, and more particularly forget about multi-legged creatures that lurked in the darkness. Beetles, ants, even wasps he could take in stride, but spiders and centipedes made his skin crawl. He started back toward the house, but realized that Beth would pick at him if he didn't get things done according to her schedule, so he located the push broom in one corner and used it to clear away all the cobwebs, poked into various corners, even shifted the bags slightly so that all of the lurking squatters would know the world was changing and that they needed to retreat to darker, more remote recesses of the garage.

Even then, he examined each bag minutely before lifting it up, and he carried them around the house and into the back yard as quickly as possible, dumped them hastily, brushing off his clothing immediately and inspecting himself to make sure that he hadn't overlooked any arachnid hitchhikers. When the last bag had been shifted, he made a cursory effort to restack the boxes he'd moved, but he was tired and hungry and besides, maybe he could just turn the kaleidoscope and find them all neatly rearranged. If he could figure out how to control the changes, he'd have one nifty labor saving device.

Beth and Samantha were washing off dishes that weren't exactly dirty but which hadn't been out of their cupboards in months. A package of chicken cutlets was defrosting in the sink. Ted considered suggesting that they use the microwave to speed up the process, but decided that if he attracted attention to himself, he'd only be assigned another chore, so he slipped quietly out the back door and pretended to be straightening up the barbecue grill and surrounding area. He glanced at the picnic table, half expecting the toilet plunger to be there, but it had disappeared.

Drawing in a long breath, he sat down at the table and tried to get his thoughts in order.

If there was a way to control the details of the changes, it probably involved knowledge that he didn't have, and wasn't likely to acquire. For all he knew there was a distinct and predictable pattern, but it was invisible to him and unless inspiration struck out of the blue, he seemed unlikely to discover it. So he decided to assume, at least for the moment, that functionally the changes were completely random. Given that situation, he could only hope that he stumbled upon the right, or at least a relatively optimal, combination of changes that he could live with. Maybe eventually he would be able to direct the power in some fashion, but not in the short run. On the other hand, what if there was a finite limit to the number of times he could change things? It would be just his luck to find himself stuck in some variation in which he and Mary were married and had the two girls as their children – or was that possible? He was too old to have fathered either of them unless he'd been very precocious indeed. His head began to ache and he stood up, feeling the need to move around.

He glanced next door and realized that he wasn't alone. Carl Rogers was diffidently trimming a row of rose bushes that crowded against this side of his house, rose bushes which Ted would have sworn had never been there before although they were so thick and tall that they clearly were not newly planted. Behind the house was a small dog house and a fenced area. The name TOBY was painted on the top rail of the fence. So that was back to normal as well. Maybe he'd reached the limit of how much change he could initiate and now things would recede back toward the original version of the world with each subsequent turn until they were back the way they had started. The possibility depressed him. To have this much power and opportunity within his grasp, and then to have it slip away seemed intolerable. No, he'd keep turning the damned thing until his arm ached before he'd let himself be trapped in the old life, which suddenly seemed to him an unbearable burden under which he'd labored for years.

Carl straightened up and dropped his shears onto the lawn, mopping his brow with the back of one hand. He must have been aware of Ted for some time, but had pretended not to notice him. Probably rehearsing a speech in his head, Ted told himself. None of Carl's conversations seemed entirely spontaneous. It was as if he had a file of lesson plans hidden away inside his brain. He'd listen to a conversation for a while without contributing while the little man in his head sorted through the files to find just the right one. Then Carl would launch into one of his perorations as though he was standing in front of a classroom. Carl took out his handkerchief and mopped his forehead, then and started walking toward him. "Getting set up for the big day tomorrow?"

Ted shrugged. "The boss isn't happy unless we're at least a day ahead of schedule. And even if we were, she'd still be lecturing me about waiting until the last minute."

Carl chuckled dutifully. "I know what you mean. Mary is the same way when we entertain. I've never understood that attitude. We get together to have a good time, so why get uptight in advance? These things always work out in the end and if there's a hitch, well, we're all friends. We're not trying to impress each other."

Ted knew that wasn't true and suspected that Ted did as well. Every time the two families got together, they were competing in some fashion, even if they weren't consciously aware of it. Mary had planted the roses in response to Beth's much more successful gardening attempts. Ted had bought the oversized barbecue grill after the Rogers put in a small patio and hosted their first mutual cookout. But it would never do to acknowledge the truth. "I gave up trying to understand the feminine mind years ago."

The back door swung open and Samantha emerged. She looked around, spotted Ted, and came directly toward him. "Beth says to remind you that we need lighter fluid for the charcoal." Her voice was a monotone and her eyes never even focused on him. Ted thought he could sense her mentally checking off another chore completed in her mental to-do list and felt insulted to have been relegated to being a task rather than a person.

He grimaced and his voice betrayed his irritation. "I already told her that I have enough lighter fluid to burn down the entire town of Managansett. Twice." But he decided he'd better check again, just to be sure.

Samantha frowned, deliberately finding offense where none was intended. "Well you don't have to take it out on me. I'm just the messenger." She spun on her heel and started back to the house, her rigid posture suggesting that she'd been mortally insulted and would never forgive him this side of the grave. Ted found himself focusing on the way her hips swayed and looked away, afraid that Carl might have noticed.

He shook his head in exasperation and Carl nodded sympathetically. "Teenagers. She's a cute kid, Ted, but I don't know if I could manage to put up with her for an entire summer. You must have nerves of steel or a capacity for charity that exceeds mine."

"I promise you it wasn't my idea." That much he was certain of. Even in this altered version of reality, he would never have suggested anything that would result in his sharing the house with two women. Even for a couple of months. Or at least not these two women. Now if it had been Jennifer and Heather, that might have been interesting. His thoughts strayed back to the kaleidoscope.

Carl seemed reflective. "Are you and Beth considering having kids of your own someday?"

Ted shrugged. "We've talked about it, but the timing has never been right. We both had jobs and we needed the two paychecks to come up with the down payment on the house, and pay the mortgage afterward. And now that I'm out of work, we can't chance Beth getting pregnant and losing our only remaining source of income. But someday, I guess, we'll reach that point." Or not, he thought to himself.

Carl was nodding sympathetically. "Mary and I were going to have kids originally. We talked about it all the time when we were younger. But I had to finish law school first and we moved around a lot during those first few years. When we finally came to Providence and got settled in one spot for a while, we talked about it again and decided that we both liked the lifestyle we'd adopted and didn't want to risk changing it. Not that there's anything wrong with children in general, of course, but it just wasn't right for us. This way we each have an office at home and there's one guest bedroom for emergencies. We like the way things worked out, even if we do have occasional regrets. I'd like to have grand kids, but only if I could skip the intermediate steps. You and Beth are still young though. You've got plenty of time."

Ted nodded sympathetically. This was the first time he had

actually felt as though he was sharing something personal with his neighbor. They had never really been friends; they didn't have much in common. Carl hated sports and loved politics; Ted was still in mourning for his Patriots season ticket, which he'd been unable to renew this past year, and hadn't voted in his life. He had never even registered.

"Maybe some day we'll take that step. Right now, I think a kid would demand a lot more attention than either of us could supply."

Carl laughed politely. "Now you sound like my wife, the economics teacher."

Ted wasn't really interested in arguing the value of having kids or choosing not to, but the mechanism of the changed world fascinated him. If the attitudes of his neighbors had changed this dramatically, were they actually the same people that they had been before? Was the reorientation absolute, or did some lingering memories bleed over from one reality to the next? Jennifer had hinted that she felt something was missing from her life, that she'd taken the wrong path somewhere. Could this be a residual attitude from earlier, when she'd been a lawyer rather than a teacher? If so, was it possible that Carl might have some vague, half memories of having had children? He hadn't sounded unhappy, so maybe even back in the first reality, he would have preferred it if they hadn't had kids. Maybe it was all Mary's idea to raise a family. If so, then Carl might well be happier now than he had been. For the first time it occurred to Ted that changing the world might help someone other than himself. On the other hand, if that was true, was Mary secretly depressed? Carl, the original Carl, would probably have described this as the law of conservation of contentment or some such.

"So you don't feel as though there's anything missing from your lives? Something you might have had at one time but lost somewhere along the way?"

Carl seemed to consider the question thoughtfully. "Naturally, I wonder sometimes what it would have been like to have a larger family. I'm sure Mary does the same. Like I said, I wouldn't mind being a grandfather, but it's all those years in between that are discouraging. Changing diapers, teaching them about sex and drugs and booze, paying college tuition, worrying about who they're going to marry. Look at Jennifer next door, for example. If she's not at the bank working long hours to earn a living, she's home trying to deal with that hopeless sister of hers. It's just not fair."

"Her sister?" Ted was momentarily confused, then mentally counted heads. "You mean Heather?"

If Carl had noticed Ted's hesitation, he gave no indication, instead settling into what Ted recognized as a familiar lecture mode. Some things hadn't changed. "Heather's not really a bad girl, I suppose. Just troubled. But that word gets applied to a lot of thoroughly bad kids as well as the ones who are actually under stress. I feel for the girl. It must be tough to lose your parents that way and then have to move in with an older sister who already has a career and plans of her own. But now even though Jennifer has readjusted her entire life to accommodate the new situation, her sister is apparently unwilling to meet her halfway and help. I look at the two of them and I think that even if Mary and I had decided to have children, and had done everything reasonable to raise them to be responsible, self sufficient, and intelligent young adults, there would still be the chance that we'd have the same kind of problems. Kids are more influenced by schools, movies, friends, and other external forces than by their parents, so it's not surprising that so many of them turn out warped. For Mary and I, it just didn't seem worth the risk."

"I suppose not." Ted's curiosity had succumbed to the usual numbness that crept over him whenever he was subjected to one of Carl's extended excursions into oration. "Look, I need to get going and finish up a few more projects or Beth will have my head mounted over the television set. We'll talk again tomorrow."

Carl stirred himself but made no effort to leave. "We'll be there. Beth and I are going to provide the dessert. I know she's a train wreck in the kitchen, but I'll be directing traffic and it makes her feel better if she thinks she's helping. I promise it'll be edible."

"Dessert?" Ted's curiosity overcame his desire to walk away.

"Yeah. I'm thinking raspberry tarts."

Ted nodded. Of course it would be. "Great. See you then."

Carl returned to his rose bushes and Ted finished puttering around as though he was actually trying to accomplish something.

As soon as a decent period had passed, he went to the back door. He needed to jot down his latest observations while they were still fresh in his mind. There might still be a pattern to the changes, if he could just accumulate enough data points. And he had another idea as well.

Beth caught him as he was about to go down to the basement. "Hold it right there! You're not going to disappear into your basement tree fort while the rest of us are doing all the work."

Ted froze, but a sudden inspiration saved the day. "I'm just going to check on the lighter fluid. You know, for the charcoal."

Beth looked dubious, but retreated with a half hearted riposte. "Well don't take all day finding it. We're falling behind schedule. Samantha and I are going out for a few minutes to pick up a few things we forgot. Are you absolutely certain you have everything you need for the grill?"

"Absolutely."

Her face said that he had better be, but she turned away without expressing an opinion verbally. Samantha was already standing at the front door, calling impatiently, and a few seconds later Ted heard the car start up.

He was in no hurry. In fact he waited until Beth and Samantha had turned out of Bailey's Court, then searched the front room and found the morning newspaper. Beth had already thrown it into a wastebasket even though he hadn't had time to read it yet. Another detail that had remained the same. He carried it down to the basement and spread it out on his workbench, then methodically began reading various articles from each section, even the political stories and social columns. Roscoe showed up and decided to sleep on one corner of the paper, and gave Ted a reproachful look when he was pushed to a bare spot on the bench.

"Sorry, guy, but I need to read this." Every few minutes his glance swerved to the cabinet where the kaleidoscope rested out of sight. He'd think for a few seconds, then turn the page and read some more. When he finally reached the comics in the back, he folded the paper and threw it in the waste bin under the bench.

"Well, Roscoe, it's obvious that I'm either completely crazy or this thing really works. I'm also pretty sure that it has a very limited range; at least I couldn't find anything in the paper suggesting that it's changing the world, or the country, or even the town. Everything's just the way I remember it. So maybe it's just us and the Rogers and Jennifer."

Roscoe didn't have an opinion on the subject.

Ted picked up the kaleidoscope and stared at it. "Assuming that I'm right and everything is the same except at this end of the street, then we don't have to worry about starting a war or anything like that. Let's call that Rule Number One – the range is very limited. I have to bring it close to something, or someone, if I want it to have any effect. I suppose I could take it to Washington and sneak up on the White House and maybe become President, but let's confine ourselves to something a little closer to home." Already he was thinking about the possibilities though. Could he take it to Eblis Manufacturing and keep turning it until he was the plant manager? Or go into a bank and shift the accounts around until he had plenty of money? He was tempted to try the latter right away, but it was Saturday and he wouldn't be able to take out any money even if his savings did suddenly balloon. "Time for that later," he told himself.

Once more he considered the possibility that the magic would run out, that he only had a limited number of tries, but he discarded the thought. This was meant to happen, he was convinced. This is the tool with which I will achieve the life that was always intended for me. It won't stop working until I've reached my goal, if then.

A door slammed upstairs and he heard footsteps. He glanced at his watch and was startled to realize that almost an hour had passed. The door opened and Beth called down to him. "Ted? Are you still down there? Did you find the lighter fluid?"

"Yes, I have it." He didn't, actually, but he had noticed two cans sitting on a shelf under the stairs. One of them had never been opened, so there was no problem.

"I notice you haven't cleaned the old ashes out of the grill yet."

Ted bit back his anger. "Don't worry. I'll take care of it this afternoon. Everything is under control."

"Well don't wait to the last minute. And don't spend all day on that yard sale junk. You know it's just a waste of time. If everything is under control here, Sam and I are going to the mall in Providence for a while. We'll get something to eat at the food court, but you'll have to fend for yourself. I'll save the chicken for supper. Is there anything you need while we're out?"

His stomach rumbled at the reminder that he hadn't eaten yet, but at the moment he was more interested in peace and quiet than food. "I'll be fine. Take your time."

He waited, expecting an answer, but Samantha was saying something that he couldn't quite make out and he heard the door close, cutting off the conversation completely. Ted breathed a sigh of relief and turned back to Roscoe. "Okay, here's Rule Number Two. Everything that changed existed somewhere already. I don't know that for sure, but we haven't seen anything pop up that wasn't here before, and it makes sense. The crystals in the kaleidoscope get rearranged but there's never anything new added. So I can't hope to sit here and turn it until I'm rich because neither of our neighbors is rich, and I can't get Sandra Bullock to be my wife unless she happens to stop by." He paused thoughtfully. "Or if I go someplace where she already is." Ted shook his head. More ambitious changes were certainly possible, but small steps were a better policy until he knew, more or less, what he was doing.

He was quiet for a while. "And finally, for now, we have Rule Number Three. Nobody except me remembers what things were like before, and as far as I can tell, I haven't changed at all. So whoever it is that operates the kaleidoscope is immune from its effects. At least I hope that's how it works. I suppose if I was changing too, I wouldn't be any more aware of it than the others. What do you think, Roscoe?"

Roscoe yawned and promptly went back to sleep. "I am overwhelmed by your enthusiasm," said Ted.

He suddenly felt the need to experiment, to exercise his new found power, but he realized that he was isolated, without transportation. On the other hand, he could walk to the strip mall easily enough. He could try the kaleidoscope there without changing anything else that directly affected him, safely out of range of Bailey's Court. He opened the cabinet and took out the kaleidoscope, weighed it in one hand. A potential problem occurred to him. If he walked into the mall carrying it openly, there was always the chance that someone would ask about it, want to look through it. It would be disastrous if someone else turned the drum because Ted himself would no longer be immune to change, and might well forget about its power.

He felt a wave of sudden insecurity. Maybe it would be best if he kept it right here in the basement. Beth almost never came down except to use the washing machine. What about Samantha? This Samantha? Did she poke around where she didn't belong? Maybe he should put a padlock on one of the cabinet doors and keep it locked inside. But if he never took it out of the house, the possibilities of change would be severely circumscribed.

It was safest in his possession. But if he went to the strip mall, could he disguise it somehow? Inspiration came suddenly. Ted poked around on the shelves under the stairs, the accumulation spot for things too good to throw away but which lacked any immediate use, until he found a zippered shoulder bag designed for carrying a laptop. It was one of his yard sale acquisitions. He slipped the kaleidoscope inside – it barely fit – and zipped it shut. The strap went over his shoulder and the case fit snug against his hip. Perfect! He went upstairs.

The shopping center was about six blocks away. It had started as a single small building, part of a chain of convenience stores, but the parent company had foundered and the individual locations became franchises for a while, then independents. This particular one, renamed Rapid-Mart, was owned by Arnold Bezwan, an Iranian who slept in the back of the store and manned the cash register sixteen hours every day, seven days a week. There were no other employees. Arnold – that wasn't his original name but he was a big fan of the Terminator movies and had had it legally changed – had added a coffee machine and fresh donuts, sprinkled a few chairs around, and had reinvented the traditional country store, at least after a fashion. He had about a dozen regulars, mostly retirees, who dropped in almost daily and often spent hours there watching television with Arnold and solving the problems of the world.

About a year after Arnold bought the property, the Rapid-Mart found itself flanked by a small Laundromat, now an auto parts store and an antiques shop, which had recently gone out of business. There was no room to expand further along Boswell Avenue, but the land behind the antique store had been undeveloped for two full blocks. A local developer had bulldozed down all the trees and built a small strip mall, but it was a terrible location and the names of the individual stores there changed almost seasonally. At the moment, there was an independent drug store, a movie rental place, a used furniture dealer, a magazine shop that actually derived most of its profit selling tobacco products, a pet store, and a Chinese restaurant way at the far end that had recently replaced Ted's favorite pizza parlor. He didn't like Chinese food.

Ted found his mood changing as he walked. The world around him was so ordinary and familiar that the events of the last few hours began to feel like some sort of bad dream from which he had suddenly awakened. There was even the faintest hint of a refreshing breeze from time to time, although the sun still beat down relentlessly. Other than a brief encounter with a dog – who ran out into the street, barked tentatively in Ted's direction, then continued onward, vanishing in the low brush that covered an undeveloped lot, Ted's walk was uneventful and he reached the exit from Bailey's Court lost in thought.

He turned left on Lowridge and walked past three houses to the intersection with Boswell. The dog wandered into view again, but seemed to have lost interest in Ted. It was probably going to try to scavenge in the dumpsters behind the strip mall.

The Rapid-Mart was directly across Boswell, and currently had two cars parked in front. Mom's Antiques was dark although the signs were still up. EZ Auto Parts was open, but none of the parking spaces in front of it were filled. Ted waited while one slow moving car approached and passed, then crossed the street.

Arnold was behind the register as he always was, talking to one of the regulars, an elderly man with a startling shock of white hair. A younger man was poking around in the milk locker and a teenaged couple was looking through the magazines and giggling a lot. Arnold nodded at Ted as he entered without so much as a waver from whatever subject he was expounding upon. Ted walked over to the newspaper rack and took a fresh copy of the Providence paper.

He read it quickly, scanned it actually, just the titles of the stories, searching for any indication that the greater world had undergone sudden strange changes that hadn't been reflected in his copy at home. As far as he could tell, everything was just as it had been. The economy sucked, the Arabs and Israelis were shooting at one another, the Europeans were arguing about currency devaluation, and Congress was trying to develop a new immigration policy. Another big city mayor had been indicted and gas prices were rising again. The names changed but the stories were always the same. The only thing at all surprising was mention that James Nicholson, his old boss, was going to be honored by the Managansett Chamber of Commerce that very day for his contributions to the community at a ceremony at the local Good Fellows Club. Ted felt that he knew Nicholson better than most, and there wasn't a philanthropic bone in the man's body. If he'd done anything charitable, it was because he expected a significant return on his investment, probably marking down a favor he could call in at some future time.

He tucked the paper under his arm, then picked out some candy bars and carried them to the register along with the newspaper. It wasn't the most balanced lunch he could have had, but it would be quick and satisfying. Arnold added up Ted's selections in his head and rang up a single entry while Ted was pulling out his wallet. "How's it going, Arnold?"

Arnold's accent had been quite strong when he had first arrived, but by now the constant chatter with his customers had polished his speech to the point where it was almost undetectable. "Not so good, Mr. Croner. Last night I had no customers for almost three hours. I might as well have turned off the lights and gone to bed."

"Things are tough all over I guess." Ted accepted his change without counting it, tucked the candy bars and the newspaper into his zipper bag.

"How's that neighbor of yours doing?" asked the white haired man.

Ted had exchanged a few words with the man in the past, but never anything personal and didn't remember his name. Hal? Harry? Something like that. "Which neighbor did you have in mind?"

The old man stirred in his seat and looked out the front window. "The wild one. You know, the youngster who's always getting into trouble with the cops. Hattie? Helen? I don't remember her damned name." Ted knew who the man was talking about and remembered his name as well. Horace.

"Heather," Ted suggested. "You must be talking about Heather." The kaleidoscope might not be able to change things beyond its narrow range, but the rest of the world apparently altered enough to recognize and accommodate those changes. That was good. It would be rather awkward if he managed to end up with Jennifer as his wife, only to discover that everyone outside of Bailey's Court still thought he was married to Beth.

Arnold remained silent, but attentive. He had always avoided doing anything that might alienate a potential customer, so he'd listen to gossip but as far as Ted knew, he never repeated it. At worst he'd shake his head ambiguously and leave you to guess what he really thought.

"I guess that's the one I mean. My wife has the police band on all the time and she tells me the girl is a real hellion. Damn thing drives me crazy, which is why I'm always over here." He chuckled and glanced at Arnold. "The conversation's a lot better."

The teenagers had moved from the magazine rack to the soda cooler but appeared more interested in a little awkward necking than in cold drinks. The other man paid for cigarettes and a package of hamburger rolls and left without speaking.

Horace seemed to have lost interest so Ted decided to nudge him a bit. It might be helpful to understand how the outside world perceived the new situation. "What's she been up to lately? I haven't been paying attention." It wasn't really a lie.

"Fights, mostly. And sneaking into places where she's not supposed to be. They've already banned her from the Loft for fighting in their bar, and she's been thrown out of a couple of other places. Bad language. Shoplifting." He dropped his voice. "And soliciting."

Arnold apparently felt compelled to intervene in defense of his customer. "Young people have no discipline. She'll grow out of it."

Maybe sooner than you think, thought Ted. "I imagine so." He nodded agreeably and left. But he didn't go far.

At one time there had been a drive in photo developing booth on a small, elevated concrete pad at the corner of what was now the tiny parking lot. It had been abandoned and the roof had blown off in a bad storm a couple of years later, so Arnold had torn down what remained and replaced it with a pair of salvaged park benches so that in nice weather his customers could sit outside, drink their coffee and read their morning newspapers. Ted dropped down onto one of them and took a deep breath, then quickly ate two of his candy bars. It didn't completely satisfy his hunger, but it took the edge off.

He glanced back through the front window, saw that the teenagers had finally approached the cash register. Now that the time had come to find out whatever it was that he thought he might discover here, Ted felt oddly reluctant. The immensity of the power implicit in the situation was unnerving, even frightening. He wasn't worried about disrupting the lives of the people around him. After all, whatever new reality emerged would feel perfectly normal to them. He was the only one who would know that changes had been made. And they might even be better off, after all. Telling himself that he wasn't actually going to harm anyone, he reached into the zipper bag with both hands and without removing the kaleidoscope managed to move the drum. It took considerable effort and it only turned about a third of the way, but it had definitely moved. Ted immediately zipped the bag shut again and glanced back at the window.

The male half of the young couple, who had a terrible case of acne, now stood behind the counter accepting money from Arnold, who held a magazine and a sports drink in his free hand. The boy made change and Arnold emerged, nodded absently to Ted, got into one of the parked cars and drove off. It was Arnold's car, Ted remembered, but he had never seen it anywhere except parked behind the store, and it had presumably been parked there when he had arrived. It was the first time Ted had ever seen it move and in the past he had idly wondered if it was a prop rather than a functioning automobile, something left there solely to advertise that the store was open.

Curiosity drove him back inside. The teenager smiled familiarly. "Forget something, Mr. Croner?" There was no sign of the old man or the teenaged girl.

"I thought I might get something cold to drink. It's brutal out there today." He walked straight to the back of the store and stood in front of the coolers, considering his choices. There was the usual variety of soft drinks and bottled fruit juice, but his eyes were drawn to an unfamiliar label. Motor oil. Ted blinked, glanced toward the front of the store, then back, shaking his head. He took out a bottle of apple juice.

A cursory walk through the store revealed two more anachronisms. The digital clock on the wall had been replaced by an ornate and clearly very elderly wooden one, which didn't seem to be working. He almost failed to notice the magazine rack, which was dominated by celebrity and teen oriented magazines, but which had a thirty year old *Saturday Evening Post* with a torn cover featuring a Norman Rockwell painting tucked among them.

Ted paid for his second purchase and stepped outside. He glanced through the adjacent window and spotted the missing girl, who appeared to be buying a fan belt. The proprietor was the same heavyset man who always seemed to glower at his customers, but just beyond his shoulder Ted could see the lottery ticket machine which he now realized was missing from the convenience store.

He wandered over to the bench, trying to decide if he had learned anything useful other than confirmation that the effects of the change were confined to a very small area. It was only then that he noticed that two of the signs had changed. They now read, incongruously, Mom's Auto Parts and EZ Antiques.

Ted's next thought was to head back home and review everything that had happened, but he was so excited by the possibilities that he was reluctant to stop so soon. All of his life, Ted had sought power. For the most part, he had done so in socially acceptable ways. When he was employed, he pushed for advancement, expansion of his authority. When unemployed, he refused to consider any position which fell short of the level of prestige – i.e. power – to which he felt he was entitled. His thirst for control had contributed to his unpopularity with his previous employers and his determination not to settle for less than an "appropriate" amount of power was the largest factor in his current job situation.

Nor was this compulsion confined to his working life. When he and Beth had first married, she had deferred to him on almost every occasion, allowing him to make the decisions that had shaped their lives together. He had consulted her as a matter of form before they'd moved to the house in Bailey's Court, but it was clear to her that the decision had already been made. It was Ted who had concluded they were not yet ready to have children. He had offered a number of reasons why it made sense to wait, but the truth was that he was put off by thoughts of the inevitable anarchy that would attend the arrival of one or more youngsters. Beth was not unintelligent and had quickly discerned his real reasons, but she had never challenged him on the subject.

Ted resented Carl Rogers in large part because his neighbor dominated conversations and held a position of authority as department head at Managansett High School – or at least had until Ted had begun meddling, but he also despised Carl because he was not the undisputed boss in his own home. Mary clearly made many if not all of the important domestic decisions. If the man had had a son, Ted reasoned, he might have been shamed into standing up for himself, but with two daughters, he was outnumbered and defeated.

Ted had lusted for power for years and now he was able to alter the lives of other people in an unprecedented and unchallengeable way. The only drawbacks were the unpredictability of the changes and the fact that no one would ever know that he was the puppet master pulling the strings because only he was aware of what was happening. Chaotic or not, the power represented by the kaleidoscope had completely seduced him. The more he used it, the more he wanted to use it.

Ted reached into his bag and touched the shaft, just to be sure it was still there. He had no conscious plan to use it again so soon, but he let his hand stay, and almost of its own volition his other arm moved and he was holding the drum as well as the shaft. It was almost as if the kaleidoscope was willing him to make use of it, although if that was the case, he reflected, it was sure playing hard to get. He strained awkwardly and was rewarded with a barely perceptible movement.

He glanced around but there were no obvious signs that anything had changed. The boy was still behind the counter, leaning back in his seat and staring idly out the front window. Then Ted realized that the magazine rack had switched places with the bread and rolls and was now on the right hand side of the store instead of the left. Horace was back in sight just inside the door, looking at one of the magazines. Ted walked across the parking lot so that he could peer through the window into the next aisle, but there was no sign of the girl there or in the auto parts store. He did notice that the latter now displayed the antique clock on the wall, but that was the only obvious difference.

The convenience store door opened and the girl walked out, apparently having stood somewhere out of Ted's line of sight, carrying a small plastic bag bearing her purchases, and crossed to the benches. She sat down, took a can of soda out of her bag, popped the top, and took a long drink. Ted walked back to the second bench, glancing at her out of the corner of his eye, and settled into the other bench. She gave him a brief, suspicious look, but made no effort to leave. Although he'd only had a quick glance, he realized she was wearing a shirt that advertised Mom's Auto Parts. Maybe she'd become the daughter of the manager. For that matter, she might already have been his daughter. Ted decided that he had to stop thinking in terms of absolutes.

It also occurred to him that he had yet to observe anything actually change. He could see the results, of course, but nothing had popped into or out of existence while he was actually watching. Maybe that was a fourth rule – that nothing changed if he was looking directly at it. If true, that would be a useful discovery. If he could find a combination with one element that was optimal, he could fix it there and then shift the others. But what if the person didn't change, exactly, but the relationship did? If he found himself married to Jennifer and used the kaleidoscope while in her presence, she might remain there, but did that necessarily mean she would still be his wife? Ted shook his head. He was coming up with more questions than answers.

Impulsively he reached into the bag, gripped the kaleidoscope with both hands, glanced up at the girl, and turned it. Or tried to. It was really stuck this time and he had to strain until the skin on his hands began to feel hot before it finally gave way.

"Are you all right, mister?"

Had he looked down at the crucial moment? He wasn't sure, but his eyes might have flicked away. Not that it mattered. As far as he could tell, the girl hadn't changed at all. He tried for what he hoped was a reassuring smile. "Just had a bad cramp in my leg. No problem."

She didn't look convinced, but she turned away, no longer

interested. Ted glanced toward the store fronts and, just as the last time, there was nothing obvious to tell him that things had changed. He stood up impatiently, walked to the front of the convenience store and looked inside. The teenager was still at the register, looking bored as he thumbed through a magazine. There were no customers. Ted was pretty sure that some of the shelves had been rearranged, but he wasn't absolutely certain.

I need a busier and more diverse environment, he told himself. And he knew the perfect place. He walked back to the antique store, turned the corner, and headed for the strip mall.

Liggett's drug store anchored the shopping center at this end, an independent that managed to survive only because the chains had yet to build within the town limits. There was a small magazine store next door that had also been forced to adapt to changing times and which derived the bulk of its income from lottery and tobacco sales. Beyond that was Martha's Movietown , which offered videogames in addition to movie rentals. Still further along, Bargain Busters sold used furniture and refurbished household appliances. Pete's Pets would probably be gone within another few months; Ted couldn't remember ever seeing a customer in the store. At the end stood the Cathay Garden, dine in or dine out. There were about a dozen cars in the lot, about average for a Saturday.

Ted felt a surge of excitement and almost reached for the kaleidoscope, but he forced himself to calm down. It was important to do this in an orderly fashion, he told himself. If he was going to learn the pattern of change, if there was a pattern, then he needed to remain calm and analytical. And the first thing to do was to establish a baseline.

He walked slowly along the line of storefronts, peering into each in turn. There was only one customer visible in the drug store, an elderly woman peering myopically at sewing supplies. A severe looking woman stood at the cash register, looking bored. Ted couldn't see the face of the clerk in the magazine store because he was reading a newspaper held high enough that the only thing visible was his left arm, which bore a tattoo of some kind of coiled serpent. There were no customers visible, although it was possible someone was in the small back room, where the adult magazines were displayed and minors were forbidden.

There were three browsers in Martha's Movietown, two teenaged girls who seemed amused by the descriptions on the backs of every DVD they examined and a middle aged man thoughtfully examining the horror titles. There was a flat screen television in the front window playing some kind of heist movie, with three hooded thieves preparing to rob a bank. There was no one visible in Bargain Busters, not even an attendant, and the rows of used furniture and refurbished appliances looked even dingier than usual.

The pet shop was clearly on its last legs. A single puppy slept in the front window. Beyond, most of the bird cages were empty and the snake in the largest terrarium appeared to be dead. There was also a tarantula, more obviously active, and Ted looked away quickly. Why would anyone want a spider for a pet? A young female clerk with a long ponytail was talking to a man and his daughter, the girl probably around twelve years old. She looked excited; her father looked resigned.

Most of the cars were parked near the Cathay Garden. A harried looking man in a sweat suit came out carrying a large bag, propped it up in the back seat, and drove off just as Ted reached the end of the sidewalk. Two large plaster dragons flanked the stairs to the door, one red with green trim, the other green with red trim. Ted paused, turned around and looked back the way he'd come. All right, here he was. How to proceed? And then a thought occurred to him. There was an ATM at the drug store. He reached around and patted his hip pocket to make sure he'd brought his wallet.

He walked back much more quickly, stepped inside the drug store and went directly to the little alcove where the ATM stood. His hands were shaking and he had to try twice before he typed in the correct password and looked at his current balance. How had it gotten that low? But that could be fixed. He withdrew his card, unzipped the bag, looked around quickly to make sure he was unobserved, and turned the drum. It wouldn't move far but it did move.

Ted forced himself to calmly zip up the bag before looking around. Nothing seemed to have changed, but then he couldn't see much from where he stood. His hands were trembling as he inserted the card again, but he managed to type the correct password on the first try this time. It seemed to take forever for the balance to appear on the screen.

It was unchanged.

Ted was disappointed but not discouraged. After all, not everything changed with every turn of the drum. He had already unzipped the bag again when he realized his error. The balance in his bank account had nothing to do with this or any other ATM. All he was doing was remote viewing information stored elsewhere. The only place where he could alter his balance would be in proximity to the master record, probably at the main bank. Or maybe somewhere else entirely. He had no idea how the system worked. Which meant that particular route to success was closed to him. No matter, he thought. There's more than one way to skin a cat. He mentally apologized to Roscoe and turned away from the ATM.

A cursory look around the store told him nothing. He hadn't been in Liggett's in months so he couldn't tell if anything had been displaced. Certainly nothing grossly inappropriate was in evidence. When he stepped outside and let his eyes wander along the line of store fronts, he was none the wiser. The configuration of cars in the parking lot had altered, but that was to be expected. A glance into the magazine shop confirmed that the kaleidoscope had worked, however. The clerk was still reading the newspaper, but she was a young woman with a long pony tail. A coiled serpent was tattooed on her arm.

The heist movie was still playing on the television at Movietown, where a rack of pet supplies nestled incongruously between the horror section and comedies. Ted moved quickly to the next window. Bargain Busters had not changed much, but the antique bird cage in one corner was no longer empty. The tarantula moved tentatively, as though aware that it was out of its element, and Ted shuddered and moved on. The pet shop seemed mostly unchanged, but the heavyset man feeding the tropical fish had bare arms rather than tattoos and there was a puppy in the tarantula's terrarium. The mutt he had seen on the walk in was sleeping in another cage. At the end of the row, Ted glanced up at the Cathay Garden, convinced that something had changed, belatedly deciding that the two dragons had switched sides, although he wasn't absolutely certain. Regardless of the details, it was obvious that the magic had worked once more. But what had he learned, if anything?

Ted was forced to admit that he was still no better off than when he had started. As far as he could tell, the changes were random. If there was a pattern, it was too subtle for him to discover. Perhaps if he could construct a totally controlled environment, he might be able to discern some underlying set of rules, but that wasn't the case here and he didn't see how he could manage it on an effective scale. He'd just have to wing it. That revelation should have disappointed him. It did dampen his spirits, at least momentarily. But then the realization of the power at his command came back like a resurgent tide and he felt elation so great that he looked around guiltily, afraid he'd somehow behaved badly in public. Another customer came out of the restaurant, glanced at him in passing, and went to his car. No one else paid even that much attention.

You're all at my mercy, he told the world at large, even if you don't know it. He felt a rush of exhilaration greater than anything he'd ever experienced. The temptation to use that power became irresistible. He glanced around quickly, as though he were about to commit a loathsome crime, then unzipped his case and reached inside. There was resistance, but the drum turned.

Ted glanced up and this time it was immediately obvious that the world had changed. For one thing, the ATM was visible just inside the door of the pet shop. The tarantula was in the window now, its glass case right next to a display of imported cigars. The elderly man cleaning out one of the cages had been shopping in Liggett's just a few minutes earlier. Ted turned and glanced back at the restaurant, which appeared to be just the same except that the sign on the wall now identified it incongruously as Pete's Cathay Garden.

Bargain Busters appeared to be much the same when he glanced inside, but the place had been so chaotic in the first place that Ted wasn't sure he would have noticed if the stock had been rearranged. Just before he turned away, a puppy ran out from behind a pock marked dresser and barked at him. The racks in the video store had been shuffled around and the television in the window was now an elderly model with rabbit ears and a dark screen. The missing flat screen set was in the window of the magazine shop, still showing the same movie. The thieves were trapped inside the bank with a group of hostages now. The young girl with the tattoo and pony tail was sitting watching it, along with the elderly woman from Liggett's and the little girl he'd seen in the pet shop. There was no sign of her father.

The two teenagers he'd spotted in the rental store were just leaving. As they got into their car – or what was now their car at least – a rickety farm truck came into the lot, parked right in front of Liggett's and a gawky, disheveled man in his late twenties got out and almost ran inside, brushing past Ted in the process. The rear of the truck was filled with crates of live chickens who were apparently so traumatized by the trip that they were mostly silent, a few of the bravest peering around but most huddled into almost unidentifiable lumps. As the driver rushed past, Ted stepped back to get out of the way, lost his balance, and almost dropped the zipper bag. The possibility that he might have damaged the kaleidoscope made him furious.

"All right, you asshole," he growled under his breath. Having completely abandoned his resolve to observe the changes clinically and logically, he undid the zipper and turned the drum again. He was expecting more resistance, but for a change the mechanism seemed completely unimpeded, and this was by far the largest single turn he'd made, almost a complete revolution. Ted wondered if the degree of change would be proportionate. It didn't take long for him to decide that it was.

For one thing, even from his limited perspective he could see that the stores had changed more dramatically this time. The Cathay Garden was now Martha's Bargain Busters and Video. The dragons were gone, replaced by two plaster tarantulas. The pet shop next door was now a Chinese restaurant. They had even put two tables out on the sidewalk and a young couple were sitting there eating Moo Goo Gai Pan. All ted could see of the next two stores were their signs, Bargain Pets followed by Liggett's Movie Rentals. Behind him the former drug store was now a generic magazine, tobacco, and pet shop.

But the biggest change was right next door. The former magazine store was now a small, dingy, unnamed drug store with a television in the window. The screen showed a Chinese couple playing with puppies. The man was smoking a cigar and the woman wore a blouse covered with interlocking red and green dragons. None of this was particularly alarming, but through the glass front, Ted could see something much more upsetting.

Someone was robbing the store. Ted hadn't realized to what extent the events of the past few hours had seemed dreamlike. Despite all the evidence to the contrary, evidence which he had accepted as true, the beliefs of a lifetime were difficult to overcome. Somewhere, beneath his conscious thoughts, he was still expecting to wake up and discover that this was all an elaborate dream, a twisted wish fulfillment fantasy. The intrusion by a clear, obvious, even mundane danger cut slantwise across his perceptions and he was suddenly terrified. So terrified that he remained frozen in place as the thieves poured out of the store.

There were three of them. The leader appeared to be a teenaged girl with a pony tail and a tattoo. She was closely followed by the elderly man and a young girl, probably twelve or thirteen. All three were armed. They were shouting and disorganized, almost panicky, and Ted suspected immediately that they were on drugs. He instinctively shrank back a step even though he was a good distance away, but he was so stunned by this new turn of events that he felt as much surprise and curiosity as fear.

He expected them to pile into one of the parked cars and tear out of the parking lot and at first that seemed to be their intention. But then the little girl ran over to where the couple were sitting outside the restaurant and started shouting that she wanted their wallets and jewelry, and a moment later another car drove into the lot and the elderly man walked over to the driver's side and gestured threateningly with his hand gun. None of the three had noticed Ted yet, but the teenaged girl was slowly turning her head to scan the area and it would only be a few seconds before she spotted him.

Ted didn't care about the money in his wallet. There wasn't enough to matter. But what if the girl thought that the zipper bag actually contained a laptop? She might take it away from him and the kaleidoscope would be gone. His first impulse was to run but that would only attract the girl's attention. He pivoted suddenly and tossed the bag up into the back of the farm truck, praying that the padding would protect its contents, and saw it drop down between two stacks of chicken crates.

He turned back toward the girl, who had finally spotted him, just as the truck's driver reappeared carrying a carton of cigarettes.

"Oh shit!" The carton dropped to the ground as the driver's eyes opened wide. Ted expected him to run back into the store but instead he bolted toward the truck, pulled open the door, and climbed up inside so quickly that neither Ted nor the ponytailed thief could react. The engine coughed and started just as the girl began to move toward them, raising her weapon. Ted suddenly realized his error and felt twin terrors. If the girl was really high on drugs as he suspected, she might well shoot him. On the other hand, if the truck driver made his escape, he'd take the kaleidoscope with him, and it would quite possibly be lost to Ted forever. He turned toward the truck, wondering if he could recover it in time, but the girl was much closer now, and the handgun looked much bigger than they did in the movies.

"Hold it right there! Both of you!"

But the driver was beyond listening. The truck backed out of its space and there was the sound of clashing metal as he shifted gears. The girl raised her arm as though she planned to shoot the driver through the windshield, but she wavered and let the weapon drop slightly as the truck jerked forward and started to turn toward the exit.

And then the sirens started up. Someone had called the police.

Instead of relief, Ted felt even greater panic. The truck wasn't stopping even though the three thieves were now running toward an elderly minivan parked in front of the drug store. Whether or not the police arrived in time, they'd want to question the witnesses and there was no telling how long it would take Ted to get away. Even then, he had no idea where the truck had come from or where it might go to before he could retrieve his bag. There was no name written on the cab, nothing to differentiate it from dozens of other vehicles in the area. Unless he acted now, the kaleidoscope would be lost.

So he acted.

He ran toward the truck, which had almost reached the street. Despite his impulsive decision to flee the area, the driver instinctively paused before pulling out into the street. His legs pumping furiously, Ted raced across the uneven pavement and managed to grab one of the ropes that held the chicken crates in place. Then he was being pulled forward and he knew his grip wouldn't last so he jumped, scrabbled wildly with his free hand, and found another rope. His feet scraped along the pavement for a second before he pulled himself up, kicking and groping until he got one foot and then the other planted on the rear bumper.

The sirens were very loud now and he glanced back, saw two patrol cars veer into the parking lot just in time to cut off the minivan. A third appeared, paused at the entrance to the lot, then leaped into motion again, following the truck. The late arriving officer must have assumed that it was being driven off by some or all of the thieves.

They hit a bump and Ted almost lost his grip. For some reason the driver still wasn't stopping, even though he had done nothing wrong. Ted pulled himself up into a more secure position, banging his shins and elbows. The road surface wasn't that well maintained, and the truck's suspension was even less so. He looked for the zipper case, but it wasn't visible from this angle. Something else was, however. Tucked in among the chicken crates were several burlap bags, two of which had been so poorly tied that the contents were visible. They weren't full of chicken feed.

It was marijuana. No wonder the driver didn't want to talk to the police. But fleeing the scene was clearly hopeless and the panicked driver had only drawn more attention to himself by doing so. If he'd done nothing at all, chances were very good no one would have looked into the back of his truck. Now, when inevitably he was forced to stop, the police would have an excellent reason for doing so. And Ted realized that his own situation was almost as difficult. How could he explain that he had simply been trying to reclaim his property? He'd have to convince them that it was some kind of valuable antique, worth risking his neck to cling to the back of a rickety vehicle traveling at excessive speed.

But they'd want to see it, examine it, and perhaps one of them would turn the drum. He couldn't very well tell them not to. Ted didn't know what he was going to do and he'd have to think of something quickly. The truck was slowing down, the driver having decided either to submit to the inevitable or perhaps to brazen it out after all.

As the pace slowed, Ted felt more secure in his perch and managed to twist his body so that he could slip between the ropes and climb into the bed of the truck. It was important to reclaim the kaleidoscope first; he'd figure out what to say to the police afterwards.

He managed to get to his knees, bracing himself against one of the crates. Several of the chickens were protesting noisily at being jostled about, but most seemed resigned to his intrusion. Ted managed a quick look back at the police car, which was so close now that he could see the dark haired police officer clearly through the windshield. They were out of the built up district now, on one of the winding roads that led eventually to the farms surrounding the reservoir north of town.

They hit a bump and Ted banged his elbow painfully. They were moving noticeably more slowly now and the sound of the tires changed as the driver edged off the paved surface onto the spotty grass and sand that lined the road. Ted noticed a man on a tractor moving slowly in their direction, but turned away quickly. He had to find his bag first. All other considerations were secondary.

For a few panicky moments, he thought it had disappeared, perhaps having bounced out of the truck when he wasn't looking. But then he saw the strap and realized it was lying between two stacks of crates, and that straw had fallen and partially concealed the case itself. He pulled it out carefully, unzipped it and checked inside just to make sure that the kaleidoscope was still there and in one piece. It was only then that he realized that the truck had finally come to a stop.

He couldn't hide; he had been clearly visible hanging on the back of the truck during the brief pursuit. Could he claim to have been terrified by the prospect of a gun battle with the thieves? It wasn't entirely untrue. Certainly they would have no reason to detain him other than for routine questioning as a witness. But could he risk the possibility that he'd be forced to surrender custody of the kaleidoscope for however long it took to straighten things out? Did he have an alternative?

The driver killed the engine and Ted heard the car door slam as the officer got out of his car. Then a male voice, authoritative, forced him to act. "You in the back of the truck! Come out where I can see you. And move slowly."

Ted took a deep breath. "All right, officer. I'm standing up now. I'm just a bystander." He stood up, the zipper bag clutched in one hand.

The policeman was standing in the road and he had his weapon drawn, holding it with both hands. "Empty your hands, sir. Do it now!"

He had no choice. He set the bag down on top of the closest chicken crate, moving very slowly. As he did so, the driver opened the cab door and stepped out, and nearly got himself shot in the process. The officer was young, and Managansett couldn't afford experienced or well trained troopers. His aim shifted toward the other man and it looked very much like he was shaking with tension.

"Stop right where you are and raise your hands!"

Ted couldn't see the driver from where he was standing, but apparently the man had complied because the officer seemed to relax slightly. The tractor sounds had been getting steadily louder and Ted glanced in that direction, saw that he'd been mistaken. It wasn't a man driving the tractor but a woman with broad shoulders, short hair, and a sunburned face. She was obviously curious and less than cautious because she was coming directly toward them, having veered from her original path.

Some of the tension drained out of the situation then. The driver must have complied, and certainly appeared no more menacing than did Ted. The officer's stance visibly relaxed, although he didn't lower his weapon. "Step away from the truck and keep your hands where I can see them." He glanced up at Ted. "Please come down from there, sir. "

Ted did his best not to look guilty. "Certainly, officer." He glanced down and decided that he'd have to turn his back in order to climb down over the rear gate to the ground. As he shifted position, he noticed that the policeman was now more interested in the driver, so he took the opportunity to retrieve his bag and take it with him as he descended. The tractor was now almost adjacent to the parked truck, the motor idling, the driver watching them with lukewarm interest. It was probably the most exciting thing that had happened to her all week, Ted thought to himself. Maybe all year.

The driver was answering questions in a voice so low that Ted couldn't hear him clearly, but he didn't care. This was his chance to get out of this situation. He unzipped the case and reached inside, then looked around nervously, feeling an odd sense of guilt. The woman on the tractor was staring right at him. His hand gripped the drum and he felt a sudden sense of confidence, winked at her, then looked down to make sure of his grip.

The drum turned, grudgingly, but it turned.

Ted looked up quickly and glanced toward the tractor. It was still exactly where it was, except that the seat was now occupied by a dark haired young man. Ted heard the truck door close behind him and turned just in time to see the police officer turn in his direction. It was the woman from the tractor, and she looked even larger close up than she had from a distance. The town's standards must have really dropped if they'd hired her, but then again, Ted had forced the issue, hadn't he?

"I'm afraid I'm going to have to ask you to ride back with me, sir." Her voice was low, gravelly.

Ted blinked. "Ride back where?"

"We'll be joining the other officers. If everything checks out, we won't detain you long, but you will need to make an official statement."

His situation hadn't really changed except superficially. He could shift the three people around him as many times as he wanted, maybe even get the truck in the field and the tractor on the road, but his basic problem remained the same. He'd just have to see it through. Nodding assent, he followed her to the patrol car.

"What are you carrying in that bag, sir?"

Ted felt sick to his stomach, told himself that he was being foolish. "It's an antique I picked up at a yard sale, officer. I think it might be worth a lot of money." All of which was true, although it wasn't all of the truth.

"Would you mind showing me, sir?" It wasn't really a question, but he was relieved to notice that she had holstered her weapon.

"No, of course not." He unzipped the bag and lifted the

kaleidoscope partway out. "It's a kaleidoscope, a kind of toy. But it's very delicate."

She didn't look satisfied, but she nodded, then opened the back door of the cruiser. Ted zipped the bag shut and slipped inside quickly, grateful she hadn't asked to examine it more closely. The door slammed shut and he realized that he was effectively a prisoner.

Ahead of them, the farm truck did a slow U-turn and started back the way they had come. The woman followed, her flashers on but siren muted. Ted wondered what would happen if he used the kaleidoscope while they were driving but decided not to experiment. If the woman disappeared and wasn't replaced, he'd be trapped in a moving vehicle with no one in control. He'd just have to wait for a better opportunity.

It took longer to get back than it had on the way out, but it seemed far too short to Ted. He still didn't have a plan.

The other officers appeared to have dealt with the three unlikely thieves efficiently enough. The old man and the young girl were sitting in the back of one patrol car, and the young woman was in the second. At least a dozen people were gathered together in one group separate from a larger crowd of onlookers, all trying to talk at once while one policeman tried to write down everyone's name and address. A fourth cruiser pulled in almost immediately with two more officers and a man in plain clothes who immediately began to take charge.

The farm truck parked exactly where it had been earlier and the police woman pulled right alongside. She got out, but made no effort to release Ted. In fact, she didn't even glance in his direction while she was handing off the nervous looking driver to another officer. Ted was tempted to try the kaleidoscope again, but since he wasn't affected by the changes, it seemed likely he'd remain trapped in the car regardless of how the external world might change. His situation was bad enough as it was; he could easily imagine alternatives that were worse. If he was going to extricate himself from this situation, he'd have to get out of the police car first.

He rapped his knuckles against the window. At first he thought the officer hadn't heard him, but her head slowly turned, as though she'd just remembered that he was there. Then she gave a quite visible sigh, walked over to the door, and opened it. "I'm going to turn you over to Detective Simonson, sir. He'll have questions to ask. If you're not involved, it would be in your best interest to be as cooperative as possible. We won't detain you any longer than is necessary."

"I understand completely, officer." He followed her, but the bag was already unzipped and he had one hand inside, resting on the drum of the kaleidoscope. Chances were good that he'd be released promptly, but he chafed at the idea of wasting any further time. After all, he had the power to change the world. Why should he be bothered by petty bureaucrats and mundane problems?

Detective Simonson glanced at him without disinterestedly. The uniformed officer was still taking down names and addresses and several of the witnesses had already wandered away, although not far. They probably wouldn't actually leave until the prisoners were taken away. Now that there was no longer any danger, curiosity had replaced fear Simonson was talking to a middle aged man whomTed couldn't remember having seen before; he had probably been inside one of the stores. Officer Olsen – he had finally read her name tag – indicated he should wait until the detective was ready for him, then walked away.

Things appeared to be winding down. Some people had actually gone back into the stores. Ted looked around, confirmed that no one was actually watching him, then reached inside the bag with his other hand and turned the drum. It jammed after only a quarter rotation but Ted persisted. He didn't want just a game of musical chairs with the uniforms; he wanted a fundamental change and he was determined to get it. Straining, he managed to force it a bit further, and then the resistance gave way and he completed almost a full turn.

He raised his head and blinked in astonishment.

The police were still there, although only one of them looked familiar. Three officers, all male, were sitting at the table outside the restaurant with plates of food in front of them. One was a complete stranger, but the one in the middle was Asian, and during his only visit Ted had seen him in the Cathay Garden, bussing tables. While he was watching, a waitress came out and handed the officers their check. The waitress was Olsen.

There was no sign of any of the three thieves, no indication that a robbery or anything similar had just taken place, and when Ted glanced at another storefront – Bargain Buster Drugs and Video – he saw that the heist movie was playing on the television again. The Cathay Garden's original building was still there – presently manifesting itself as Martha's drugs – but it had moved to a corner of the parking lot. Its original site was now bare pavement with an ATM in one corner.

Ted had no interest in picking out any additional changes. Right now, he just wanted to go home and catch his breath. Since the robbery had not occurred, no one appeared to be interested in him or in preventing him from leaving. He zipped the bag shut, took a deep breath, and set out for home. Just before he crossed the street, the farm truck pulled out and passed him. The driver was a young woman with a ponytail.

It seemed to take forever to get back to Bailey's Court. He was tired, physically and emotionally, and also somewhat depressed. Sure, he might have more power than anyone else in the world, but what good was it if he couldn't control it, shape the changes, choose the best possible future? Was he really going to have to rely on chance to get what he wanted?

He was so caught up in his thoughts that he almost walked right past his house. There was no car in the driveway so Beth and Heather hadn't come home yet. They'd still be together, of course, since they were out of range of the last few changes. Ted went inside, glanced around discontentedly. The house had never seemed so dingy before. How could he have let his life come to this?

He wanted a beer. No, he wanted something stronger than that. There was a bottle of wine that someone had given them as a present at Christmas. Ted didn't like wine unless it was sweet and Beth rarely drank anything, so it hadn't been touched. But where had they put it? Ted poked through several cupboards before remembering that he had taken it downstairs with some vague idea that it ought to be kept cold. He'd put it on a shelf in the far corner, where they stored their Christmas ornaments and unused wrapping paper.

He carried the zipper bag downstairs, intending to retrieve the wine, but it wasn't there. Instead there were two bottles of expensive brandy.   Carl Rogers liked brandy. Or at least, the original Carl Rogers had liked it. Ted wasn't fond of it himself, but today he'd make an exception. He twisted off the cap and drank right from the bottle.

It was stronger than he expected, burning his mouth and throat, and he hastily lowered the bottle. The liquor coursed through his body and he felt his shakiness subside, then began to feel light headed instead. He glanced down at the label, wondering just how strong it was, but decided he'd had enough in any case. He would have to think clearly if he was going to figure out what to do next. One thing was certain. This wasn't his ideal world. Far from it. And it was time to do something about it.

"I proclaim this present version of reality as less than optimal and so I banish it." He realized belatedly that he didn't actually know very much about his current situation. Perhaps Beth had a good job and was making enough money to support them both in the style he'd like. But she was still Beth, and if he was going to change things, he might as well play for the whole pot. After all, if he didn't like the next rendition, he could always change it again. Ted raised the kaleidoscope to one eye and, with considerable effort, managed to move the drum another quarter turn. As he did so, he heard the station wagon turning into the driveway. "Just in time," he whispered to himself, realizing that he should have waited to be sure they were back. The kaleidoscope could not change their relationship to him if they weren't within its range.

Another few minutes passed before Ted found the courage to venture upstairs. He remembered his intention of recording all of his observations and comparing them. Part of his mind insisted that there had to be some underlying order, but another part believed there was no pattern for him to detect, or if there was, it was too subtle for his perceptions. There was very little risk, he told himself. He had nothing to lose that he couldn't recapture, even if it took a while to do so.

He emerged from the basement cautiously, called "Hello" several times, but there was no answer. The house remained silent and felt empty, and he realized that he hadn't heard anyone come inside. Just to be certain, he walked around and looked into each room. He paused in the den, noting that the still life was back on the wall, but in a different position, the first evidence he'd seen that there had been new changes, and it occurred to him to wonder if he could restore the original settings by turning the drum in the opposite direction for exactly the same distance as it had traveled since he'd owned it. Not that he had any intention of going backward, of course, but it was an interesting question. He would have to try it at some point, just to find out if the results were any different.

Someone had left the television on and it was showing some kind of horror movie. Ted noticed that a dark clad figure was chasing a young girl across a poorly lit lawn, but he wasn't interested and turned the set off immediately. He checked the kitchen next, and felt a surge of excitement when he noticed that the stove and refrigerator had swapped places. Impressive as these shifts of physical objects might be, they had no material effect on his life, however. He was looking for something more fundamental.

The doorbell rang just as he was starting toward the den. Ted cursed under his breath and went to answer it. Samantha was standing outside, dressed conservatively for a change, once again wearing her unflattering glasses and with her hair – back to brunette - done up in a pony tail that made her look younger than she was. She was holding a large roasting pan and looking bored.

"Hi, Mr. Croner. Mom sent me over with this. She said Mrs. Croner wanted to borrow it for tomorrow."

Ted was mildly disappointed. At first blush, things seemed to have returned to a reasonably close approximation of their original configuration. Could there be a fairly rigid limit on the degree to which the kaleidoscope could alter reality? He supposed that made sense, otherwise the houses would be trading rooms, people would have arms growing out of the top of their heads, and so forth.

"Okay, come on in." He opened the door wider. "I don't know where she is right at the moment but I suppose if you put it out in the kitchen, she'll find it when she gets home." He hesitated. "I don't suppose you know where she's gone? My wife, that is." He didn't refer to her by name, because he wasn't sure just who his wife was at the moment.

"Beth? She's over next door, talking to Mrs. Hastings. They're out on the patio. Do you want me to tell her that you're looking for her?"

"No! No, that's all right," he said hastily. "I don't want to bother her." So he was still married to Beth and Jennifer still lived next door. This was all starting to look very familiar.

"I'll just put this in the kitchen then." Samantha eyed him rather warily as she passed, having detected something odd in his manner or the tone of his voice. Ted was barely aware of her, lost in his own thoughts. She vanished into the kitchen, then reappeared a moment later, heading straight for the front door.

Ted decided to fish for more information. "How are things at home, Samantha? Everyone okay?"

She hesitated and the wary look was stronger than ever. "Sure, why wouldn't they be? Dad still hates his job at the bank and Mom still can't talk him into looking for something else." There was a hint of sarcasm in her voice. "And then there's Heather…"

"Your sister?" He tried not to make it a question but his voice rose at the end almost of its own volition.

"Unfortunately. No one's speaking to her right now, although I suppose she won't actually get disowned. She used some of her tuition money to buy herself a sports car and Dad says she's going to have to get a full time job if she's really not going back to college in the fall. He also wants her to pay rent if she lives with us. And her new boyfriend Arnold is creepy." Samantha seemed poised to expand the list of her sister's faults, but Ted intervened.

"What does your mom have to say about all this?"

Samantha shrugged. "She's trying to work out a compromise like she always does. Secretarial school or something."

"Maybe that's the right choice. You can't decide how someone else should live their life. Everyone has to make his or her own decisions." Although that wasn't quite true, he realized. He wasn't just affecting his own life by turning the kaleidoscope. Things changed for everyone around him. For just a brief moment, he felt a twinge of guilt. He was, after all, abrogating to himself the right to shape the futures of other people. Guilt was almost a novel experience for him, but he had no difficulty in suppressing it.

Samantha had relaxed slightly but was still obviously uncomfortable. She edged toward the door. "I guess. I really have to go. I'm supposed to be taking Toby out for his walk.

Heather's too busy, of course."

"Okay. Thanks for the pan." He closed the door behind her.

Ted completed his survey of the house, then returned to the kitchen. Most of the major appliances were back in their proper places, but the kitchen witch was still missing. Most notably, an aquarium had been crowded into one corner of the room, even though it was so large that it was now impossible to sit at the closest end of the table properly. The master bedroom had also been rearranged and there was a night table he didn't remember ever having seen before. The shower curtain in the bathroom had also changed and clashed horribly with the rest of the room.

He was picking at a rather dry chicken breast he'd found in the refrigerator when he heard voices growing gradually closer. The back door opened and, after a short pause, closed with a bang. Ted left the kitchen just in time to see Beth and Jennifer entering the den. Jennifer was wearing a rose patterned blouse and a pair of rather ugly eyeglasses. Beth was wearing a THINK tee-shirt and was smoking.

Ted hesitated in the doorway as Jennifer sat down on the couch. Beth seemed more animated than he remembered. "There you are, Ted. Did you remember to bring up the galvanized tub from the basement while I was out?"

"Not yet," he answered automatically. "There's still plenty of time."

Beth turned to Jennifer. "Ted enjoys the suspense of letting everything wait until the last minute. Sometimes I think he does it just to tease me."

Jennifer laughed politely. "I'm sure everything will be fine. It's not as if there was a schedule we have to keep."

Beth's tone grew more serious. "It might be better if we did. Some people would benefit from more structure in their lives." She turned back to Ted. "I'm going to take Jennifer shopping with me today. She's temporarily without a car."

Ted had a sudden vision of himself carrying more grocery bags into the house. His arm ached in precognitive sympathy. He turned toward Jennifer. "What happened to your car? Accident or breakdown?"

Jennifer looked flustered and wouldn't meet his eyes. "Neither. It's pretty embarrassing as a matter of fact. I must have parked it somewhere while I was out last night but I couldn't remember where it was so I walked home, but it's the strangest thing. I usually park right in front of the Houghton's house when we meet there, but I vaguely remember walking a couple of blocks this time. I just can't recall where I left it and I was too tired to walk around looking for it last night."

Ted smirked. "Either someone stole it or that must have been some party."

She looked at him directly then and there was confusion, perhaps even fear in her eyes. "But it wasn't a party at all. It was just a dull dinner meeting with the other department heads to decide how we were going to attack some curriculum problems next year. I only had one glass of wine. I thought about calling the police except that I would have felt foolish telling them I couldn't remember where I'd parked."

"I'm sure it will turn up," said Beth. "You aren't the only person on Bailey's Court who has sudden lapses of memory. Ted can forget a dinner engagement, an errand I've asked him to run, and our anniversary, all in less time than it takes to talk about it. Come on, Jen. We need to get going." She looked at Ted. "We'll be back in an hour or two. Would you do me a favor and go over to see Mary? She's going to loan us one of her roasting pans."

Ted glanced back toward the kitchen. "It's already here. Samantha brought it over a little while ago."

"Great. That's one less thing to worry about."

Jennifer stood up, smiled faintly, and slipped past Ted. Beth followed, but without the smile.

Ted trailed after them into the front room and watched through the window as they walked to the station wagon. Jennifer was wearing jeans and he had trouble looking away until she climbed inside and shut the door.

As far as he could tell, most of the major elements of his life were very much back to the way they had been when this had all first started. It occurred to Ted that he could throw the kaleidoscope away and carry on in a manner that was pretty close to the one he was used to. The alternative was to risk making things even worse, on the chance that they might get better. After a few weeks, or months, he might even convince himself that he had imagined the whole thing. After all, a magic kaleidoscope that changed the real world was pretty farfetched. And if it did exist, why would anyone have put it out for a yard sale? On the other hand, it was broken and wouldn't turn when he'd found it, so maybe the former owner hadn't realized what it was capable of. But someone must have known at some point. Someone had built the kaleidoscope and endowed it with its magical properties. It obviously wasn't new, but neither did it give the impression of being unusually old. How had it ended up in a box of junk at a yard sale?

Ted decided it served no useful purpose to consider questions he couldn't possibly answer and turned instead to the more interesting task of trying to decide what to do next. Several transformations had led him back to a life very much like the one he had started with. Some of the interim changes had been interesting, but he had to confess that none of them had been any more and one or two were distinctly less pleasant than his former life. So he could stop where he was and continue much as before or he could take a chance and roll the dice again.

It really wasn't a difficult decision to make. Ted hadn't been very happy with his life during the past few years and the present state of things promised only more of the same. He was still married to Beth and she was still the cool, uninteresting, faintly resentful woman she'd become since the wedding. Jennifer Hastings was still untouchable and he had no doubt that Carl Rogers was as tedious as ever, even if his subject matter had changed. Banking wasn't likely to be that much better, or even particularly different, from theoretical economics. And Ted still didn't have a job and he very much doubted that the stack of unpaid bills had gone away. For that matter, was Beth employed now and, if so, was she making a decent wage?

He was still hungry and a cursory exploration of the kitchen turned up nothing that didn't need cooking except another half box of stale crackers. He dumped the chicken bones in the trash, then ate a few of the crackers, washing them down with the last cup of coffee from the percolator, but he still felt only marginally satisfied.

If only there was some way to control the specific elements of reality that were affected by the changes. He supposed that the crystals or plastic beads in the drum might have some direct correspondence to specific items in the surrounding area, but there was no practical way that he could think of to determine which were which. Even if he could, there was no method that he could imagine that would control which of them shifted position inside the drum, and he couldn't risk disassembling it in order to experiment. No, it would have to be hit or miss, pot luck, the draw of the cards. His one advantage was that, as far as he could tell, he had unlimited chances. Or was that even true? He began to wonder again whether or not there was some limit on the use of the kaleidoscope. Maybe you only got three wishes, or five, or whatever. He tried to remember how many times he had used it already, but he wasn't certain that he'd counted correctly.

Ted stood up abruptly. Could that be it? Had the world returned to something close to the original because the magic was almost used up? Would subsequent turns restore more and more of the familiar, erasing the changes he'd made? One way or another, he had to know. If that was the case, he wouldn't be any worse off at the end of the cycle than he was now, so he really had nothing to lose. Without washing out his cup and putting it in the sink – Beth would be silently reproachful when she found it sitting on the table – Ted walked briskly to the staircase and descended into the basement.

Roscoe was asleep on the bench, curled up next to the kaleidoscope, but he stirred when Ted picked it up and stared at it thoughtfully. "Well, Roscoe, it's time to try again. Let's see if we can find something better this time. Hope to see you there."

Ted raised the kaleidoscope to his eye and turned the drum. Or at least that's what he intended to do. It seemed to have frozen in place again, and increasing the pressure didn't help this time. "Damn it!" His hands were sweating and his grip kept slipping. Frustrated, he rummaged through a drawer and found one of his rags, wiped his hands, then wrapped it around the drum. "All right now," he said firmly and tried again. This time, reluctantly, the drum moved.

When he set the kaleidoscope back down, Roscoe was nowhere to be seen. "Sorry, Roscoe, but there are bigger issues at stake just now." But then he realized that it was entirely possible that Roscoe had just wandered off.

Ted went upstairs feeling both curious about what might

have changed this time and nervous that he might find himself worse off than before. He went directly to the den, and was relieved to see that the mirror was back on the wall, so obviously the magic wasn't used up yet. The television was on, showing a scene from a horror film that looked vaguely familiar, but Ted was more interested in the large aquarium that stood beside it, partially blocking the screen because it was much too big for this room. How had the present version of Beth – assuming it was Beth – justified such an odd arrangement? The couch and the chair had switched places as well.

Ted crossed to the television and leaned over to turn it off. As he did so, the young woman running across the darkened lawn turned toward the camera and screamed. Ted was momentarily stunned because the presumed victim to be was very clearly Samantha Rogers. Despite the torn, revealing clothing, and unusual hair style, she was clearly recognizable. He watched in fascination as she turned away, still running, only to stumble and fall headlong on the grass. A dark shrouded figure towered over her and Ted saw an axe rise into the air, hovering, and then the action was interrupted by a commercial for canned hams. The spell broken, he reached out and turned off the television, shivering a little. Was Samantha an actress now or was this a more fundamental change?

There were minor differences in the kitchen as well, and the furniture in the master and guest bedrooms was intermixed between the two rooms. The bathroom and Beth's sewing room appeared to be unchanged. There was no one else in the house. Ted crossed to the front room and stepped outside into the bright sunshine. It was hotter than ever, oppressive and damp without a hint of a breeze, and sweat ran down his face and made his shirt cling to his body. He glanced to his left and noticed that both the SUV and the sports car were parked in the Rogers' driveway, but the station wagon was nowhere to be seen. The birdbath was back in front of his house, but it was upside down.

The familiarity of the scene outside, despite the minor inconsistencies, was both reassuring and unsettling. At the back of his mind there lurked once again the thought that this was all a product of some complex and unusual delusion, that he'd lost his mind and was imagining all of these changes. And if that was true, it was equally likely that he didn't know which of the various realities was the real one. In fact, he couldn't be quite sure what he thought he remembered as the real world. What had originally been hanging on the wall in the den? Who really did fall and break their arm? Or was all of this an illusion? Was he actually confined to the restricted ward of some mental institution, lying in a coma in which he imagined his entire life as a suburban dweller with an unhappy marriage and a sexy but untouchable neighbor? Maybe he was actually an economics professor himself, or a movie actor who grew too immersed in the parts he was playing.

Ted tried to ignore his doubts. What the hell, if he was crazy he had nothing to lose, and if he was sane, he had everything to gain. He glanced at the Rogers house and shook his head. No, this time he was going to go for the gold. He turned and walked directly to Jennifer Hastings's front door.

No one responded immediately when he rang the doorbell. There was no car in the driveway, but it might be in the garage. Ted shifted his weight from one foot to the other, nervous, and was about to ring the bell a second time when there was a faint sound from inside and the door began to open.

Heather was standing there, her blonde hair done up in a bun, wearing a tee-shirt and cut off jeans. "THINK" was stretched over her breasts and Ted had trouble moving his eyes away.

"Hi, Ted. Sorry to take so long but we were down in the cellar. Come on in. Don't mind the mess. It's moving day."

She opened the door wide and stepped back so he could enter. Once across the threshold, he found himself standing in the middle of chaos. Cardboard boxes, wicker baskets, paper bags, and other containers were strewn about Jennifer's living room in apparently random profusion. Some of the boxes had been opened, others had not. A large axe had been laid across the coffee table. Ted noticed Beth's kitchen witch lying in one of the wicker baskets, but nothing else looked familiar.

Heather walked past him to the kitchen and shouted in the general direction of the basement door. "Jennifer! Ted Croner is here!" She turned back and smiled.

Ted picked his way through the debris. "What is this? Spring cleaning? Getting ready for a yard sale?"

Heather tossed her head. "Nothing so easy. I'm moving in.

Jenny and I have been talking about this forever. You know, making it official. It's a pretty big step in a relationship, but I think we're ready."

"Relationship?" Ted was confused.

Jennifer appeared, crossed the room to stand beside Heather, her arm insinuating itself around the younger woman's waist. Heather neither flinched nor looked surprised and Ted realized he had just received the answer to his question.

"We weren't going to say anything until the cookout tomorrow, but we've decided that there's no point in waiting any longer. It didn't make any sense for Heather to keep her apartment when I have plenty of room for her here." She glanced at the disarray around the room. "Or at least I think I do. She has more stuff than I realized." They both laughed. "There's an extra bedroom where she can put her computer and law books and do her studying. In return I get help with the housework and the mortgage payment," she pulled Heather closer, "not to mention the purely physical benefits."

"Actually," said Heather coyly, "I'm mostly interested in the gourmet cooking. I could burn boiling water. If I didn't have a microwave I wouldn't cook at all, and if I keep depending on fast food I'm going to look like a blimp by the time I'm old enough to vote."

Jennifer pretended to be offended. "What? This is all just about the food? You aren't drawn by my personal charm and aura of intense sexuality?"

"Well, maybe just a little." Both of them laughed again. Ted felt as though he might be sick. The two most attractive women on the block, both completely out of his reach. There was an awkward moment during which he tried to think of something to say, but his discomfiture eased when Toby ran through the room, apparently chasing shadows, making it unnecessary for him to speak.

The two women separated at last. Jennifer gestured toward the kitchen. "I was just about to put together some lunch. Would you like to stay and have something with us? Nothing fancy. And I have cold beer."

His stomach growled softly, reminding him that he still hadn't eaten an actual meal today, but just at the moment he couldn't think of anything he'd less like to do than spend an hour or so in the company of these two. At least under the present circumstances. Why couldn't they have become raging nymphomaniacs?

"No, no thanks." His voice sounded a bit hoarse and he cleared his throat. "I ought to be getting home. I just wanted to find out…I mean I wanted to make sure you were both still planning to come over tomorrow."

"We wouldn't miss it," Jennifer assured him. "Is Mrs. Rogers' sister still coming?"

"Her sister?"

Jennifer looked puzzled. "I thought you'd already met. I talked to her just the other day and she seemed quite nice. She's spending a few weeks with them while her arm is healing up. She was in an automobile accident and can't fend for herself."

"Oh, yeah. Sorry, my mind was somewhere else. As far as I know, yes she's coming."

"I figured. I mean, you wouldn't expect Mary to come without her."

"No, of course not. Everyone has been invited." Samantha was pretty young to be Mary's sister, he thought, but it's not completely impossible. Half sister maybe. "Look, I'd better leave the two of you alone or you'll be unpacking until midnight."

Heather glanced around. "At least."

Jennifer put her arm around Heather's waist again. "Oh, I think we'll find something more interesting to do before midnight."

Ted turned and started for the door. Jennifer broke her hold and followed him while Heather went out into the kitchen. She kept her voice low. "I want you to know we really appreciate your inviting us, Ted. Most people around here wouldn't be so open minded. This is still a pretty small town and we haven't made a secret about our being partners."

He hesitated, dredged through his thoughts to find something appropriate to say. "Everyone has to decide for himself, or herself, what road they're going to travel. That's always been my philosophy." And I certainly didn't choose this road, he thought, and I won't be on it for any longer than is absolutely necessary.

He started to open the door but Jennifer hadn't finished. "I should warn you that Heather insists on contributing something tomorrow. She tries hard but she wasn't exaggerating when she said she was a horrible cook. And naturally she wants to make a good impression."

Ted smiled. "Let me guess. She wants to bring a fancy dessert."

Jennifer nodded. "I tried to talk her into making a salad or something, but she's convinced she can follow a simple recipe. I'll try to make sure we don't get food poisoning or anything like that."

Ted laughed, but not because of Jennifer's little joke. "I'll bet she's planning to make raspberry tarts."

Jennifer looked startled. "How in the world did you know that? Did she say something to you already?"

"No, I'm just psychic. Catch you later." And he left before she could say another word.

Ted didn't run back to the house. Not quite. But he walked as quickly as he could. He didn't go directly to the basement because he was still curious. Was Samantha now Mary's sister or was it Beth? Did that mean that he was a bachelor? He went to the master bedroom and opened the closet. His clothing was there, but it was spread out from one side to the other. No female clothing at all. So he was unmarried. That had some possibilities, but with Jennifer out of reach and with no job, he didn't like his chances of making this into the world of his dreams. He wanted more than just an acceptable state of affairs; he wanted something with positive energy, something exciting. No, this just wouldn't do. He would have to take destiny in his hands once again.

Down in the basement he looked around for the cat. "Roscoe? Did I lose you again? Well, maybe you'll be back next time." He picked up the kaleidoscope, feeling a rush of anticipation. Would the next turn be better or worse? Was there yet some way that he could influence the outcome? Maybe if he concentrated even harder on what he wanted. He closed his eyes, trying to rearrange things mentally. Ideally he'd like to end up married to Jennifer. It would be nice if she was a lawyer again, with a good income. That way he wouldn't have to work at all.

There were a few other things he'd like to change as well, but he could live with a lot less.

He opened his eyes, looked into the kaleidoscope, and – with the usual difficulty – managed another slight turn.

When he lowered his arms, Roscoe was sitting upright on the desk, regarding him curiously. "Welcome home, buddy. Where were you last time, I wonder?"

Roscoe didn't answer but a voice called down from him from the top of the stairs. "Ted, are you down there again?"

It was a question he'd heard Beth ask many times in the past, with the same petulant, irritated tone. But it wasn't Beth's voice. It took a few seconds for Ted to realize who was calling him. It was Heather.

"Ted?" The voice called again. "Would you come up here please? I need to talk to you."

He still didn't answer. Instead he looked at Roscoe and winked. "Heather?" He spoke barely above a whisper. "Well, that might work." And if it didn't, he could always shuffle things around again. He went upstairs.

Heather wasn't in sight, but the television was on in the den and he followed the sound. The same clip from the horror movie was playing, but this time the victim never turned to face the camera. Ted hesitated, watching the screen intently, but the familiar commercial cut off the action. A vase of cut roses stood on top of the television. Heather wasn't there so he turned toward the kitchen and raised his voice. "Heather? Where are you?"

She appeared immediately, coming down the hall from the bedroom. She was wearing a ratty looking night gown and her hair was up in curlers. Without makeup, her complexion was pale with an asymmetrical patch of freckles. She had a cigarette in her mouth and her expression was one of mildly angry boredom. He hardly recognized her.

"There you are. I told you hours ago that I'm hungry and you promised to go out and pick up a pizza or something." Her voice shivered with the same whine he'd heard her use with her father when he'd insisted that she walk the dog.

Ted's stomach had given up growling for the moment, but the thought of food set it astir once again. "Pizza? Yes, I can do that. Mushroom and pepperoni?"

110

"Oh, let's have the works. I'm eating for two after all."

Ted's eyes trailed down to Heather's belly, but the billowy nightgown concealed the shape of her body. "You are? I mean, you are."

Heather looked offended. "As if you didn't have something to do with that. And while you're out, don't forget to pick up the charcoal and stuff for the cookout tomorrow. Unless you've thought of some way we can call the whole thing off." She sounded hopeful.

"I thought you were looking forward to having people over." He was treading on unknown ground here, but it didn't seem likely that they'd be hosting a party that they had both dreaded, and since he knew it would never have been his idea, she had to have suggested it.

"That was before," she pouted. "It's not going to be much fun with my parents all bent out of shape like they are. Dad was just starting to get used to us living together and had started talking to me again, but when they found out we were pregnant, he just blew his top. I guess he thought we were just having a fling and things would get back to normal eventually. Mom's not as bad, but she looks like she's going to burst into tears all the time. And my sister's getting a big kick out of becoming the favorite now that I've disgraced the Rogers name."

Ted struggled to follow this latest turn of events. "Samantha has always been a little jealous of you, hasn't she?" he offered.

"Samantha?" Heather was clearly confused. "What does she have to do with anything? I'm talking about Jennifer, my charming big sister. You know, the chain smoker with the sports car who goes out with a different guy almost every weekend and sometimes doesn't come home until the following morning. You'd think my parents would be happy that I made a serious commitment and moved in with you instead of sleeping with every jerk with an over active prick in town." She barely paused for breath. "But no, they're all hung up because I dropped out of school and we haven't gotten married yet and now I'm knocked up. They were always bragging about how easy going and understanding they were and how they think it's important for me to make my own decisions, but when I finally do something that they don't happen to agree with, it's like I slapped them in the face, dragged their name through the mud. They're just a couple of hypocrites is what they are."

Ted raised his hands and managed to cut off the flow of words. "All right, I get it. Why don't you go finish your hair and get dressed while I go for the pizza and when we get back, maybe we can have our own little party." He winked.

Heather was not amused. "In your dreams. That's how I got into this mess in the first place." She patted her belly. "We sleep in separate beds until the brat is born. That'll give you plenty of time to have a vasectomy so this doesn't happen again."

Ted felt his groin contract. "But don't you want more kids someday?"

"I didn't want this one, remember? How are we going to pay for diapers and baby food when neither one of us has a job? We're going to have to take out an equity loan on the house just to pay next month's bills." She turned away. "And hurry up with that pizza. I'm starving."

Ted waited until she had disappeared into one of the bedrooms, then quietly opened the door to the basement and hurried downstairs. The rest of the changes this time might be wonderful but none of them could possibly have made up for what he'd already seen. He was breathing quickly when he reached the bench and sat down, his legs shaky. Roscoe looked up to see if he had brought anything edible with him. "Well, Roscoe, that certainly didn't work out the way I had hoped it might." He picked up the kaleidoscope. "I'm sure things will be better next time. They could hardly be worse." No one had ever warned Ted against challenging fate.

Without even looking through the eye piece, Ted turned the drum on the kaleidoscope, then set it back down, relieved that it had moved relatively easily this time. Roscoe was gone again, either having blinked out of his current existence or just having run off when Ted's back was turned. Ted nodded to himself, took a deep breath, then started for the stairs.

As had become his habit by now, he checked the den first. The furniture was almost back to the way it had been early that morning, as far as he could remember. The television was off and the aquarium was gone. There was a mirror on the wall, but he couldn't quite remember if that was right. The kitchen, however, was still all jumbled. The food dish was in its proper place and said ROSCOE, although there was no sign of the cat. There was a bowl of fruit on the kitchen table and the kitchen witch was still missing. A canned ham, unopened, sat on top of the stove, which had swapped places with the refrigerator again. The dishes and other tableware were in the pantry cabinet rather than the cupboards, which were filled with packaged and canned food, cleaning supplies, and for some reason the extra pillows that should have been in the bedroom closet. The kitchen table was gone, replaced by the wicker one from Jennifer's patio. The bedroom rug was on the floor, badly stained near the sink and stove. The countertops were grimy and the sink was filled with dirty dishes, some of which were quite obviously long term residents. The house in general felt dusty and badly kept.

"Not so good," he muttered under his breath. But where was his wife, whoever she was at the moment?

He poked his head into each of the two bedrooms, but no one else was home. A quick look in the closet told him that he was married again, or at least cohabiting, but he didn't recognize the clothing, which didn't necessarily mean anything. There was a landscape painting on one wall that he was pretty sure had been elsewhere in the house at one time, and some of the other furniture had been rearranged, although not as radically as in the kitchen. The rest of the house seemed relatively normal although when he glanced out into the back yard he noticed that the grill and picnic table had both been relocated.

Ted walked back through the house and out the front door. His driveway was empty and the garage was open. The familiar stack of yard sale items was still there, but there was no station wagon. The birdbath was visible where it had been pushed into one corner so that it was out of the way. He could see a sports car parked in the driveway in front of the Rogers house and, when he turned around, he spotted the tail end of the SUV just inside Jennifer's garage. The sound of a door slamming interrupted his thoughts and he turned again to see Samantha, attractively dressed in jeans and a tight fitting top, emerging from the Rogers house. Samantha noticed him standing there and changed course, walking directly in his direction.

"Hello, Mr. Croner. Is it okay if I hang out over here with you for awhile?" She was clearly flirting a little. Ted felt uneasy. Her sister was at least technically an adult; Samantha was still just a kid.

"Sure, I guess. What's wrong? Problems at home?'

"Well, my mom's really mad at my sister because she's probably going to flunk out of college, but does she yell at Miss College Slut? No, of course not. Jennifer's her favorite. So she takes it out on me. I haven't been able to do anything right for weeks, according to her. It's not fair."

"Your sister Jennifer?" Ted was moving puzzle pieces in his mind. So did that mean he was married to Beth again, or was he still living with Heather? It couldn't be Mary because she was the only one old enough to be Jennifer's mother.

Ignoring him, Samantha launched into a catalogue of woes that was self sustaining and didn't really require an attentive audience. Ted tuned her out as she recounted being yelled at for sleeping too late, for forgetting to wash out her coffee cup, for misplacing the toilet plunger, for playing her music too loud, for not picking up her room, and so on. "Jennifer spends all of her time partying instead of studying, but I'm the one who gets lectured about wasting my time hanging out with the wrong people. It just isn't fair!"

Samantha pulled a crumpled packet of cigarettes from her pocket and automatically offered it to Ted. "Smoke?"

Ted shook his head.

"Mind if I do? I can't smoke in the house because Jennifer says she's allergic." She rolled her eyes to express her opinion of her sister's supposed frailty.

"Be my guest. Are you and your sister both coming to the cookout?"

Samantha lit her cigarette and took a deep draw before answering. "I don't know if ANY of us are going to be coming." She took another couple of puffs, then threw the cigarette down and ground it out with her heel. "I don't know why I smoke. I hate the taste."

"So what's the problem about tomorrow?" Ted was genuinely curious. "I thought everyone was looking forward to it."

Samantha looked away, obviously ill at ease. "At first,

114

maybe. But that was before Mom and Dad found out that you'd invited Heather from next door."

Ted grew more cautious. "What's wrong with Heather? She seems like a nice enough person to me."

Samantha shrugged her shoulders. "You know, the way she dresses. And all those guys she has coming to stay over with her all the time ever since her parents died and left her the house. Mom didn't much like her even before that, and now she has a long list of things that are wrong about her. I'm not even supposed to say hello to Heather if I run into her some place, as though whatever is wrong with her is catching."

Ted was about to ask for more detail when he heard Mary's voice calling from somewhere out of sight, confirming his assumption about her. "Samantha Rogers! Where are you?"

Samantha grimaced. "I guess I'd better go see what she wants. First she chases me away and then she gets mad because I'm not within reach. It's just not fair. Thanks for listening to me, Mr. Croner."

"Any time, Samantha." He stood and watched her trudge back to her front door and vanish into the house.

Ted was about to go back inside as well when he heard a car turn into Bailey's Court. He shaded his eyes and recognized the station wagon, coming directly toward him. Presumably Beth had been out shopping and was just returning. That probably meant lugging bags into the house again, but at least he could probably trade manual labor for a solid lunch. The cold chicken had just whetted his appetite. Eventually he'd figure out what the pros and cons of the current reality were and decide whether to stick with it for a while or switch to another right away.   Things probably couldn't remain as they were, of course, even if it was indeed Beth and not Mary who was his wife. They'd still be in financial trouble and stuck in a loveless marriage. And what good was it to find a miraculous device if he wasn't going to use it to better himself?

But it wasn't Beth driving the car. Nor was it Mary. It was Carl Rogers. He pulled into the driveway when Ted stepped out of the way and killed the engine. He was wearing a tee-shirt labeled THINK.

"I see the troglodyte has finally ventured out of his den."

Carl slammed the car door and walked around to open the tailgate. "We have groceries galore to unload and I stopped at the hardware store and picked up an axe so we could get started on removing that stump in the back yard. Give me a hand with these."

Ted was so stunned that he didn't move. He'd been checking off names in his mind, fitting them into what he thought was their new arrangement, but he couldn't figure out how to fit this new piece into the pattern. How could he be sharing a house with Carl?

Carl, who had already taken one bag from the car, promptly provided the answer. "Get a move on, lover. We have ice cream and a nice fresh ham and various frozen vegetables all defrosting into inedible mush. I made room in the refrigerator for everything before I left. Oh, and I bought a bottle of champagne that we can chill and open for our anniversary tonight."

Ted felt his gorge rise and was almost physically ill. He could not have spoken to save his life. Instead he turned, ran into the house and down the stairs to the basement, almost losing his footing in his haste. He staggered and almost fell again as he crossed to the workbench, half afraid that the kaleidoscope would be gone. Drawing a deep breath to steady himself, he raised it to one eye and turned the drum.

Or at least he tried to turn it. It was stuck again. Ted frowned and exerted more force, but the drum remained obstinately fixed in place, even when Ted strained so hard that he felt his muscles trembling. Desperate, he shifted his grip and tried again, but the drum remained stubbornly immovable. He even tried reversing the direction for the first time, but with no better luck. He dropped his arms, panting softly, sweating profusely.

Carl's voice drifted down the stairs, concerned. "Ted? Are you down there? Is everything all right, love?"

Ted glanced toward the stairs. "Everything's fine," he called shakily. His voice dropped to a whisper. "No, everything is most definitely not all right. Everything is very fucking wrong." He tried to turn the drum again, and once again failed to budge it.

Carl was obviously not satisfied with his answer. "Ted? Your voice sounds funny. Are you sure you're all right? I'm coming down."

"No! I'm good. Just hold on a minute. I left the jigsaw

running and screwed up a project I'm working on. Give me a chance to fix it and I'll be right there."

One of the rags was lying on the bench top. Ted snatched it up, wrapped it around the shaft of the kaleidoscope, and began securing it in the vice as he had before.

"Well hurry it up," called Carl. "I swear you spend as much time in the basement as you do in bed. That's no way to build a strong relationship."

Ted shook his head, glared at the kaleidoscope. "There is no fucking way you're going to leave me in this mess." He took down the wide mouthed wrench and fastened it on the drum, not bothering to provide a protective wrapping this time. Using both hands he applied full pressure.

At first he thought this wasn't going to work either. No matter how much pressure he applied, there was not even the faintest hint of movement. It was as though the drum had been soldered to the shaft. He tried steady pressure and he tried jerky thrusts with both hands. Neither tactic was effective. Ted could hear footsteps overhead and his pulse quickened as he wrapped both hands around the wrench and tried again. This time there was the faintest hint of movement. It might have been an illusion, but Ted chose to interpret it as progress. He shifted his feet to improve his leverage and applied himself again.

Whatever had been providing the resistance failed all at once and the drum head turned so suddenly that Ted lost his balance and almost fell. He was certain this time that the drum had turned, but he had also heard the dismaying sound of metal giving way under pressure. His hands were sweaty and his palms hurt; he lost his grip and the wrench fell to the floor with a clatter, narrowly missing his foot. His heart was beating so rapidly that it felt as though it was trying to burst out of his chest.

Ted leaned forward, put both hands palm down on the bench for a few seconds while he caught his breath, forced himself to calm down. Somewhat more collected, he turned at last to examine the kaleidoscope. The drum had certainly moved; he was quite sure of that. But this time he had damaged it in the process. Where before it had been a perfect circle, the drum was now more than slightly oval and the metal was faintly rippled where the jaws of the wrench had gripped it. He examined the drum carefully and could find no place where it had split or torn, but it had definitely been warped into a new shape. Fearing what he might see, Ted removed it from the vice and peered through the eye piece. The familiar mosaic display was there, but it also had become elongated and flattened.

The distortion made him feel suddenly ill. What if he'd somehow broken the spell, or whatever force was at work here? What if he was stuck in whatever reality now existed? Had it changed at all, for that matter? He dreaded the thought of walking upstairs and finding Carl sprawled on the couch, perhaps with his shirt off. The image made him feel nauseated and he tried to expunge it from his mind. He thought about trying to force the drum back into its original shape, but he was almost afraid to touch the kaleidoscope now. It had been a magical toy, but it was also an object of immense and unknown power, power which might not have worked to his benefit at all this time.

Several minutes passed before he finally found the courage to investigate, minutes during which Ted paced back and forth nervously, unable to settle his thoughts. No one called down to him, which he chose to interpret as an encouraging sign. In fact, there were no sounds from upstairs at all. Carl must be gone then. But who might have taken his place?

Finally, cautiously, he went upstairs.

The house was silent. He went immediately to the kitchen this time rather than the den. If there'd been no change, Carl would be unpacking groceries. As much as Ted feared finding him there, he knew he would not be able to think clearly until he knew one way or another. The kitchen, however, was deserted and there were no bags of groceries in evidence. The refrigerator was gone, however. An aquarium stood where it had been. Roscoe's food dish was also there, but it was sitting in the middle of the table, and it was filled with fruit. There was a dead mouse in the sink.

The stove was on, something in the oven. The smell of cooking meat reminded him that he still hadn't eaten anything substantial since breakfast and he was suddenly famished. He was about to reach for the oven door to open it and peek when the connecting door to the garage opened and Beth appeared. She looked much as she usually did, but she was wearing the THINK tee-shirt. The lettering, however, was reversed. She had a small rose blossom threaded in her hair.

"Oh, there you are," she said brightly. "I thought we were going to have to launch a search party. Lunch will be ready in ten minutes. You just have time to run next door and return these." She raised her hand, offering him a pack of cigarettes. He accepted them automatically.

"Sure." His voice shook a little. "Whose are they?"

"Jennifer's, of course. No one else in the neighborhood smokes." She sounded surprised but not alarmed.

"Right, I wasn't thinking. I'll just drop them off and come right back."

Ted stepped past her and was halfway out the door, his mind racing, when he realized that Beth was still talking to him. "Hold on a second. I just remembered something else. Come with me."

He hesitated, then followed her into the den. The couch was missing and the refrigerator stood in its place. The television was where it was supposed to be, but it was lying on its side. Someone had left it on and the familiar horror movie scene was unfolding. He couldn't see the faces of either figure, but the woman was dressed as the kitchen witch.

Beth was peering around the room, apparently puzzled, then walked over to the refrigerator and reached behind it. She withdrew her arm, dragging out a familiar looking axe. "Here it is! I borrowed this from Jennifer a week ago and I keep forgetting to return it." She turned and handed it to Ted. "As long as you're going there anyway, you might as well bring it back. I won't have time to finish with it before the cookout."

"Sure," he answered, trying to keep his voice under control, refusing to ask just what it was that Beth had planned to do with the axe. "Anything else?"

"Not that I can think of. Tell her hello for me."

Outside, Ted paused just inside the garage and set the axe down, breathing heavily. Things had changed again, all right, but he could already sense that something new and strange had been added to the mix. The switches he'd seen before were sometimes unsettling, but they'd all made some kind of sense. This time was different. Some of these changes were clearly bizarre. For the first time he realized that the forces he was manipulating might not be under even as little control as he had supposed. What had seemed to be a delightful and potentially profitable game was becoming an increasingly risky and unpredictable proposition.

His first instinct was to go back to the basement and use the kaleidoscope yet again, but he knew that was foolish. In its present condition, it would be more likely to make things worse, perhaps much worse, than to improve them. He wouldn't take that risk until he had to, until he knew more about this current reality. And he didn't really want to face Beth again just at the moment, at least not this version of her. There'd been something in her manner that made him very nervous. Even at her most irritating and sarcastic, she'd always been deferential. The Beth he'd just spoken to was self assured and assertive, a lot like Jennifer had been. He could sense the difference and it made him uneasy.

He picked up the axe, checked to make sure he was still holding the cigarettes, and walked across the lawn to Jennifer Hastings's front door. He looked around for the birdbath, but it was nowhere to be seen, and there were no vehicles parked in any of the three driveways. Where was the station wagon? Did he and Beth own one in this reality? He raised his hand to the door bell and hesitated. Was this Jennifer's house now, or had she swapped with the Rogers family? He glanced at the mailbox, but it had a street number, no name. Well, he had an even chance anyway. He pressed the buzzer.

To his great relief, Jennifer answered. She was wearing a dark, tailored suit, complete with necktie. Smiling broadly, she gestured for Ted to come inside, apparently pleased to see him. There was a strange fixity about her expression, but no sense of menace so Ted followed her in. He raised both hands to show what he was carrying, while hurriedly glancing around the room. "Beth asked me to return these." The furnishings seemed almost normal, except that the couch and chairs were all facing the wall and the birdbath stood in one corner with a television mounted on it. Over the couch, a large painting of the Rogers' SUV covered the wall. The curtains looked as though they had been made of wicker.

Jennifer took the cigarettes, almost snatched them from his hand. "I was wondering where I'd left these." She shook the pack, took one out, and crammed it into her mouth, chewing furiously.

Flakes of tobacco spilled from her lips and fell to the floor. "I've been craving one ever since I got up this morning." Her words were slightly slurred and her eyes didn't quite focus.

Ted suppressed the urge to turn and run from the house. "Where do you want this?" He indicated the axe.

"In the kitchen, of course." Her voice had changed, become faintly seductive. "Where else would I keep an axe? Come on, I'll show you."

The kitchen was more cluttered than he remembered it. In one corner, several ratty looking pillows had been stacked against the wall beside a food dish that read SAMANTHA. A hook had been attached to the wall above the dish and a heavy leash dangled from it, ending in a spiked leather collar. Ted glanced away, noticed a fruit bowl full of dead mice in the middle of the table.

He had to try twice before he could find his voice. "Where do you want me to put it?"

Jennifer was watching him with frank appraisal and her voice was low and suggestive. "Just put it in the sink. I have to wash it before I can use it again."

One of Ted's favorite daydreams opened with him returning something to Jennifer's house and having her come on to him. The reality – this reality anyway – made his skin crawl even as other parts of his body responded to the stimulus. He set the axe down carefully on the counter beside the sink, which was filled to overflowing with freshly cut roses. Their thorns seemed unusually long and he would have sworn that those closest to his hand had moved slightly, as though reacting to his proximity.

"Can I offer you something to drink or do you have to get right home?" He might have imagined the flirtation in her voice earlier, but there was no doubt about it now. She was watching him with openly displayed lust, her head tilted slightly to one side, her hands on her hips, her fingers moving slowly as she pressed them against her skin. Ted was simultaneously tempted and repelled. His mind was telling him to run for safety but the rest of his body had a very different agenda.

"I suppose I could stay for a few minutes. Just to be neighborly."

She licked her lips and he felt his pulse quicken. "I don't think you've seen the rest of the house since I redecorated." Her voice was thick, husky.

"No, I don't think I have." So was his.

"Then I think it's time you had the grand tour."

She started toward the rear of the house without glancing back, confident that he would follow. Ted hesitated for a moment, but his eyes were drawn to the sway of her hips and any lingering uncertainty was washed away by a tide of sexual arousal.

Jennifer's house was all on one level with the bedrooms down a short corridor that ran along the back wall of the living room. The central air was running, but wasn't making much headway. The hallway was short and dimly lit, but the first door on the right opened into a master bedroom which, he was happy to note, was laid out quite conventionally. The curtains were drawn and the bright daylight was filtered into a grainy dimness that concealed much of the detail. It wasn't until he had stepped inside that he noticed that some of the shadows and lines in the walls and furniture were actually skeins of undisturbed spider webs. The bed had been turned down, but neatly, and on a spindly table to one side a small portable television had been left on, but with the sound turned down so low it was just a faint murmur. He glanced at the screen just as a white clad figure raced from left to right, closely pursued by a larger one brandishing an axe. Ted looked away before the axe fell for the first time.

Without saying a word, Jennifer had turned to face him, raising both hands to undo her necktie. At that precise moment, Ted thought it was probably the sexiest thing he had ever seen, enticing enough that he could momentarily forget even the spider webs. He had followed her into the room but he stopped now just inside the door.

Her voice was like liquid velvet. "You don't mind if I change while I'm here, do you? I just got home from work and this suit is much too hot for this time of year."

Ted's mouth was dry and various answers suggested themselves, most of them involving offers to help. Despite his long standing admiration of Jennifer, he had to admit to himself that he was still slightly in awe of her. She had a self contained sense of her own dignity that made him feel inadequate and uneasy, as though she was laughing at him from behind her face. Nor had he been able to completely put the spider webs out of his mind. Every time a shadow flickered he found himself glancing that way to make sure it wasn't some many legged creature scurrying across the wall.

"Maybe I should just wait outside until you're done." He regretted the words immediately; they were an admission of his own cowardice. Ted honestly believed that he was an effective, competent person at work, at home, in every situation he faced. His defeats were forgotten or edited into elaborate conceived strategic repositioning. His victories in small matters were magnified into victorious campaigns. He considered himself brave but not foolhardy, innovative but not enamored of change for its own sake, a strong manager who had empathy for his subordinates but who made hard decisions when it was necessary. He was wrong on all counts.

"Don't be silly. We're both adults and I'm not shy." The tie was gone and she started unbuttoning her shirt. "But I'll turn my back for this next part if it bothers you." Enough of her shirt was open to reveal that she wore no bra before she turned around and presented her back. Ted discovered that he was holding his breath and slowly exhaled. He wanted to leave. He wanted to stay.

Jennifer started to slide her arms out of the sleeves of her shirt and the collar slowly slid down her back. As it did so, a tattoo was exposed. Ted didn't really find tattoos a turn on, but he ordinarily wasn't repelled by them either. In this case, he took an involuntary step backward and his gut tightened. At first there were just indistinct points which formed lines and then became identifiable appendages. He knew what was coming even before the bulbous body was revealed as it crouched between her shoulder blades. It was an oversized spider, rendered in such detail that it seemed to Ted that it wasn't a tattoo after all but some hideous living creature that had fastened itself to her back like a leech.

He staggered back a step, then another, barely stifling a cry of fear and disgust. He retreated into the hall, his hands shaking, his knees wobbly. "I really have to get going." His voice was a hoarse croak. "Beth was just taking lunch out of the oven and she'll be furious if I don't get back."

Jennifer had half turned, far enough that he could see her face, not far enough to completely conceal the lurking horror on her back. "But I have so much I want to show you. Why don't you just call and tell her that you're helping me move some heavy furniture? I'm sure she'll understand."

"Some other time. Sorry, I have to go." He retreated a few steps, unwilling to turn away until he was at the end of the hall. Then he bolted through the house and out the front door. He paused outside, leaned over and grasped his knees, retching and coughing. Eventually he felt more in control of himself, straightened up and started back to his own house without even glancing behind. This reality was another wipeout, he realized, and he couldn't get away from it fast enough.

Samantha Rogers was sitting on her front steps. She spotted him, stood up, and started walking deliberately across her lawn in his direction as he approached, clearly planning to intercept him before he reached his door. Although she looked perfectly normal, he had no desire to talk to her again and picked up his pace, hoping to just wave and go inside before she could stop him.

He thought he was going to make it. There were only a few steps left to take before he would be at the door when she called to him. "Mr. Croner! Hold up a second."

"What do you want, Samantha?" His voice was a compound of impatience, irritation, and trepidation, but Samantha had either missed his tone or didn't care whether or not she was welcome.

"Have you seen my sister anywhere? I've been looking for her all morning."

Ted definitely wasn't in the mood. "Not recently, no. I don't think I've seen her since yesterday. Maybe she went for a walk." An amusing thought struck him. "Maybe she had an accident and broke her arm and someone rushed her to a hospital. That seems to happen a lot around here lately."

"She already broke her leg, Mr. Croner, not her arm, and that was a week ago." Samantha was quite close to him now and he realized she was wearing gloves and earmuffs, despite the temperature, oddly paired with shorts and a filmy halter top. "She can barely make it back and forth from her bedroom to the bathroom and I, of course, have to fetch and carry for her highness. It's not fair, but what can you do?" She came to a stop and looked at him directly. "Are you sure YOU are all right? You look like you have a fever or something."

"I'm fine. I've just been very busy lately." He wanted her to go away; he wanted a chance to think and decide what his next step should be.

"I really need to find her. It's kind of important."

"Well, maybe one of her friends came and picked her up. I haven't seen her and I don't have a clue where she could have gone to. Listen, Samantha, I'm sorry but I can't stay and talk. Beth will have lunch on the table and she's not going to be happy with me if I show up late. I'm sure your sister is just fine and she'll turn up any time now." He actually wasn't sure of that at all. He wasn't sure of much of anything just at the moment.

He turned and put one hand on the doorknob, but she moved closer, into his line of sight again, and he found it impossible to ignore her.

"I almost forgot. Mom wanted me to ask if you had an axe we could borrow."

Ted paused, flustered. "What does she need an axe for?"

"You know. Chopping things." She jerked her right arm up and down to illustrate the point. It reminded Ted of the scene from the horror film and his stomach lurched slightly.

He suppressed a shiver. There was something in Samantha's attitude that suggested he didn't really want to know any more. "No, sorry. I don't have one." Inspiration struck. "But Jennifer next door does. Why don't you ask if you can borrow hers?"

"Sure. Good idea. Thanks, Mr. Croner. I'll do that."

"No problem." He watched her walk away toward Jennifer's house, shook his head, and went through the garage and into the kitchen.

The table was set for three. Beth was fussing over the stove and Heather, her leg in a walking cast, was sitting awkwardly at the table. She was wearing an off one shoulder top that provided a good view of her cleavage and Ted couldn't resist looking, although his recent experience with Jennifer kept him wary. His eyes dropped to her belly, which appeared perfectly flat. Had she been pregnant all along, concealing the fact from her parents? Or was that part of the reason Carl had been so obviously displeased with her that morning? Or had someone else been pregnant and traded her condition? Not Mary, surely, or Samantha. Maybe Jennifer had had more time for a social life than she'd let on. Then a really scary thought occurred to him. Could Beth – the original Beth - have gotten pregnant? She was supposed to be taking the pill, but she might have missed one.

"Hi, Mr. Croner." Heather gave him a little wave, breaking his chain of thought.

Beth glanced over her shoulder. "Oh, there you are. I was beginning to wonder if Jennifer had locked you in her basement like she did with Carl. Heather stopped by to borrow some cat food and we got talking, and since there's plenty of food I invited her to stay for lunch. We should be ready to eat in just a minute or two."

"Hi, Heather. Catfood, huh?"

"Yeah. We were going to make soup later."

Ted let that one slide by. He glanced toward the basement door, but his stomach was growling again and the prospect of lunch seemed a more immediate concern than escaping into yet another, possibly even more distorted reality. He slid the closest chair out from beneath the table but didn't sit down. "Did you know your sister is looking for you?"

Heather rolled her eyes. "Again? She just wants me to play another dumb game with her. To be honest, I'm kind of hiding out over here for a while. The last time we played, I got this for a prize." She made a fist and rapped the side of her cast. "And she was up late last night sharpening all the kitchen knives so maybe it's better if I stay out of sight until she loses interest."

Ted's pulse accelerated. "That must have been some game."

"Yeah, well, she cheats, you know. If she hadn't sawed through one of the steps, I would have made it out of the cellar okay. I told her no more booby traps, but she never listens."

Beth carried a bowl of salad over to the table and placed it near the center. Ted examined it surreptitiously, still undecided about whether he should wait long enough to eat or just go downstairs and turn the kaleidoscope again. The salad looked perfectly ordinary, but he had never been fond of what he thought of as "rabbit food," preferring meat and more substantial

126

vegetables.

"The casserole should be just about ready. I baked some potatoes and carrots with it." Beth turned off the stove and began putting on a pair of oven mitts. Ted caught a whiff of the roast and his stomach rumbled. It smelled good.

There was something in Beth's manner that disturbed him, but he couldn't quite put his finger on it. It reminded him in a weird way of Jennifer's intensity while she'd been undressing. Hungry or not, he felt the urge to escape and took a step toward the basement door. "I just need to go downstairs for a minute. I'll be right back."

Beth made a weary sound. "Not again. I swear you spend more time down there than you do upstairs. If you go down now, we won't see you again until supper time. At least sit and have something to eat first. I went to a lot of trouble to prepare a nice dinner and reheated leftovers are never as good as when it's first served."

She had opened the oven door slightly and the aroma of roasted meat filled the kitchen. Ted felt his stomach clamoring for satisfaction. It smelled delicious. "Well, actually I am a little hungry." He glanced at his watch. Somehow it had gotten to be the middle of the afternoon already. "I didn't realize how late it was." He sat down next to Heather, directly across from Beth's seat.

Beth removed the roasting pan from the oven and set it on top of the stove. "I'll let you do the carving, Ted. You're so much better at it than I am."

"It smells delicious, Mrs. Croner," said Heather, and Ted had to agree.

Beth turned and crossed to the table, set the pan down on a wicker trivet shaped like a rose. Ted blinked, his mind refusing to accept the data provided by his eyes. The slab of meat in the pan, garnished with potatoes and carrots, was unmistakably Roscoe the cat. He hadn't even been skinned and his fur was singed into tight little knots. For a few seconds Ted remained frozen in shock, then his eyes began to open wider and his lower jaw dropped. He fumbled behind his back for the chair as he stood up, pushing away from the table, but he was too uncoordinated and it tilted back, falling to the floor with a clatter.

127

Apparently little disturbed by his reaction, Beth took her seat. "What's the matter, Ted? You haven't turned vegetarian on me, have you?"

Ted had to try three times before his voice would work. "That's Roscoe!"

"Of course it is. He was just the right age. If I'd waited much longer, he'd have been tough and stringy and you know how you hate it when your meat is dry and full of gristle."

Heather was nodding enthusiastically. "You should talk to my mom, Mrs. Croner. She says Toby won't be ready to eat until next winter. She's saving him for Christmas dinner."

Beth shook her head. "You know, I never understood why she bought such a small dog in the first place. Toby would be enough for Ted and I, but there's never going to be enough meat on him to feed all four of you. She should have gotten a young Labrador retriever, or a German shepherd."

Ted took another step back from the table, felt the wall behind him. The room seemed to be tilting and he wondered if he was going to faint.

Beth gave him an impatient look. "Do sit down, Ted. And if you're not going to carve, then I'll do it."

"I...I have to go downstairs. For just a minute. I'll be right back." It was as if someone else was operating his vocal chords. He wanted to look away from the broiled corpse, but it was as though his eyes were physically tethered.

Beth didn't argue this time. "All right, do what you have to do. We'll start without you. But you'd better hurry it up. Cat never tastes right once it cools down."

Ted nodded as though this made perfect sense, suppressed the urge to laugh hysterically, and bolted for the stairs.

His legs were unsteady when he reached his workshop and he bent over the waste bin, gagging heavily, thankful for the first time that his stomach was nearly empty, then succumbed to a wave of nausea when he remembered the lunch he'd been offered. Once his spasms had passed, he sat down at the bench, his legs wobbly, sweating heavily. His hands shook when he picked up the kaleidoscope and they were so damp that he could not exert enough pressure to turn the drum. Reason finally displaced imminent panic, however, and he set it down, waited until he felt more in control of himself, then wiped his hands on a rag, wrapped it around the kaleidoscope drum, and began to exert pressure. It didn't move at first and the ghost of his earlier panic began to return, but then there was the slightest of shifts, followed by a full half turn.

He placed it carefully back down on the bench and tried to relax the muscles in the back of his neck. Somewhere along the line he'd developed a raging headache and his hands were shaking again. After a few minutes, he decided that his legs would support him and stood up. The smoothness of that movement reassured him somewhat and he walked to the stairs, climbed almost all the way to the top, then paused, listening for any tell tale sounds from beyond the door.

Eventually he slipped through into the narrow hallway, moving as quietly as possible, then paused again. He could hear the kitchen clock ticking but the house was otherwise quiet. Rather than reassuring him, the silence made Ted more nervous than ever and he moved very cautiously to the kitchen and poked his head inside. There was no one in sight, and the table no longer was set for a meal, was bare except for a fruit bowl made of wicker. He sniffed, but there were no cooking smells either, just a vaguely sour odor as if something had died in the walls. The stove was in its proper place, but the refrigerator was still missing.

The aquarium remained in its place, but it wasn't an aquarium any longer. It was one third filled with sand and contained a few varieties of cactus, as well as a medium sized, currently motionless spider. It wasn't a tarantula, just an enormously oversized garden spider. Somehow that was even more horrible. Ted shuddered when he saw it and gave that side of the room a wide berth, edging around the table. Almost absentmindedly he plucked an apple from the fruit bowl, examined it closely, and began to eat it. His stomach was still knotted but eating something seemed to help. When he reached the corner of the table, he saw a food dish on the floor, filled with chunks of unidentifiable, but bloody meat. The name on the dish was BETH.

He tried the den next. It looked almost normal, except that the painting on the wall was a still shot from the horror movie. An unidentifiable female recoiled from horror as a black jacketed villain prepared to hit her with an axe. Her face reminded him of

Charles Munch's *The Scream*. The man bore a strong resemblance to Carl Rogers. The area rug under his feet was upside down and the television was turned to face one wall.

Obviously the world was still badly out of whack. Ted felt trapped. The damage he'd done to the kaleidoscope was having terrible, bizarre repercussions. When he'd started, there had been the alluring possibility that he would eventually hit upon the perfect combination, or near enough, and that it was just a matter of running through the different permutations of reality until he found one that suited him well enough. Now it seemed that each of the elements of reality was also subject to wild distortion. The best he could hope for in the short term was to find one that would afford him time and safety enough to decide what to do next. He might be able to restore the kaleidoscope to its original shape, or close enough, if he was careful. Then he could find the first reality that was even reasonably acceptable and lock the kaleidoscope away some place and never use it again. Or it might be possible to turn it in the opposite direction and progressively undo all of the changes until he reached the base reality. At this point, he reluctantly acknowledged to himself that he would be happy with that outcome. He and Beth would make it somehow, or they wouldn't. Even the job at Eblis didn't look as unappealing as it had only hours earlier. Sometimes, he realized, you have to make do with the best that's available, at least until something better comes along.

When nothing untoward turned up during his tour of the house, Ted regained some of his self confidence. He walked to the front door, opened it, and cautiously stepped outside. His driveway was empty again and the station wagon was parked in the street in front of the Rogers house. He turned the other way and saw the SUV in Jennifer's driveway. It had been repainted, the side facing him emblazoned with a horned demon, a three armed candlestick with dripping black candles, a goat's head, and a cowled figure, all mixed together into a psychedelic collage. A sinewy rose vine was wrapped around the downspout at the nearest corner of her house, but the flowers were a dark, bloody red and looked like gaping mouths. Okay, he thought to himself, I'm not back in Kansas, let alone Bailey's Court. At least, it wasn't the Bailey's Court that he remembered. Even the silence seemed heavy, oppressive.

He was not tempted to visit the neighbors this time and was about to go back inside when he heard shouting from the Rogers house. Curiosity got the better of his judgment and he stepped out further into the yard just as something heavy crashed against the bay window across the way. Glass exploded outward like a bursting bubble and rained down on the grass and Mary's elaborately constructed cobblestone walkway. The voices grew louder, angry, shouting, muffled at first but more audible as the front door was thrown open and a figure emerged. It was Carl, retreating in obvious haste while facing back the way he had come, his arms raised defensively. Carl was wearing a sweat suit that said THINK across the back of his shoulders.

"Keep away from me, you crazy bitch!"

Carl slowly retreated, followed almost immediately by Jennifer Hastings, who stepped outside with the axe held tightly in both hands. "I told you and told you to stay away from my things, didn't I?" She stepped down into the yard and Carl backed further away, halfway to the street. "But no, you had to mess with them anyway. You couldn't just leave well enough alone. Now they're ruined and I'm going to have to start all over again. Do you know how angry that makes me?" She raised the axe above her head to illustrate. The gesture seemed familiar to Ted and he interpolated what must happen next. Except that it didn't.

Carl's voice changed as he tried to placate her. "Be reasonable, Jenny. I only ate a couple of them. There are still plenty left for tomorrow."

If anything, Carl's words only seemed to make Jennifer angrier than ever. "They were supposed to be a set, you imbecile! They have to be properly balanced on the tray. If the presentation is sloppy and unprofessional, you end up looking like a fool! Is that what you want? Do you enjoy making a fool out of me?"

"Don't you think you're over reacting just a little bit?" There was a hint of anger in Carl's voice now. "There's no reason to make this into a federal case. They're just goddamn tarts, after all. They're supposed to get eaten."

Jennifer made a little rush toward Carl, waving the axe, and he danced back out of range. "You're not going to keep on getting away with this. I've put up with more than my share already. I'll catch up to you sooner or later, you bastard." She lunged forward again.

Carl back pedaled and avoided a not very well coordinated swing, the blade coming nowhere near him. "Later works for me, dear."

She gathered herself together, obviously preparing to renew her attack. Carl glanced to the side and saw Ted for the first time. "You're making a bad impression on the neighbors, darling."

Jennifer raised the axe. "I'm planning to make a bad impression, all right." But she also turned, saw Ted, and gave him a broad smile that he found grotesquely inappropriate. "But not on the neighbors." Slowly, reluctantly, she lowered the axe to the ground, with one hand around the end of the handle. "Sorry if we disturbed you, Ted. Carl and I are having a little family dispute."

Carl edged away from her and toward Ted. "Hey there, Ted. How about I come over and we open a couple of beers while the wife is cooling down?"

Ted most definitely did not want company. If he had wanted company, it would not have been Carl Rogers. If it had been Carl Rogers, it would not be just after his wife tried to cleave him in two with an axe. "I'm not sure that's a good idea right now. I'm kind of busy and the house is a mess."

But Carl kept coming and before Ted could draw away there was a hand on his arm. "Don't worry. It's only me she's mad at and she'll get over it in a while. And you promised me a beer this morning, remember? I've got a powerful thirst just now." He glanced at Jennifer, who was watching warily. She didn't say anything, but she raised the axe, gave it a half hearted shake as if to warn Carl of retribution to come, then stalked back toward the house and disappeared inside. "See? She's already cooling off. You know women. They get overly emotional at times. Raging hormones."

"I'm really tied up just now, Carl. Getting things ready for tomorrow. You know, the cookout." He tried to pull away but Carl's grip was firm.

"Just a beer. I'll stay out of your way if there's stuff you have to get done. I just need to keep out of sight until the little woman has a fresh batch of tarts underway. She never thinks about anything else when she's cooking, particularly when it's her specialty - ham tarts."

"Ham tarts?" Carl ignored him and started toward Ted's front door, finally relinquishing his grip. Ted sighed and resigned himself to the inevitable. Now that he thought about it, he could use a beer himself. He only hoped there was some in the refrigerator. If he could find the refrigerator.

He had to hurry to catch up to Carl. "Is the game on?" Carl headed directly to the den. Ted shook his head and followed, found the refrigerator standing next to the couch. He opened the door cautiously and was relieved to discover various normal looking groceries, a few leftovers, a pair of pliers, several pairs of neatly folded socks, and a six pack of beer. He also noticed a bowl of dead mice covered with plastic wrap. "Nice," he whispered under his breath. "Party snacks, no doubt." He took two beers and turned around to hand one to his visitor.

Carl had apparently forgotten the television, which was still facing the wall, and had wandered out into the kitchen. Ted followed and found him knocking on the glass side of the terrarium instead. The spider was ignoring him. Carl turned as Ted entered. "Roscoe here looks like he's gained a little weight. Have you been feeding him caterpillars again?"

Ted handed Carl one of the beers without replying and both men twisted off the tops and took long, slow pulls. It tasted all right, really good in fact, but Ted was too tense to enjoy it.

Carl made a loud, unpleasant, appreciative sound and smacked his lips. "I like the new arrangement, by the way."

Ted frowned. What was Carl talking about now? The furniture?

"It seems to be working," he answered cautiously.

"I tried to get Jennifer to do something similar once, but you know her temper. She wouldn't last a day."

So this was about Beth. Where was Beth anyway?

"When does she get home?"

"Beth?" He had no idea how to answer the question. "I'm not sure," he said truthfully.

"I suppose the hospital will make her talk to the police before they release her." Carl turned away, clearly not really interested, and walked toward the den. Ted followed him.

Carl turned on the television, even though the screen was

still facing away, and settled into the one chair still present in the room. Ted leaned against the door jamb and drank some more, feeling slightly better.

Carl had settled back in an awkward sprawl and when he talked. He gestured with the beer can, spilling some in the process. "Beth has been acting funny for a while, hasn't she? I said something to her a couple of days ago and she almost bit my head off. I wouldn't have blamed you if you'd chopped her up and buried her body in the basement."

"She's just been very busy getting ready for tomorrow's festivities. You know how it is. Everything has to be just right or it's a major disaster. The usual stuff."

Carl made a disgusted sound. "Huh! Usual for you, maybe. Jenny hasn't cleaned the house in so long that the spider webs have spider webs on them. Samantha's room is so bad I won't even go in there any more."

"Samantha? Your daughter?" Ted knew he didn't want to ask the next question, but it was a compulsion so strong that he couldn't resist. "Why can't she clean her own room?"

Carl frowned and gave him a look laced with anger. "That's not very funny, Ted. You know she hasn't been able to take care of herself since the accident."

Ted retreated hastily. "Of course. Sorry. I wasn't thinking. I've been a little absent minded lately."

The doorbell rang. Both men turned to look toward the front of the house. Carl stood up and moved the curtain away from the narrow window that provided an awkward view of the front lawn. Ted started to leave the room but Carl held up one hand. "Wait! Don't answer it. It's just that witch from next door." He let the curtain fall back.

"Jennifer?"

"No, the other one. You know, Mary what's her name. The lawyer."

The doorbell rang again. Ted was one of those people who was physically incapable of ignoring a ringing telephone or doorbell. "I really should answer that."

"Well, I wouldn't have anyone like that in my house, but this is your place. You do whatever it is that you want to do." Carl took another pull of his beer and settled back into his chair.

"You wouldn't have another of these, would you?"

"In the fridge." Ted walked back through the front room to the door, hesitated, took a deep breath, and swung it open. Mary Rogers stood on his doorstep, her face pinched in an expression of deep concern. She was dressed like the kitchen witch, complete with broom and pointed hat. Ted took a sip of his beer to conceal his expression, which mixed astonishment with levity.

"Hi there," he managed. "What's up?"

Mary's voice was intense, tinged with suspicion. "Is your wife home?" She spoke barely above a whisper and her eyes kept moving back and forth, peering past him into the house, as though she expected something lurking there to leap out at her.

"No, not at the moment anyway. Is there something I can help you with?"

"When will she back?"

"I'm really not sure. I can tell her you were here if you want."

Mary seemed to be considering the situation with considerable care. Ted was almost ready to believe she wasn't going to answer at all when she finally nodded her head. "Perhaps you can help. Do you mind if I come in for a minute?"

Ted sensed once again that things were wobbling out of his control. "Sure. Why not? Come on in." He opened the door wider and Mary stepped into the front room, looking around furtively. Her knuckles were white where she clutched the broomstick.

"Could we talk in the kitchen please?"

Ted was past being surprised. "Sure. Follow me."

He led the way with Mary following so closely that she nearly stepped on his heels. Once there, he turned to face her. "Can I offer you something? Tea? A beer? Maybe a cold mouse?" The urge to laugh, to giggle actually, was rising once more. He had to get rid of her, and Carl, and sit down to think.

If Mary detected anything strange in his manner or words, she gave no sign of it. "No, thank you. I'm fine." She gave a deep sigh and visibly relaxed. "I feel so much better now. I always find it easier to talk in a kitchen, don't you?"

"I can't say that I've ever noticed either way. What can I do for you, Mary?"

"Well, the thing is, I was going to do my shopping today, but I can't seem to get the van to start. I've called my mechanic, of course, but he can't come out to look at it until tomorrow and there are a couple of things that I really need to have right away. I was wondering if I might borrow some from you, just until I can get to the store."

"I don't see any reason why not, if we have them." And if he could find them. "Just what do you need?"

"Well, first of all, I need some rope. Clothes line would be fine, but I'll make do with whatever you have so long as it's reasonably strong."

"I think I can help you with that. Follow me." As he led her out into the garage, he wondered if he should have put her off. He kept an extra coil of clothesline in the garage, but it might be hidden under the bed now, or on the roof, or in Jennifer Hastings's oven. He opened the cupboards where he kept outdoors tools and began rummaging through them. Some of the contents were familiar, others not. He would never have stored the stack of dinner plates here, for example, or the hair curlers, or the package of toilet paper. And he had never even seen the bowler hat before. Or the stuffed owl.

"Of course, handcuffs would be even better, but I don't suppose you'd have any of those. At least none to spare."

Ted blinked but his voice never changed. "I don't think we have a set. Sorry."

"That's all right. I'm sure I can improvise with rope. Or maybe some heavy copper wire if that's the only thing you have. I tried to use an extension cord once, but it just wasn't adequate."

He thought about what she'd just said. Instinct told him to ignore it, but Ted never had been a very disciplined person. "Mary, why exactly would you want a pair of handcuffs?"

"Well, for Heather, of course. She broke the lock on her door last night and got out and caused heaven only knows what kind of trouble. She was in quite a state when she got back home this morning. You know how she gets when she's in one of those moods of hers. It's disgraceful!"

Ted continued his search and found the clothesline tucked into a corner. "Here you go. Brand spanking new."

Mary seemed disproportionately delighted. "This will do

wonderfully. Now I need some raw, red meat, beef if you have it. About a pound, I think, should be enough."

Ted felt the artificial smile freeze on his face. "I think there are some hamburger patties in the freezer. I didn't see anything else in the fridge." Except mice, he thought. Is their meat red?

"Oh dear, it would be so much better if it was fresh, you know. But I suppose I'll just have to make do."

Ted led the way back inside and into the den where the refrigerator now lived. Mary and Carl ignored each other, at least at ostensibly, although once when Ted glanced in their direction he caught them winking at one another. The rest of the time Carl stared intently at the side of the television, occasionally sipping at his beer; the television was on but the sound was so low that Ted couldn't make out what program it was. It sounded as thought someone was shouting or screaming. Mary glanced toward Carl again, her face slipping into an expression of naked lust for just a second, then looked away. The patties were in the freezer, along with two frozen salmon fillets which Mary declined to take. "The meat must be bloody, you know. It just won't do otherwise."

Ted was anxious to get rid of her and his manner became brusque, although she didn't seem to notice. "Is there anything else I can get for you?'

She paused thoughtfully. "I don't suppose you have a chainsaw?"

Ted grimaced. "Uh, no. Sorry. Fresh out of chainsaws."

"Well then I think this is everything. Thank you so much. I can't imagine how horrible things would be tonight if I wasn't prepared."

Suppressing a twinge of curiosity, Ted escorted her to the front room, would have nudged her along except that he felt a deep aversion to touching her. She gave him a final, exaggerated smile just before he closed the door. Ted stood there, massaging his temples with both hands, then slowly turned around. Carl was standing in the doorway, waving an empty beer can.

"Forget about me? I could really use another of these."

"Yeah, sure. I thought I told you to help yourself." He considered having a second as well, but the first had hit him hard on his relatively empty stomach and he decided to forego the beer in favor of a banana from the fruit bowl. When he took it, he noticed that there was a pack of cigarettes at the bottom of the bowl. It was held closed by Roscoe's collar. He shuddered, wondering where Roscoe was now. Alive? Eaten?

Carl had returned to the den. Ted followed and was trying to think of an excuse to eject him, when he heard a faint sound behind him. It hadn't sounded like Roscoe, but something had moved in the darkened end of the hall leading to the bedrooms. He turned and peered around the corner. Someone was crouched down in front of the bathroom door. When his eyes focused, he realized that it was Heather, with her arms wrapped tightly around her body, her head down so that he could barely make out her face.

"Heather?"

She looked up, then stood quickly. "Sshhhh!" She took a step forward, still half concealed in shadows. Her clothing looked odd, as though she'd been rolling around on the floor and had wrinkled and soiled it. There were small tears and large, streaky stains. "Who's in there?" Her eyes drifted toward the den; her voice was a raspy whisper.

Without understanding why, Ted lowered his own voice. "It's just Carl from next door. What's wrong?"

"Is she gone?"

"Who? Mary? Yes, she's gone home. Why are we whispering?"

Heather ignored his question and looked toward the den. "Can you get rid of him?"

"Carl? I guess so. Come out where I can see you." Her secretiveness was contagious; he couldn't bring himself to raise his voice.

Heather moved toward him and his eyes widened. Her hair was a mess, unwashed and unbrushed. She was wearing a heavy dog collar with spikes. One of the sleeves of her blouse was torn off at the shoulder, revealing a black bra strap. There were tears in her jeans as well, but they didn't look as though they were stylishly intentional, and there was a dark patch that might be dried blood on one thigh. She was holding one arm tight against her body, as though it was injured, and she had a black eye.

"What happened? Did someone attack you?"

"No, it was just her. She does this all the time. She never

lets me have any fun." Heather sounded irritated rather than frightened. "She still treats me like a child."

"Mary? Mary did this to you?"

"She's just jealous because no one wants her any more." Heather had become defiant. Even her voice had risen. "They want me." She rearranged herself into a position which was probably intended to be provocative, but which Ted found more appalling than appealing. "Tell him to go away and I'll show you why." She gestured toward the den.

Ted licked his lips. This didn't fit the scenario of any of his erotic fantasies, and he still had trouble thinking of Heather as a woman and not as a child. On the other hand, she was not bad looking, even in her mildly battered state. If anything, the implied vulnerability was something of a turn on. "I'll see what I can do. Stay out of sight."

He found Carl still sprawled in the chair, staring at the television, even though he had apparently turned it off. "Here you go." Carl accepted the beer with an offhand nod, never turned to look at Ted.

"Look, Carl. Like I said, I'm really kind of busy right now. I have a whole list of things that I have to get taken care of before tomorrow. I hate to be a bad host but..."

"But you'd really like me to hit the road." Carl turned to look at him at last, his expression neutral.

"Yeah, that's pretty much it. Sorry. Maybe your wife has calmed down by now, or you could walk up to the Rapid-Mart and shoot the shit with Arnold." Too late he remembered that Arnold no longer managed the Rapid-Mart, but his unwelcome guest didn't seem to have noticed.

Carl took a sip and stood up slowly. "That's all right. I think Jenny's had time enough to cool down. She doesn't hold a grudge long. I'll say that much for her. And if she's still mad, she won't remember why and probably won't blame me. She doesn't even remember what she did to Samantha any more." He took another drink and started toward the doorway.

Ted stepped to one side to allow him to pass. "We'll see you all tomorrow, then?"

"Sure. I'll probably bring Samantha over early and get her set up in the back yard. She doesn't get enough sun in her room, particularly since Jenny boarded up the windows, so it'll be a good chance for her to get out for a while. She's as pale as a maggot."

"Great! It'll be nice to see her." Ted hoped he sounded at least minimally enthusiastic.

He followed Carl to the front door and watched him walk away across the grass. Obviously he was going to have to use the kaleidoscope again. Maybe it was time to seriously try moving it in the opposite direction. But before he did that, he was going to find out just what it was that Heather was offering. After all, he deserved some kind of compensation for all the difficulties he'd been put through during the last few hours, didn't he? And it wasn't as if it would really have happened once things got shifted around again, right? Ted had never experienced any difficulty in constructing a rationalization for doing whatever it is that he wanted to do, and this was no exception. If he felt the faintest sliver of guilt, or worry, he swept it away carelessly.

He turned and found Heather standing only a few paces away, watching him intently. She was leaning against the doorjamb leading to the kitchen, her pose awkwardly provocative. "Alone at last," she said quietly.

Now that the moment had come, Ted felt a sudden uneasiness. There was something in Heather's manner that wasn't just seductive. It was almost predatory, reminding him of those unsettling moments in Jennifer's bedroom. She looked at him the way Roscoe watched an unsuspecting mouse, just before he pounced. He remembered Mary's request for handcuffs and wondered if, just possibly, there might not have been a very good reason why she wanted them.

And then his stomach growled and he realized that he was feeling light headed. The beer was really getting to him. "What say we have something to eat? I'm so hungry I'm ready to fall right over." He tried a small laugh, but it sounded so awful that he cut it short.

"I'm hungry too," she said slowly, caressing each syllable. "But not for food."

"Well, you can watch me eat if you like." But he made no effort to turn away. The more he watched her, the more nervous he became. She probably hadn't deliberately placed herself so as to block the door, but unless she moved he wouldn't be able to get past her without initiating physical contact, and even though he was still half turned on, he was also half turned off. With Beth, he had always been the aggressor. He wasn't sure he liked this role reversal. He preferred to be in control. A surge of anger stiffened his back and he moved forward, intending to brush past her and prove that he was not as malleable as she apparently believed.

"I can think of something much better you can do with your mouth." When he tried to step past her, Heather pushed away from the doorway and put one hand on his chest, as though to restrain him. Ted fought down the urge to pull away. It was suddenly very important that he not reveal his growing anxiety. Heather looked as though she smelled his fear already, and he was reminded once again of Roscoe, playing with his prey.

"So can I, but I'll enjoy it a lot more if I put something solid in my stomach first."

Her face fell, but it was an obviously deliberate pout and she didn't drop her hand. Instead her lower body swayed and he felt her hip press against his. His body was sending very mixed signals now. The sexual tension was palpable, but there was still something very wrong.

"I don't think you like me, Mr. Croner." She had switched to a little girl's voice that set his nerves on edge.

"Sure I like you." He didn't want to burn his bridges yet, but he could already feel his anticipation ramping down. Alarm signals were going off in his head. "But maybe this isn't the right time and place. Carl might have heard you talking. You wouldn't want him to tell Mary that you and I were doing something naughty, would you?" It cost to say that, because he was thinking about several very naughty things he'd like to be doing with her right that very minute. Caution – not to mention fear – was winning its battle, dampening his enthusiasm. He trusted his instincts, and they were telling him to run away. On the other hand, he told himself, you're a lot stronger than she is, and her body was definitely not that of a child.

Heather seemed to realize that she had overplayed her hand and that he was backing off, mentally if not physically. She leaned back against the door frame again, her expression dour, arms crossed resolutely across her chest. "You're teasing me. I don't think you like me after all, and I'm not sure I like you either."

"Well, I'm sorry you feel that way. Maybe under the circumstances you should just go home. We can talk about it again later." His pulse was slowing and he began to wonder why he'd found her so alluring only a moment earlier. He felt something close to revulsion now.

Heather's face screwed up in an expression of disgust. "Back to that old witch? Not on your life." She dropped her arms and tried to look like the forlorn waif again, but achieved only awkward petulance. "She'll just lock me up in my room, or maybe even worse. You don't know how evil she is. I want to stay here with you. I can hide down in the basement, maybe. If you don't tell her where I am, she'll never find me there."

"Not the basement!" He involuntarily glanced toward the cellar door. "You wouldn't like it down there. You'd just feel locked up again."

She swayed toward him and wriggled her shoulders so that the damaged side of her top fell a little lower, exposing the top half of one breast. "Are you sure you don't want me to stay? We could have a lot of fun together if I moved in here with you. I'm sure Beth wouldn't mind. She and I get along just fine and there's lots of things that three people can do that two people can't."

Ted's internal battle threatened to boil over once again. "What exactly did you have in mind?" His voice was hoarse.

"I know you gave her some rope. Do you have any more?"

"Probably. What do we need rope for?" Wicked images began flashing through his mind.

She moved forward and he retreated toward the kitchen, but somehow she maneuvered him so that his back was to the near wall. He could almost feel the heat coming off her body. She put one hand lightly on his chest again and her touch seemed to slash through the shirt into flesh. "Well, if you have some more rope, you could tie me to the bed. Or I could do you if that turns you on." She touched him with her other hand, running her fingers lightly up over his ribs. He shivered, but didn't know whether it was passion or revulsion. He was tempted, very tempted, but those alarm bells were still going off somewhere deep in his mind and he wanted to step back for a minute, think about what he was doing. It was never wise to jump too quickly. If he had acted on impulse, he would've taken that job at Eblis even though he knew it wasn't satisfactory, and then he'd have been stuck until he could find a graceful way out. Oh, he could always quit, of course, but prospective employers weren't reassured when they saw that kind of thing in your employment history. It suggested something was wrong.

And something felt wrong here. Something in Heather's demeanor bothered him and his sense of self preservation pushed back against his physical craving. "Maybe we should talk to Beth about that first."

"What is wrong with you?" Her voice deepened but her hands moved up to his shoulders. "Don't you want me?" She touched his cheek. "I know I want you."

Ted raised his hands, took hold of her forearms, and deliberately pushed her away. Not roughly, but firmly. He smiled to take the sting out of it and tried to look apologetic and infatuated and commanding all at once. The result was insincerity and sly indecision. "All right, what have I got to lose? Why don't you go ahead into the bedroom and get ready? I think I have some more rope downstairs. I'll just go and get it."

"You won't be long?" She was clearly suspicious.

"I'll practically run down the stairs." And he would too.

Heather started toward the bedroom, but paused and looked back at him, her eyes sharp and clear. "You won't make me wait, will you?"

"I'll only be a minute or two. I promise." Technically, it wasn't even a lie, because in a minute or two, she would have no memory of this conversation, probably wouldn't even be in the house. All he had to do was banish her with a turn of the kaleidoscope.

He was breathing hard when he reached the workshop, but not because he'd run. Knowing that Heather was upstairs in his bedroom and not following her was one of the hardest things he'd ever done, but fear had triumphed over lust.

Not without considerable regret, he picked up the kaleidoscope. Now the question was whether to go forward or to try to backtrack - if the latter was even possible. Although he only had a hazy idea how an ordinary kaleidoscope worked, he was pretty sure that you couldn't recapture old patterns simply by turning the drum in the opposite direction. The crystals would just fall into another new configuration. He stared at it thoughtfully, wondering if perhaps he might not be better served by attempting to reverse some of the physical damage he'd done. The drum was noticeably misshapen and it made sense that if the mechanism was distorted, so too would be whatever changes it generated. He was probably lucky that he hadn't ruptured it and destroyed its magical properties altogether.

"Maybe if I straighten this out a little," he said to himself. The metal wasn't actually torn and if he was careful, he ought to be able to restore it to something close to its original shape.

There was a noise from upstairs, probably Heather growing impatient. Ted shivered and took the drum between both hands, attempting to force it back into its original circular shape. As far as he could tell, the effort did no good whatsoever. He hadn't really expected that it would.

It had taken a wrench to do the damage; it would probably require the same again to undo it. He carefully wrapped rags around the kaleidoscope and secured it in the vice. More sounds from upstairs, obviously footsteps crossing the floor. He heard the door open at the top of the stairs.

"Are you coming or not?" Heather sounded angry.

He turned and shouted toward the staircase. "In a minute. I haven't found the rope yet."

"Well, we can use something else. I haven't got all day, you know."

"Just wait a little. If I don't find it pretty soon, I'll come up."

She didn't answer, but the door slammed.

He had the wide mouthed wrench now, and carefully closed the jaws so that they gripped the drum firmly. Ted knew that he had to be very careful. If he applied too much stress to the metal, it would split, and that way lay more uncertainty than he cared to risk. Very slowly, he closed the jaws until he felt resistance, took a deep breath, then continued, applying more pressure. There was the faintest sound of metal under stress. Ted stopped, opened the vice and unwrapped the kaleidoscope. It was still misshapen, but it looked as though he distortion had decreased slightly and there was no sign of a break in the smooth surface of the metal. He wrapped it again and started the process anew.

Half a dozen cycles later, Ted decided he'd done just about as much as he dared. The results were far from perfect, but the shape of the drum was clearly more circular than it had been when he'd started. He was considering one more round when he was interrupted.

Heather opened the door again. He hadn't even heard her footsteps this time because he'd been concentrating so intently. "Ted, if you don't come up here right now I'm coming down to get you. No one keeps me waiting like this. No one. It's just not fair!"

Her voice was brittle with fury and Ted decided that he didn't want to be anywhere near her while she was angry, perhaps not even when she was happy. He gave the kaleidoscope one more quick examination, noting a slight flattening here, the hint of a wrinkle in the metal there. Bad as it was, it would have to do. He could hear the top step's familiar creaking sound as Heather started down toward him. "Did you hear me, you asshole!"

Ted raised the kaleidoscope to his eye and turned the drum. Or rather, he tried to turn the drum. It wouldn't budge. "God damn it to hell!"

"What did you say to me?" The voice dripped with menace. Ted glanced toward the stairs, saw Heather's legs up to her knees. They were actually quite nice legs. She was halfway down and, apparently, had taken off her jeans. Maybe everything else as well. Ordinarily he would have looked forward to seeing the rest of her, but instead he felt close to panic. He tried to turn the drum again, but it still wouldn't move. Apparently his attempt to repair the damage he'd done had had unintended consequences. Either that or the damned thing was just acting contrary again. His palms began to sweat and he almost dropped it.

He realized that he would have to use the wrench to move the drum, if even that would work, but when he picked up the heavy tool, it slipped from his shaking fingers, bounced off the bench, and caromed away into a corner. Ted put the kaleidoscope down, slid off the stool, and retrieved it, but when he stood up and turned back to the bench, the kaleidoscope wasn't there. He blinked several times, dumbfounded, before a slight sound to one side suggested the solution.

Heather was standing just out of reach, completely naked,

holding the kaleidoscope close to her face. There were bruises and scratches on her body, and on one thigh the tattoo of a battleaxe. "So what's the deal with this old thing?"

Ted licked his lips, terrified, told himself that if he couldn't turn the drum, Heather certainly would not be able to. "Nothing special. It's just something I'm trying to fix. I think it's an antique and it might be worth a lot of money." He stepped toward her and raised his hand, but she backed away warily.

"It has to be more than that if you're willing to play around with this instead of playing around with me."

"Heather, please give that back. It doesn't even belong to me. I'll be in big trouble if anything happened to it." More trouble than she could possibly have guessed. Ted realized that he was babbling and forced himself to stop, saw from Heather's expression that he had not been particularly convincing. He switched to what he hoped was a more confident, less anxious tone. "Just hand it over and I'll put it away and we'll go upstairs. I'm sorry that I got distracted." His eyes ran up and down her body and he genuinely was sorry. Sort of.

Abruptly, Heather hid the kaleidoscope behind her back. "No, I don't think so. I think I'll just keep this for a while. If you want it back, you're going to have to do something for me. Something really dirty."

All sexual desire left him in a rush. His immediate fear was that Heather would damage the kaleidoscope beyond repair and that he'd be stuck in this inexplicable and very unpleasant reality for the rest of his life. Then a more frightening thought occurred to him. What if Heather managed to turn the drum somehow? Then he'd be one of the variable items, no longer the center of events. He might not even remember what the kaleidoscope was and never even try to get it back.

"All right, I'll do anything you want. But you have to let me have that back first or I'll never be able to concentrate."

"No." She drew the word out like a dying breath. "I like having the leverage. It'll give you some incentive to please me." Ted took another step toward her and she danced back all the way to the foot of the stairs. "Now, now. If Teddy wants his reward, he has to make little Heather happy first."

"Damn it!" Fear and fury filled his voice. "I said give it

146

back to me and I meant it!"

Heather recoiled as though he'd hit her. "Don't you yell at me! Don't you dare! That's what she does! She does it all the time and I don't like it! I very much don't like it!"

Ted tried to moderate his tone, but his voice still came out raw and angry. "Then just put it down on the bench and I won't be angry any more. Come on, we'll just forget about it and go upstairs. You must be chilly down here." Probably not, since he could see the sweat glistening on her body.

She brought her arm out from behind her back, then raised the kaleidoscope over her head. "If you want it that badly, why don't you come and get it?"

Ted immediately lunged forward, grabbing at the kaleidoscope, but his foot slipped and he missed with his first grab. He regained his balance and tried again, and Heather slapped his hand aside, surprising him with the strength of her countermove. Then she was running up the stairs and he was following her, but she was light on her feet and was through the door before he was halfway up. He heard the faint patter of bare soles across the floor as he reached the door, but in his haste he tripped, banging one shin against the threshold, and fell forward. By the time he had recovered and stood up, there was no sign of her, and he couldn't hear her either.

"Heather? Where are you?"

He tried the bedroom first. The blankets had been turned down and her ruined clothing was lying in a heap on the floor, but she wasn't there. He didn't find her in the guest bedroom or the bathroom either. A hasty glance into the den was equally unproductive, and the kitchen was empty and silent. Ted felt a glimmer of despair, then heard the distinct sound of the latch on the back door.

When he stepped out into the back yard, he thought at first that she'd vanished. Then she stepped out from behind the barbecue grill, still naked, and waved the kaleidoscope at him. "Time to play, Teddy! Come and catch me if you can!"

Ted didn't waste his breath trying to reason with her this time. He charged across the lawn, expecting her to freeze in surprise or perhaps turn and run away. She had long legs and could probably out distance him for a few seconds, but Ted fancied that he'd kept himself in good shape, that she couldn't stay out of his reach for long, particularly out in the open. His conviction that he was physically fit was another of his secret vanities that had no basis in fact. He'd put on weight in the wrong places, his stamina had suffered from his indolent life style, and he hadn't exercised regularly in years. She could probably have run rings around him for the rest of the afternoon.

She enjoyed teasing him, letting him get almost within reach before darting away. Sometimes she danced in toward him rather than fleeing, catching him completely by surprise, and when he tried to catch her by the arm she did a graceful little sideslip and ran past his outstretched arm. When he charged, she retreated, letting herself be driven back to the line of dense underbrush at the rear of his property, then slipped past him and ran back toward the house.

Within a few short minutes Ted was breathing hard and his heart was pounding. "Stop playing games, Heather," he shouted hoarsely. "Just give it back and I won't be mad at you any more."

She laughed at him. "But I like it when you're mad. Maybe if I let you catch me, you could spank me and tell me what a bad girl I've been. Or I could spank you for being so mean."

He wanted to do a lot more than just spank her, but he realized now that she could keep out of his reach indefinitely. It might prove smarter to play along, at least for the moment. "You've sure been bad all right. Now let's stop playing games before someone sees you like that."

Heather glanced down at her body as though she didn't understand what he was talking about. "Like what? Don't you like the way I look?"

"You're gorgeous." He couldn't quite keep the sarcasm out of his voice. Heather had dropped her arms and her pose was more relaxed; she didn't react when he took a couple of slow steps toward her, closing the gap between them. "Look, if you don't want to give it to me, just put it down some place safe and we can go back to the bedroom." If she wanted to be tied up, he'd oblige, then recover the kaleidoscope and make his escape.

Heather seemed to be considering his suggestion. She turned the kaleidoscope over and over in her hands. "What's so important about this old thing anyway?"

"I told you, it's a valuable antique. So just put it down before you break it, okay?"

"Valuable? This thing? It's just a piece of junk, a toy."

"But it's old, Heather. Probably hand made." He took another step forward and this time she took a matching one back. "Please just put it down."

Her face grew animated again and she backed away a couple of steps. "I don't think so."

"Look, what do you want for it? I have some money." He stopped where he was, afraid that any further advance would spook her into running off again.

Apparently the prospect of ransom appealed to her because she abruptly dropped the playful look and grew more serious. "How much money are we talking about?"

Ted felt a flash of hope. "How much do you want?"

"A million dollars."

Ted took another pace forward. "You know I don't have that kind of money. Be reasonable." He was almost close enough to risk lunging toward her. "How about a hundred? That's all I have in cash." Actually, he had less than twenty in his wallet, but Beth kept about fifty dollars in coins in an old fishbowl in their bedroom. If it was still there.

"Why would you give me a hundred dollars for this old thing?" She waved the kaleidoscope disdainfully. "Do you have it on you?"

"Some of it's in my wallet. The rest is in the house. I told you it's an antique. Look at the date stamped on the bottom if you don't believe me."

There was no date, of course, but Heather tried to figure out what part was the bottom so that she could look, and that was as much of a distraction as he was likely to get. Ted leaped toward her and caught her free arm as she tried to spin away. He felt his grip slipping as she dropped one shoulder and tried to break free. His finger slid along her forearm to her wrist, but her skin was slick with sweat and he knew he'd lost her. Heather threw herself backward, wrenching her arm free, staggered a few steps and recovered her balance more quickly than he could. Ted planted both feet and lunged toward her. She eluded him easily again, back pedaling and laughing, but her foot slipped and she almost fell.

Ted almost had her then, but somehow she recovered and managed to stay just out of reach. Then she turned, obviously preparing to sprint away. Desperate, Ted threw himself forward and shoved her hard in the back. She stumbled, managed to maintain her balance for only a few of steps, then went sprawling face first onto the grass.

Ted crouched over her, trying to grab the kaleidoscope, but she rolled away, laughing, and kept it out of his reach, shielded by her body. When he tried to straddle her, she lashed out with one long leg and hit his right knee hard enough to bring tears to his eyes. He cried out and danced back awkwardly, recovering quickly when he saw her scrambling to her feet.

"No you don't!" He tackled her from behind, wrapping both arms around her waist, and they hit the ground together hard. Under other circumstances, Ted might have found wrestling with a naked college student exciting and pleasurable but just now it seemed like the latest in a string of nightmares. His only thought was to recover the kaleidoscope and engineer an escape from this horrific reality.

She was stronger than he expected and determined not to give up her prize. Or maybe she just enjoyed the rough housing. She switched hands when he managed to pin one arm down, and her constant squirming made it impossible for him to set his legs and gain sufficient leverage to control her. At one point a flailing hand hit his nose and he swore at her, and that brought a delighted laugh. She tried to drive her knee into his groin but he blocked the blow.

"God damn it! Lie still!" Ted slapped her. He did it without forethought and was a little bit shocked by what he'd done. Heather seemed to have been taken by surprise as well. She lay back, motionless at last, the kaleidoscope held just above her head. The rage he'd felt subsided quickly and he was about to apologize when he saw the expression on her face. She was smiling.

"Now that was more like it, lover." There was a purr in her voice that reawakened his faltering lust and for a second or two they were both motionless. "Kiss me and I'll give you anything you want."

It wasn't clear to Ted which was the greater motivator just

at that moment, the kaleidoscope or the sex. He placed his hands on the ground on either side of her face and slowly lowered his head, closing his eyes as he felt the heat of her body against his. Maybe he could have both after all.

And Heather swung her arm up and hit him across the side of the head with the kaleidoscope.

Ted didn't immediately lose consciousness, but it felt as though his brain had been disconnected from the rest of his body. He was aware of the fact that he was falling, that Heather had rolled out from under him, flipping him over onto his back in the process, but there was no sense of alarm. He felt suspended in time and space and the world seemed to flicker around him. He could see a single, large, oddly shaped cloud drifting across his field of vision. It looked a lot like a birdbath. Then Heather's face came into view, twisted by lust, but it wasn't sex that drove her now, he realized, but violence. She raised both arms above her head, holding something he'd been trying to take away from her, but he couldn't recall exactly what it was or why he had wanted it.

She was going to hit him again. He accepted that with no real sense of alarm. He had settled into numbed resignation, almost looked forward to losing consciousness. He thought about closing his eyes but decided to keep them open. He wanted to see this, to find out how his story finally came to its end. But before the blow could fall, another shape appeared behind her, dark, indistinct, and a loop of rope fell past her face and tightened around her throat and then she was gone, pulled out of his line of sight, and the weight on his chest was gone. But it didn't matter because the sky was growing dark anyway and he closed his eyes and let his awareness fade away.

It was almost full dark when Ted regained consciousness. The fight with Heather came back to him almost immediately with all of its implications and he sat up in sudden terror, then regretted having done so. He had a terrible headache and felt dizzy. Several minutes passed before he even considered his next move. The first attempt to get to his feet was a miserable failure; the second was slow, tentative, and when he was finally erect, he wasn't sure he could walk. He reached up to touch the side of his face and felt dried blood, not a lot of it, but even a little was enough to make him queasy again. He'd always been a bit squeamish about blood, particularly when it was his own. Dispassionately, he realized that he'd lost the kaleidoscope, for the second time today, and this time the prospects of recovering it were not good. But it was hard to muster enough emotion to care about anything except his head just at the moment. As soon as he felt steady on his feet, he made his way back to the house and into the bathroom.

The man in the mirror looked familiar, despite the unruly hair and a face plastered with sweat and blood. He ran cold water and carefully washed, then examined the cut that ran from the side of his temple down to his cheek. It had stopped bleeding and didn't look like it would need stitches, but he put some antiseptic on it and a bandage across the worst part. There was considerable bruising as well. Damn it! She might have given him a concussion, particularly if the second blow had landed. Fear gave way to fury. He felt angry, almost angry enough to forget his terror.

He was also ravenously hungry.

A more thorough search of the refrigerator turned up a bizarre variety of items. There were light bulbs in the vegetable crisper and several pairs of socks in the freezer. Most of the remaining contents were food, or appeared to have been food at some time, although some of it was moldy, some was mixed with other items that were inedible, and some was just unidentifiable. He did find a few raw carrots and the remains of a stick of cheddar, both of which he wolfed down with a beer chaser. The pantry cabinets were similarly chaotic. There were more than a dozen boxes of Red Rose tea, as well as a bottle of antifreeze, the long missing remote for the television, and several cartons of cigarettes. Ted found a not quite stale loaf of bread and ate several slices while completing his search, but with the worst of his appetite abated, the gnawing in his gut gradually ceased.

He began to feel a bit stronger, but his hands were still shaking and his pulse was elevated. He thought about the kaleidoscope and the possibility of its recovery. He could still remember everything that had happened, or at least he thought he did, which suggested that Heather hadn't used it yet, unless his memories had somehow survived another transition. In either case, he could still recapture the initiative if he could reclaim it soon enough. Heather might even have discarded it after knocking him unconscious. But where had she gone and why hadn't she delivered that second blow? He remembered the vague shape he'd seen just before blacking out, the rope. Had Mary come to his rescue? If so, she'd just left him to recover in his own good time. But where was the kaleidoscope if that was the case? Could she have left it outside?

Ted went out through the back door and made a thorough search of his back yard in the waning light, but the kaleidoscope was nowhere to be found. He felt a wave of despair that almost sent him back into the house for more beer. Where was Beth? He hadn't seen her, or her current version, since the last change, and it appeared that they were together again.

He worked his way around the house, searching in the shrubbery and every other out of the way spot he could find, just in case Heather had thrown the kaleidoscope away when she'd been attacked. Sometimes he looked in places he had already checked thoroughly. Sometimes he was so distracted that he couldn't remember where he'd looked and where he hadn't, which meant he had to back up and search an entire area again. The sun seemed to drop suddenly below the horizon, leaving him in increasingly inky darkness, and he was in the process of retrieving a flashlight in order to continue when he realized there just wasn't any place else to search. At least not here. He needed to look where he should have started. Heather, or possibly Mary, had obviously taken it with her. Had they gone home or left the neighborhood entirely?

If it was the latter, he wouldn't even know where to start. That left only one alternative. Resolutely, he turned and started walking toward Jennifer's house, or what had once been her house back when this had all started. Now, apparently, it belonged to Mary and Heather.

He was headed for the front door but he stopped suddenly when a sports car turned into Bailey's Court, moved far too quickly to the turnaround, then pulled into the driveway ahead. It was dark enough for Ted to step into a shadow and be effectively invisible. He could see the driver clearly when the outside light snapped on. It was Carl Rogers. He didn't get out of the car, or even turn off the engine, just waited. Perhaps another minute passed before the front door opened and Mary came out, still wearing her witch outfit. She went around to the passenger side and got in. They didn't speak. Carl never even looked in her direction. But his earlier antipathy toward her was no longer evident. He backed the car out into the street and they drove off together. If either of them spotted Ted standing between the two houses, they gave no sign. Were they having an affair? Had their earlier diffidence all been an act? Ted shook his head. He didn't care, and if he succeeded in his mission, it wouldn't matter. That's how he thought of it now. It was his mission.

As soon as they were out of sight, Ted went directly to the front door and pressed the bell. He heard it buzzing inside but there was no other sound. There was a light on in the front room but what he could see of the rest of the house appeared to be completely dark. He rang the bell twice more before opening the screen door and, very carefully, trying the inner door. Not surprisingly, it was locked.

He stepped back and looked around. If necessary, he was fully prepared to break a window and enter that way. The damage would presumably disappear once he turned the kaleidoscope, if he found it. Or it would at least be displaced. Jennifer had talked about installing a burglar alarm a while back, but had never gotten around to it. Presumably that still held true here. The Rogers didn't have one. Ted walked around the perimeter of the house, examining each window, trying to decide which would be the easiest to force. Then he reached the back door and decided to try that as well.

The knob turned in his hand and the door opened.

Ted stuck his head inside. The interior of the house was completely dark except for a dim glow that filtered in from the front room. There wasn't even a nightlight in the kitchen. He could hear a clock ticking somewhere, but there was no other sound. The air conditioning was off, or broken down, and the air was stale and hot. There was an unidentifiable odor that made him think of moldy food. "Hello? Is anyone home?" He waited for an answer, not entirely certain that he wanted one. He called again, then slipped inside and closed the door quietly behind him, wishing he'd thought to bring a flashlight after all. It was full dark outside now and the clear sky and nearly full moon provided limited light. "Heather? Are you home?"

He checked the kitchen and front room without finding

anyone. Some of the furniture was arranged oddly, but otherwise nothing seemed too distorted. Nothing that he could see anyway. Satisfied that no one was hiding in the shadows waiting to pounce on him, he started down the hall toward the bedrooms.

When he reached the corner, he tried the first door. It was obviously in use as a bedroom, but he couldn't see any details until his eyes focused and he was afraid to turn on the light. No one was there, but a large straw broom lay across the bed. The wall paper appeared to be interlocking roses. He backed out and closed the door. The adjoining bathroom was also deserted, but light flickered under the bottom of the door to the next room. He hesitated, knocked softly, and thought he heard a rustle from inside. "Heather?" There was no answer.

Ted gathered what remained of his courage, told himself that anything he did now was reversible once he'd reclaimed the kaleidoscope, grasped the knob, and swung the door open.

It was another, smaller bedroom. The flickering light came from perhaps a dozen candles scattered randomly about, together providing enough light that he could see the shape if not the texture of the chaos that reigned there. Clothing, books, makeup containers, left over food, dirty dishes and silverware, and general debris covered most of the floor, the flat surfaces on the furniture, and accreted into unpleasant and shaky looking piles in the corners. He sensed rather than saw faint movement and imagined roaches and ants scurrying about, and then thought about spiders and shuddered, almost withdrawing into the hall. Every available surface was covered by the mess except for the bed. There was only one object on the bed. It was Heather, tied spread eagled with the clothes line that he had loaned to Mary. She'd been gagged with a soiled dish towel. He was relieved to see that she was no longer naked, although the terrycloth bathrobe was disarranged and still provided a distracting view.

Thoughtfully, Ted sat down on the bed beside her. Her eyes were alert and calm, almost unblinking. She was obviously fully conscious and recognized him but she gave no indication of alarm, hardly reacted at all. He watched her face for a minute or two, organizing his thoughts, then reached down and pulled the gag out of her mouth. "Hello, Heather."

"Hello, Mr. Croner." It was a little girl voice, but she

smiled at him seductively, apparently still playing the same game she'd adopted earlier. "I hope I didn't hurt you too badly. I didn't mean to hit you so hard but I kind of got carried away. That happens sometimes even when I don't want it to." The last sentence sounded almost wistful.

"I'll survive." He managed not to let his simmering anger seep into his voice or face. "Where's the kaleidoscope, Heather?"

She smiled. "Untie me and I'll show you."

Without thinking, Ted raised his hand to touch the wound on the side of his head. "No, I think it would be best if you stayed just the way you are, at least for the time being. Tell me where it is and once I have it, then I'll untie you."

"If you untie me, I can think of much nicer things we can do than play with that old thing." There was only a hint of her earlier enthusiasm. Heather seemed to realize that she had already played that card.

Ted was surprised to realize that he felt not the slightest hint of sexual arousal this time. Heather had ceased to be a desirable young woman as far as he was concerned. She had become a thing, an artifact of this horribly contrived alternate reality, and the thought of having sex with her roiled his stomach. It was disturbing just to be this close.

He struggled to keep his voice level. "I think this time we'll play by my rules. Yours are a little bit too rough for me. Now tell me what you did with it." Heather's eyes flashed and she pressed her lips together, obviously unwilling to cooperate. Ted sighed. "I don't want to hurt you, Heather, but I will if I have to."

"Is that a promise?"

Ted felt his face flush and made a fist, showed it to her. "I'm not joking around."

"I never thought you were. But I don't think you have the balls to actually do anything." She was still smiling and her voice was still playful, but there was a hard edge in it. "When push comes to shove, you're just another wimp who can't get it up without help."

He almost hit her then, but at the last minute he relented and his fist slammed into the pillow beside her head. Heather never even flinched. "Missed me." She laughed at him, but it was an ugly sound completely devoid of humor.

"Tell me where the goddamn thing is!" He wanted to hit her, knew that it would give him immense satisfaction to wipe that coy smile off her face, break her nose, blacken her eyes, but he wasn't sure he could do it. It wasn't chivalry; it was a deep rooted fear of doing anything that might get him into trouble.

Even as a kid, Ted had always talked a better fight than he was capable of waging. He had an inventive imagination and had developed more than one elaborate plan of vandalism or theft or just general mayhem with his peers. Sometimes he had even talked others into carrying out those plans. But he had never been willing to put himself, his own reputation at risk, and he always found an excuse not to become personally involved in the execution of his pranks. If Ted had been more prone to self examination, he might have realized this explained why he had come away from school with no real friends, why he missed no one he'd ever worked with and why few of them could even remember his name. He had never really shared danger with anyone.

Frustrated, he turned away and drew a deep breath. "Please tell me where it is, Heather," he pleaded. "I can't tell you how important it is to me." There was the hint of a whine in his voice. He heard it and despised his own weakness.

Heather's eyes narrowed in contempt. "Find it for yourself, you pathetic turd." Ted's head whipped around and he saw her expression. Her eyes were hard now, her jaw set. "I thought it might be kind of fun to screw you, but it's more fun to screw with you, if you get my meaning. I don't know how Beth ever put up with a dickless wonder like you."

The urge to strike her had become almost overpowering. Ted literally shook with rage for which he could find no outlet. Finally, he pulled the pillow out from under her head, then pressed it down onto her face, holding it there with both hands. At least this way he couldn't see those mocking eyes or hear what she was saying. Heather started to struggle, but the ropes were tight and there wasn't much she could do to resist. Ted leaned forward, pressing down on the pillow, watched as her struggles became weaker and weaker. At the last minute, realization of what he was doing came to him and he lifted the pillow away. Heather coughed hoarsely and continuously for several seconds, her eyes unfocused, and only slowly regained her composure.

Ted didn't say anything until he was sure she was paying attention. "It's not so funny now, is it?" Once again, his voice sounded unnaturally calm. She was wrong. He was stronger than she could possibly understand. Nothing could touch him, at least not once he'd recovered the kaleidoscope. "Now where did you put it?"

"Maybe I stuck it up your ass. Why don't you take a look? I'm sure there's plenty of room for your whole head." There was no coquetry in her voice, no amusement. He felt her hatred as a solid force, but all of the emotion seemed to have drained out of him. What remained was deadly resolve.

He pressed the pillow over her face again, this time calmly and deliberately. He used one hand to hold it in place and the other to fondle her body. There was nothing sexual in it. He felt nothing. It was an expression of the power he held over her, an unspoken threat of what might follow if she didn't do what he told her to do. He didn't relent this time until she stopped struggling, and when he removed the pillow, he feared for a moment that he'd waited too long. Even in the dim candlelight he could tell that Heather was pale and in distress. Her first few breaths were raw and labored, and when she tried to spit at him, she failed miserably.

"I'm waiting for an answer," he said calmly. "I can keep this up all night if you want. You'll tell me sooner or later."

"You don't have the balls." There was still anger in her voice, but something else. Respect, maybe? Or just fear. He really didn't care which. If he got the kaleidoscope back, this Heather would be gone forever and it wouldn't matter what she thought of him. Or what he'd done to her. Ted gave a theatrical sigh and covered her face again. He counted inside his head, waiting until she was motionless, then a little longer because he knew she was just pretending. When he finally moved the pillow away, Heather's renewed breathing sounded so hoarse that he felt a twinge of sympathetic pain. But it was a very small twinge.

"Where is it, Heather?"

The silence stretched and he reached for the pillow. Her eyes followed his movement this time and her face twitched. "Will you untie me if I tell you?" She sounded conciliatory, but he

158

didn't trust her. Everything was a game with her, and she was the only one who knew the rules. At least until someone else changed them.

"Yeah, sure. As soon as I know you're telling me the truth, I'll untie you. But no more tricks. No more games. Just tell me where it is, I find it, you get loose."

"What happens then?" Her voice was sly again, but it was almost as if she felt obligated to play a part. Her heart was no longer in the role.

"I'm sure we'll be able to think of something that both of us will enjoy." He was lying. His flesh crawled at the very thought of touching her. He didn't know if he'd ever be able to look at her again without remembering.

Heather considered her situation, apparently concluded she had very few options. "All right. I think it rolled under the bed. I dropped it when Mary was tying me up."

Ted's heart skipped a beat. If she'd broken it, he really would kill her. On the other hand, the blow to his head was much more likely to have caused damage. "I'll take a look." Ted slipped off the bed, knelt on the floor, and began groping in the darkness with one hand. There wasn't enough light to see but it was a single bed and it wouldn't take long to search. His fingers touched cool metal almost immediately and then the kaleidoscope was back in his hand, and it appeared to be all in one piece. The feeling of relief made him momentarily lightheaded. He stood up and turned toward the door without a glance at Heather.

"Hey! What about untying me?"

He looked at her but kept his distance. "I don't think so. I think it'll be safer for both of us if you remain right where you are for the time being."

"You promised!"

"So I did. And I'll keep my promise. A few minutes from now, you won't be tied up any more. All right? Just be patient. I have to go home first."

Heather looked up at him speculatively. "What? Have you got another toy there we can play with?" She tried to shift her body seductively, but without success. "Come on. I'll play nice."

But Ted wasn't listening. He had already left.

Ted stepped out through the back door. He felt physically

and emotionally drained and his knees were shaking. There was no sense of guilt about what he'd done to Heather, but the violence he'd resorted to had had consequences. He felt nauseated and his head hurt. Instead of immediately heading home, he walked over to the chaise lounge and dropped into it, holding the kaleidoscope in his lap. He let his head fall back and took several deep breaths. The anger he'd felt moments earlier was still there, pumping adrenaline into his body, but it was hard to keep it directed at Heather. She was, after all, a product of his own manipulation, however inadvertent.

From where he sat, he could see the lights of downtown Managansett over a stand of low pine trees. The rest of the world would be just as it had always been, he realized. It was only here on Bailey's Court – and at the strip mall - that things had changed so radically. He wondered how that was possible. Mary had implied that Heather had gotten into trouble in the past. Did that mean that the changes were retroactive? That must be the case, he reasoned, because marriages and other relationships had changed. So in that sense, the range of the magic was not limited to the immediate area as he had originally concluded. But the objects to be changed apparently had to be in close physical proximity.

Headlights swept past and he glanced in that direction, saw the station wagon coming toward him. Beth and Samantha were back. Ted stood up, but he was in no hurry to greet them. In his present mood, he knew he'd snap at them and that would be counter productive. It was time to move on to something else, hopefully something better. He even had one hand on the drum when it occurred to him that there was one thing more he needed to do first, something that he could take care of right away, something where it wouldn't matter if it went wrong. In fact, in one sense, the more wrong it was the better he'd like it. And it would give him an outlet for his anger because it would be aimed at someone who really deserved it.

But first he'd need the station wagon.

He took his time returning to the house and when he reached the kitchen all of the bags of groceries were in the kitchen and being distributed to cabinets, the refrigerator, the shelves in the small pantry, although for some reason the fresh vegetables were going into the dishwasher. Ted didn't ask. Beth glanced in his direction for a second, but turned back to her work without comment. Samantha didn't even look around. She moved with sudden, jerky movements that made it quite obvious she was angry about something. Presumably she and Beth had argued.

"I need to take a quick run into town. Is there anything we need?" He didn't really want to run any errands but the words were so automatic they came out without conscious volition.

Beth didn't turn her head, but she did respond. "We just got back from shopping, Ted. Does it look like we need anything?"

"Just thought I'd ask." Ordinarily he would have been annoyed by her tone, but Beth – at least this version of Beth – wasn't going to be around much longer so he was able to be charitable. He walked across the kitchen and retrieved the keys from their hook. His hand was on the doorknob, but he didn't quite make the escape he'd hoped for.

"As long as you're going out, you might as well drop Sam off at the Corrigans. She's going to sulk all weekend if we don't let her visit her precious boyfriend."

Ted only vaguely knew Milt , had never met the wife, and hadn't been aware that they had a teenaged son. He also didn't know if Samantha had had a boyfriend in any of her previous incarnations. But most of all, he didn't care.

"I don't know if I'll be going that way."

"They're on Morrisson Avenue. It's right on the way." Samantha's voice was an uneasy mix of irritation and hopefulness.

Ted couldn't think of any way to get out of it. "All right, get a move on." He set the kaleidoscope carefully on the floor in the back seat where it would be out of Samantha's reach. As soon as her door closed, he started the engine. Although he considered Samantha's presence a temporary annoyance at best, curiosity got the better of him as he backed out the driveway. "So how long have you two been together?"

Samantha was looking out the window and didn't turn her head. "A few weeks. What do you care?"

"Just curious." He switched gears and they started out of Bailey's Court. "So have the two of you been fucking?"

She turned her whole upper body and gave him an appraising look. She was surprised but not shocked by his crude

161

language. "Like rabbits. Do you want details?"

"Not particularly." His voice shook slightly. He'd meant to shock her, but she'd taken it in stride. This was definitely not the same Samantha who had blushed whenever Ted swore in her presence. He turned onto Morrison Avenue after a short, uncomfortable silence. "Which house is it?"

"The red one on the right. The one with the birch trees out front and the ivy climbing up the side."

In the darkness, her description wasn't entirely helpful, but he slowed to a crawl until she indicated he should stop. The house was faux brick and looked out of place among its neighbors. Ted eased over to the curb and stopped. There was a lemonade booth facing the street with piles of paper cups and a scrawled sign that said "Lemonade 50 Cents", but no one was there. "Looks like your boyfriend's an entrepreneur," Ted suggested.

"It's his kid sister's," came the huffy reply. "She's a brat." Samantha opened the door and started to slide out.

"You're welcome for the ride," he said sarcastically. "Just ask, any time."

"Whatever." She didn't even look back, almost ran across the lawn to the door.

Ted watched her go, started to pull away, then stopped in front of the next house. Impulsively he released his seat belt, twisted around and retrieved the kaleidoscope. He glanced up at the Rockwell house thoughtfully. "What the hell," he told himself, and turned the drum, which had lost its previous balkiness. Maybe the hit on the head had been beneficial after all.

There was nothing to indicate that anything had changed, but he was confident that it had. For all he knew, Samantha was now Samuel, and she might be the brother of her former boyfriend. If so, he'd be rid of at least one annoying distraction. If not, well, he would be no worse off than he was already. He dropped the kaleidoscope onto the seat beside him and drove off.

He was able to park only one block from the Good Fellows Club. Apparently there hadn't been an overwhelming turnout for the ceremony honoring James Nicholson. Ted had worked for the man for almost two years at Ward Products, and had come to loathe the very sight of him. Nicholson was in some ways quite brilliant. Even Ted would admit that the man had excelled in many ways as director of Manufacturing Support. He could be charming when he wanted, had a gift for talking people into adopting his point of view, and certainly he understood the intricacies of the production process. But to those who worked for him, Nicholson was a tyrant subject to fits of frightening rage, prone to arbitrary decision making, and quite evidently a sadist who enjoyed humiliating his subordinates. Nicholson had run through four secretaries in a single year, three of whom had been reduced to tears on at least one occasion.

Ted was good at his job in production planning. Not great, maybe, because he didn't find the work either interesting or fulfilling. But his schedules were always finished on time, he had the lowest error rate in the department, and he fancied himself as lead scheduler even if he didn't technically have the title. When Nicholson superseded old Jameson following the latter's retirement, he had hoped to finally be recognized.

Nicholson had crushed him within the first few weeks, criticizing him unfairly, demanding that schedules be reworked for no good reason, and he'd found fault with everything from the arrangement of Ted's desk to the way he dressed. When Ted received the first bad performance review in his entire career, he'd had no choice but to quite. Beth hadn't quite understood the logic, but if she'd been there, if she'd known Nicholson the way Ted did, she wouldn't have questioned his decision.

And now Ted hoped to get his own back.

With the kaleidoscope clutched tightly in one hand, Ted walked directly to the front door of the club and opened it, avoiding a homeless woman in worn clothing who had pushed a shopping cart full of her few possessions up against the side of the building while she paused to have a smoke. There was a narrow, dimly lit vestibule inside, beyond which a hallway led to the main function room, from which the murmur of voices was clearly audible, and to a staircase that led to the offices on the second floor. To the right, a good sized coat room stood open but unused; it was much too hot for even light jackets and the racks were forlornly empty.

Ted had hoped to slip inside and join the crowd, but an elderly man sat at the door with a clipboard and a list of names, many of which had checkmark next to them. Obviously attendance was by invitation. Fortunately, Ted had been in the building on several previous occasions and knew his way around. Acting as though he had a perfect right to do so, he went immediately to the staircase and climbed to the second floor. No one challenged him.

There was a smaller conference room on the second level, as well as several offices, the club's rather laughable library, and a few other rooms whose purpose Ted didn't know. He was more interested in a kind of balcony that ran along one edge of the meeting room below. It had been closed off some time ago for safety reasons, but there wasn't enough money available to pay for more than a cursory safeguard. It was easy enough to climb over the makeshift barrier.

Even from this distance, Ted recognized Nicholson easily. There was an arrogance in his posture that was unmistakable. He sat to the right of a white haired man who was apparently still singing Nicholson's praises to the assembly. As Ted had suspected, the turnout was light. Only about half of the seats that had been set out were actually filled and many of the attendees looked bored. Ted recognized the speaker, though not by name, as one of the bigwigs at Eblis Manufacturing, the chief employer in Managansett, although the factory had fallen on hard times and had recently reduced its staff by almost a third, another argument against his having accepted their job offer. It was still in much better shape than Ward Products, however, which was rumored to be contemplating bankruptcy protection. The prospect that Nicholson might soon be unemployed was satisfying, but not satisfying enough. Nor was it personal.

Ted hefted the kaleidoscope, determined to enjoy this moment. He felt a resurgence of the sense of power he'd experienced earlier. This time it was Nicholson who was the pawn and he, Ted, was the one in control. It felt good. It felt great. All of the difficulties of the last several hours receded into insignificance because now, at long last, he was going to get his own back, at least in some small way.

He savored the moment. The white haired man was a poor speaker but Ted was able to follow the gist of what he was saying. Nicholson was being thanked for participating on the steering committee of some unnamed charity and for providing resources from his employer to one special event or another. Ted knew how that worked. Obsolete or slow moving items were donated and the company took a full write off of the retail value of the item, even though the actual cost was half as much. Nicholson volunteered clerical services from time to time and passed the work along to his subordinates, who had to handle this additional load without falling behind in their regular duties, for which service they were neither rewarded nor thanked.

Ted let his anger grow, enjoying the anticipation. He didn't know exactly what would happen, of course, but Nicholson was riding high and almost any alternative would be undesirable, from his point of view at least. The only downside was that Nicholson would never know what it was that he had lost. The waiters moving quietly from table to table were all male; the possibility that Nicholson might switch roles with one of them seemed so perfect that Ted could wait no longer.

He took the kaleidoscope firmly in hand and turned the drum.

The tableau below did not at first appear to have changed at all. The white haired man was still speaking and Nicholson sat beside him, appearing to listen attentively. Ted ran his eyes over the crowd and noticed at least one change; the homeless woman he'd passed outside was now sitting at a table with two gentlemen, one of whom had been waiting on a table just a few seconds earlier. Otherwise nothing seemed to have changed.

The speaker shifted position and his words were suddenly much easier to follow. He was still gushing thanks, but not to Nicholson any longer. He was thanking the Chamber of Commerce for their kind words. Ted blinked, uncomprehending at first, then realized that the white haired man was now the honored guest instead of the principal speaker. Which presumably meant that he and Nicholson had switched roles. That was hardly the outcome he'd hoped for. It left things virtually unchanged.

A few seconds later, he realized that the situation was even worse than he had thought. Nicholson was now a Vice President at Eblis Manufacturing, not Ward Products. And he was also president of the Chamber of Commerce. Rather than avenge himself, Ted had managed to put his old enemy into an even more enviable position.

This wouldn't do at all. Ted almost dropped the kaleidoscope in his waste to retrieve use it again. But before he could do so, fate intervened.

"Excuse me, sir. May I ask what you're doing in there?"

Ted was so startled that he almost dropped the kaleidoscope. Behind him, a young man wearing a blazer with a Chamber of Commerce logo on the pocket was standing attentively, a disapproving expression on his face. Ted hastily slipped the kaleidoscope behind his back, hoping that the makeshift barrier through which he'd climbed had concealed his hands, and smoothed his face into what he hoped was a reassuring expression.

"Sorry. I just wanted to hear the ceremony and I didn't have an invitation." He ducked and stepped through the strands of yellow tape. "I used to work for Mr. Nicholson."

The young man looked only marginally less wary. "You're not supposed to be in there. That's why we have the tape up. It's dangerous."

"Sorry," Ted repeated. "I thought it would be all right if I was careful."

"I'm going to have to ask you to go back downstairs. The second floor is off limits to unauthorized personnel." His tone had switched from wary to annoyed. "If you want to see Mr. Nicholson, it'll have to be after they break up. You can wait in the lobby if you want."

Ted thought that "lobby" was a bit of a stretch given how small it was, but he wasn't about to argue. "I don't suppose you'd know how much longer they'll be in there?"

"I couldn't say, sir."

Ted sidled toward the stairs, trying not to make it obvious that he was concealing anything. Although what did it matter if the man saw it? It was only a kaleidoscope after all. "Well, I suppose I'll just have to try another time. I'm really sorry to have bothered you."

"That's all right, sir. It's for your own safety, you understand." There was a note of deference in his voice now. Possibly he was wondering if Ted was someone to be reckoned with, someone he shouldn't irritate, someone with power. Well, thought Ted, that's exactly what I am, but you'll never know just how powerful I really am.

Downstairs he considered using the kaleidoscope again before leaving, but the young man was watching from the top of the stairs, and his first attempt had gone seriously awry. Even worse, he wouldn't be able to tell what effect, if any, it had on Nicholson. No, he thought. There will be other times, other chances to shift the balance. He would be patient.

A shopping cart full of coathangers had been left in the lobby and Ted had to maneuver around it in order to leave the building.

Most of his remaining anger dissipated during the drive back. It hadn't been a disaster, he told himself, just a setback. Nicholson might have temporarily benefited from the change, but sooner or later Ted would have another chance and next time his former boss might find himself homeless, or waiting tables, or maybe something even worse. Ted concocted unlikely plans in which he lured Nicholson to a local prison, or the intensive care ward of some hospital. See how much power you have as a convicted pedophile or with AIDS, he told the phantom enemy in his mind.

He was almost home when another thought occurred to him and he changed course, turning into Morrison Avenue. If Samantha was still his sister and law and he didn't want to be stuck with her indefinitely, he'd have to get her back within range of the kaleidoscope the next time he shuffled Bailey's Court. Which meant he'd have to pry her away from her boyfriend.

Although he had expected to have to go up to the house and ring the bell, he was spared that effort when he saw Samantha sitting at the lemonade stand in the front yard. She was with her boyfriend and when Ted was close enough to recognize him he was so startled that the car swerved. It was Arnold, from the Rapid-Mart, except that he wasn't from the Rapid-Mart any more. Then the pieces fell into place. The teenaged boy who had swapped places with Arnold earlier that day must have been the original Corrigan kid. Was Samantha dating him even then? If so, he'd been cheating on her because he'd been there with another girl, and they hadn't acted like casual friends.

Ted swerved across the road and parked, illegally, facing the wrong way, directly in front of them, then rolled the window down. They had hung a gas lantern on a pole so that the lemonade stand was brightly lit. It was only then that Ted noticed that Samantha had changed clothing. She was wearing some kind of tight leotard with an ivy pattern. He couldn't be sure but he thought Arnold's shirt and pants strongly resembled the outfit she'd been wearing when he had dropped her off.

He also noticed that it was not lemonade they were selling – or trying to sell. Instead of paper cups, there were shot glasses, and beside them stood bottles of gin, vodka, brandy, and other liquors. The price had gone up to $2.00 per shot. He was almost tempted.

"Time to go home, Samantha." Ted didn't even look at Arnold. He was almost old enough to be the girl's father. How in the world did he fit in with the Corrigan family?

"I'm not done here." Her voice was sullen, but with an element of uncertainty. Ted sensed that there was something wrong and wondered if enough of the girl's original personality survived that she felt out of place. He'd always sensed a strength in her that was missing from the rest of her family, as though she was the only true adult.

"Beth will be worried about you, and we've got a lot of work to do before tomorrow, remember?"

"Yeah, the cookout." Ted was relieved to see that she was standing now, moving around the side of the stand toward the car. Then she spoiled even this minor triumph by turning back toward Arnold. "You're still coming, aren't you?"

Arnold, who hadn't spoken a word, nodded without enthusiasm. "I told you I would, if you really want me there. If your family won't mind."

Ted opened his mouth but Samantha was too quick for him. "There's going to be plenty of food and Beth's always telling me she wants to meet my friends. I'll call you in the morning, just so you don't forget."

"All right." He gave a little wave and an apologetic nod to Ted, then turned away.

Ted felt a twinge of regret. He'd always liked Arnold, who was respectful, knew his place, always tried to be pleasing. It was a shame that his life had been disrupted. But then again, Ted thought, maybe he was better off, happier in this scenario. Maybe some time in the future, Ted would have time to take a closer look and nudge him into something else if it appeared that he was unhappy. That soothed his conscience and he put all thoughts of Arnold out of his mind.

Samantha was in a semi-sulk. She was pretending to be mad but even Ted's less than sensitive radar about other people could tell that she was working hard to keep up the pretense. "How are things going with you two?" He didn't really care, but it seemed like an appropriate icebreaker. How did you talk to teenagers anyway?

"Okay, I guess. He's going to have to look for a new place. His sister's pregnant again and they're going to need the room he's using."

Ted did some fast interpolating. Arnold wasn't the Corrigan's son, apparently. He was the wife's brother. That made more sense, although Arnold still had a hint of his accent and Ted wondered how that had been parsed into the equation. Maybe he'd spent his childhood abroad. Or was Mrs. Corrigan an immigrant as well? Ted had never met her, and had spoken to her husband only once or twice.

"I'm sure he'll find a place."

"Yeah, well, he needs a job first. He was supposed to start at Bargain Busters next week, but they called and told him they're cutting back."

"Did they say anything about the robbery?"

"What robbery?"

Ted thought back. No, he'd undone the robbery a while back. It was getting hard to remember what was real and what wasn't. Maybe he should have been taking notes, just to establish some kind of a baseline. He'd do that from now on, he told himself.

Predictably, Beth was not happy when they arrived home. "I have all this work to do and the two of you are gallivanting around as though we didn't have guests coming tomorrow."

Ted and Samantha exchanged looks. It had, after all, been Beth's idea for him to take Samantha with him, and she hadn't objected when he'd said he was going out. Nor had it been that long since they'd left. There was no point in arguing. Ted took the line of least resistance, stowed the kaleidoscope in the hall closet, and he and Samantha spent the next half hour completing minor chores from a list Beth had compiled in their absence.

The evening seemed to pass quickly. Ted had been considering his options while he worked and when Beth recruited Samantha to help prepare a late supper, he retrieved the kaleidoscope and descended to his workshop. He was anxious to try another reality, but he remembered his earlier resolve and waited until he'd had time to write a brief description of his current situation, the relationships as he understood them of everyone in Bailey's Court, even the locations of key items of furniture. He couldn't possibly know everything that had changed or that would change in the future, but this seemed the best way to ensure that he didn't cast himself completely adrift.

When he was done, he took the kaleidoscope back upstairs, making as little noise as possible. Beth and Samantha were talking in the kitchen, too preoccupied to notice as he walked through the hall and slipped out the back door. It had cooled down a bit with the coming of night but it was still warmer than Ted really cared for. He supposed the weather covered too big an area for it to be affected but it would be nice if they had a working air conditioner.

"Okay, this time how about something a little more pleasant, if you please." He raised the kaleidoscope and swept it across the sky until he found the moon. This time when he tried the drum, it cooperated immediately, rotating almost a full one hundred and eighty degrees before it jammed again. He lowered his arm and looked around, but as far as he could tell, nothing had changed. But it had changed, of course. He was absolutely certain of that.

Now that he'd acted, he felt oddly reluctant to discover just what he had accomplished this time. Although he still believed he had found the key to a better life, he was starting to feel alienated from his environment, set adrift in a series of nebulous alternate realities. It wouldn't have been so bad if there had been a clear route back, a way to undo the changes he'd already caused and begin with a fresh slate. The people around him were becoming grotesque caricatures rather than people and Ted, who had always been wrapped up in his own preoccupations, suddenly felt a new emotion – loneliness. If only there was someone he could share this all with. Of course, he could tell Beth or any of the others what happened when he turned the kaleidoscope, but it's not likely they would believe him, and even if they did, their conviction might not survive the next turn of the drum. No, he was in this by himself, at least until he reached the end of his personal road and stopped using it.

But would he stop? Did he have to? If he found the ideal life for himself, an adoring, sexy wife, independent means, whatever else he wanted, he might not use it again in Bailey's Court, but there was nothing stopping him from taking it elsewhere, was there? He might go to Washington and shake up Congress. Hell, he could go on a White House tour and change Presidents. Of course, it might be the White House cook who ended up in the oval office, but then again, she probably would do as good a job as any of the other buffoons who got themselves elected. The possibilities cheered him and he turned around, determined to go back inside and find out what was what.

Before he reached the door, he was caught in the beam of a flashlight from the opposite side of the yard. Ted froze, raised his hand to shield his eyes. "Who's there?"

"Mr. Croner? Could you help me please?"

Ted peered closer. He couldn't see anything in the glare but he recognized the voice. "Samantha? Is that you?" It appeared that he was back to being a neighbor instead of a brother in law.

"Yes. Could you come over here please?" She sounded as though she might be on the verge of tears.

Against his better judgment, Ted trudged across the lawn. Samantha was kneeling on the grass beside a huge stand of rose bushes that crowded against this side of the Rogers house. They towered over his head and had spread to both corners of the building like a thorny wall out of a Walt Disney cartoon. "Are you all right, Samantha?" He didn't want to get too close until he understood the situation. His encounter with the previous version of Heather had made him wary.

"I'm fine. It's Toby." The flashlight beam moved away from him and he was able to see more detail. "He's all tangled up and I can't get him loose."

Ted stepped forward, blinking, and saw the problem. Toby was lying right at the edge of the rose bush, his leash thoroughly tangled in the vines. The dog lifted its head and whimpered and even in the darkness, Ted could see that one foreleg was bleeding.

"I was just taking him for a walk and he took off and pulled the leash right out of my hand. Before I could catch up with him, he was all tangled up in this and I think he cut himself on the thorns. No one else is home and I don't know what to do!" She was crying now.

"Okay, just calm down. It doesn't look too serious. Give me that light for a minute." He set the kaleidoscope down on the grass and used the flash to examine the tangle in more detail. Satisfied that he understood the problem, he handed it back. "Just hold it pointed there so I can see what I'm doing."

Wary of the thorns, Ted managed to work a short length of the leash free, but the branches seemed to contract around the rest of it. He pricked himself slightly and drew his hands back, sucking on the injured thumb.

"What happened?" asked Samantha, a bit more composed now.

"Damn thing bit me!"

"It's just a rose bush, Mr. Croner."

Ted shook his head. "Lately I've come to think that nothing is just what it seems, kid. There's always a twist you're not expecting."

Samantha had turned her attention back to Toby. "So what do we do now? Do you think you can get him loose?"

Ted was tempted to tell her that it wasn't his problem, but he relented. "Yeah, we'll just unclip the leash from his collar and worry about it later."

Samantha made a disgusted sound. "I should have thought of that."

"Yeah, well us old folks still have something on the ball."

"You're not that old, Mr. Croner."

Ted glanced at her, wondering if there was a hidden meaning, but Samantha seemed intent upon the dog and he told himself he was getting paranoid. It only took a minute to unfasten the leash.

Samantha leaned closer. "I think he may have a broken

172

leg."

"I don't see how that could have happened but you're going to have to take him to a vet for some stitches."

"I guess. Can you bring him inside for me? I'll put him in his bed basket so it's easier to carry him around."

Ted had hoped to disentangle himself from Samantha and go home to evaluate his latest situation. "I really need to get back to the house."

"Please. I can't hold him and the flashlight and I'm afraid I'll trip over something in the dark and drop him." Her voice suggested that she was ready to burst out crying at any moment.

Ted sighed. "All right, but I can't stay."

It took a couple of tries before he could get both forearms under Toby and lift the little dog without hurting him unnecessarily. Toby was licking the injured leg but seemed otherwise undisturbed and Ted wondered if it was really more than just a scratch. Not that it mattered.

Samantha led the way, lighting their path to the front door, and opened it when they arrived. Ted followed her inside and glanced curiously around the room. It looked perfectly ordinary, and quite unfamiliar. He recognized some of the furniture, including a lamp that Beth had bought the week they were married and a coffee table that he'd seen in Jennifer's living room just a few hours earlier. It was mismatched, but otherwise arranged much as you would expect, except that one painting was hanging with its face to the wall and there was a measuring cup full of artificial flowers in the front window.

"I'll take him now." Samantha had set the flashlight down on an end table and was holding out both arms. Ted carefully transferred Toby to her and she turned away. "I'll just put him in his bed."

"Right. I'll be going then." There was no sign of the rest of the family, but Ted was more interested in his own situation than in Samantha's.

The teenager had already disappeared from sight, but her voice drifted back. "Thanks, Mr. Croner."

He had turned back to the door and was about to leave when he heard the groan. Ted froze, waited a few seconds, but the sound didn't repeat itself. "Is anyone there?" he asked quietly.

The sound was repeated, a bit louder this time, and Ted was able to determine that it came from the darkened kitchen that opened off the living room. He picked up the flashlight that Samantha had discarded, hefted it as though it was a weapon, and moved slowly across the room to investigate. His instincts were telling him to get out of the house, but he had to know what this reality had in store for him, and if there was something particular unpleasant he might as well find out about it now.

There was a light switch just inside the door; when he flicked it up there was a faint click but no light. He turned on the flashlight and swept it through the darkness. At first the room seemed even more ordinary than the living room. Stove, refrigerator, cabinets and sink, a table and four chairs in the center of the room, microwave on the counter. Everything appeared to be in it proper place. Then he noticed the indistinct muffled shape in one corner, half concealed by the bulk of the refrigerator. Even with the flashlight, he couldn't make out much detail from this distance so he stepped into the room.

He was halfway across the intervening distance before he could identify the object, a gray cocoon made of cottony fibers. There were spider webs connecting it to the walls and ceilings, intricately patterned, glittering moistly where the light touched it. The central mass resembled an oversized tent caterpillar's nest and it was larger than an adult human, which wasn't surprising since it was draped around the upright body of Carl Rogers. His face was lightly swathed with webbing but recognizable. Carl's eyes were closed, but when Ted focused the light there, they popped open, staring blindly, and then the moan was repeated, desperate, hopeless, and miserable. Ted stumbled back a step and the flashlight dropped from fingers that no longer had the strength to hold it. Shocked, disgusted, and suddenly terrified, Ted turned and fled the house.

He made it home without incident, but with no memory of having crossed the intervening space. The front door was unlocked and he slammed it behind him, caught his breath, then deliberately turned and threw the bolt. He was shaking so badly that he lowered himself into a chair and held his knees with both hands, waiting for his pulse to slow down to normal.

Someone called from deeper in the house. "Ted? Is that

you?"

He recognized the voice. It was Jennifer. Could it be possible that he had finally hit upon a combination where they two of them were together? It would almost have been worth seeing that horrible apparition in the Rogers kitchen if that was the case. "Jennifer?" he answered tentatively. "Yes, it's me."

"Aren't you coming to bed, darling? I've been waiting for you forever." Her voice was sultry, inviting.

He had to try twice to get the words out. "I'll be right there." He resisted the temptation to rush right in. He needed to compose himself. First impressions were important. Of course, in this reality he supposed it wouldn't be a first impression, if he and Jennifer were married, or even if they were just living together. But for him it would be the first time even if Jennifer thought otherwise. And then another thought occurred to him. What if they weren't married? What if he was still married to Beth, or Mary for that matter, and his real wife was away for the evening? No, that wouldn't work. If she wasn't somewhere in Bailey's Court, then she wouldn't have been changed and they'd still be married. He remembered Jennifer's homicidal attack on Carl – not this particular Jennifer, he told himself – and his pulse began to race. It's not fair, he told himself. We're finally together and I have to worry about some crazy alternate version of Beth discovering them, maybe with an axe in her hands.

What the hell, he thought. Even a clandestine affair is better than nothing, and if things got sticky, he could always use the kaleidoscope again. But first he checked the rest of the house to make certain they were alone, locking all the doors. His last stop was the bathroom, where he quickly checked himself out in the mirror beside the front door, then marched off to the bedroom.

He paused at the door and cautiously surveyed the room. As with the Rogers' living room, it was conventionally laid out – except for the frying pan hanging over the dressing table – but not entirely familiar. He didn't spend much time looking at the furniture this time. Jennifer was lying in bed, naked – at least from the waist up, and he was pleased to see that she measured up to his expectations. The lower half of her body was covered by unfamiliar rose patterned blankets. She had a book open which she obviously had been reading, but immediately set aside when she saw him. She looked every bit as good as he had imagined and he felt his body stirring with admiration. It was almost too good to be true, but after all the bad luck he'd had during the last twelve hours or so, he figured he was due to get at least one break.

"Why are you standing way over there? I've been waiting and waiting. I thought you'd never get home. I still don't understand why you had to go out tonight." She was pouting, but her body language was an open invitation. Maybe Ted could live with giant spider webs next door after all, if this was part of the package.

"I'm sorry but it was something I just had to take care of. But it's all done now and I'm at your command for the rest of the evening."

Jennifer smiled, sat up a bit straighter, and Ted's pulse jumped. "Well now it's time for you to rescue me from that boring old book. I don't know why I read legal thrillers anyway. They're always too technical for me."

"I can think of a few better ways to pass an evening." He started across the room toward her.

"I'll just bet you can." Her smile faded a bit. "Where were you anyway? I thought you said you'd only be a minute."

"I had to help one of the neighbors with a little problem."

Jennifer's face stiffened and Ted froze where he was, almost within reach. "Not that bitch Beth again? She's been trying to get her claws into you ever since she moved in next door."

So he didn't have to worry about being surprised by an enraged wife. Even better. "No, I haven't seen her tonight," he lied soothingly, if it was a lie. "It was Samantha. She was having a little problem with Toby. No big thing, but I felt bad for the kid."

"She's big enough to take care of her own problems." Her eyes trailed down his body to his crotch. "And it looks like you're big enough to take care of some of mine. Why don't you get rid of those clothes? You'll be more comfortable in this heat without them."

Ted fumbled with the buttons on his shirt, telling himself to take it slow. There was no reason to hurry. Obviously he and Jennifer were married – or at least living together - and the doors were locked, so they weren't going to be interrupted. Even if he ultimately decided that this reality wasn't suitable either, he could at least enjoy himself for a few hours before moving on. It's not as if anything he did would have irremediable consequences.

He was on the very last button when Jennifer straightened up and dropped one hand to the top edge of the blankets. Smiling, she whisked the covers back to reveal the lower half of her body.

Ted gasped. His expression must have changed dramatically because Jennifer looked suddenly alarmed. "What's the matter, lover? Is something wrong?"

He didn't answer, couldn't answer. All he could do was move his eyes along the length of her body, the large full breasts, the slight mole just below her navel, then the hips, which were covered with tiny, overlapping scales, dark at first but growing lighter as they marched down over her thighs and knees, or to where her knees should have been. From the hips down to the bifurcated tail, Jennifer was more fish than human. Thoughts of mermaids raced through his head, but he knew this was more than that. The misshapen drum was no longer just shuffling attributes around from person to person, object to object. Now it was mixing human and inhuman subjects, in this case with monstrous consequences. Wherever the aquarium was now, did it hold a fish with tiny human legs?

"Are you sick, Ted? You're very pale." She half raised her upper body. "Can I get you something?"

Ted imagined her flopping across the floor like a landed fish, or maybe she just balanced on her tail somehow. His stomach lurched. "Nothing's wrong." He was surprised that the words had actually been audible, that they almost sounded normal. "I just forgot something. The front door. I need to go lock the front door."

"Don't worry about that! No one is going to come in here without an invitation after what happened to Heather when she sneaked in that one time. She screamed loud enough to wake the dead."

"Well, you can never be too careful. I'll just be a second. I won't be able to concentrate if I don't take care of it." Ted knew that the words were coming from his mouth, but it felt as though some other entity had seized control of his body, preventing him from screaming and running from the room.

Jennifer settled back, clearly miffed. "If it takes that little to distract you, then maybe you don't find me attractive any more. Maybe you'd rather it was Beth in your bed."

Ted shook his head – although at the moment, that's just exactly what he did want. "It's not that. You're beautiful, honest." It was a half truth. The top half.

"Well get it over with and come to bed. And as long as you're up, take the cat out of the refrigerator so it can thaw overnight."

Ted walked unsteadily out of the room. By the time he reached the top of the cellar stairs, his hands were shaking. He opened the door, then remembered that the kaleidoscope wasn't in the basement. In fact, he didn't know where it was. He broke out in a sudden cold sweat and had to press one hand against the wall to steady himself. Where had he put it? How had he managed to forget about it? He had taken it outside this last time, and then Samantha had called him and he'd gone over to see what she wanted. It was still in his hand then, he remembered with absolute certainty. Then he'd gotten involved with rescuing Toby and carrying him into the house, and somewhere along the line he'd lost it.

He must have set it down while he was dealing with the dog. He had no clear memory of doing so, but he was sure he hadn't been carrying it when he was inside the Rogers house. He remembered having the flashlight in his right hand when he went into the kitchen, and he'd groped for the light switch with his left. Then he'd dropped the light when he'd bolted from the house, but he was quite sure both hands had been empty by then. It had to be outside somewhere, probably near the rose bush.

Ted went out through the garage instead of the front door and grabbed the large flashlight he kept mounted there, heaving a small sigh of relief that it was right where it should have been, and hadn't been replaced by a plunger or a broom or something even more exotic. He thought he heard Jennifer's voice calling but he shut the door behind him and hit the switch to open the outer door, trying to expunge all memory of those moments in the bedroom from his mind. Escape was the only priority now. Escape into yet another reality. Ted seriously wondered if he was just going to make things worse with each new turn, but if he couldn't go back, he had to continue forward until he found something that would be bearable. His life with Beth hadn't been all that bad. Maybe if they had both made a little effort, they might have managed to hold onto more of the good parts. But it was too late now.

The garage lights had come on when the outer door started to rise, and Ted didn't have to look hard to realize things had changed dramatically. The yard sale boxes were all gone and the SUV was parked in their place. An axe was mounted on the wall next to other outdoor tools, as well as a few inappropriate items including several of his neckties, a picture of Roscoe mounted upside down, and what looked to be a string of very old, dessicated hotdogs or sausages. Two of the cabinet doors were open and a quick glance told him they were similarly full of sensible and nonsensical items. He turned the flashlight on as he walked toward the driveway and felt a wave of relief when a beam of light shot out obediently. He'd half expected it to play music or do nothing at all. He rounded the corner and went directly to the towering stand of rose bushes.

For the first few seconds he thought that either he'd been mistaken or that someone else had come by and taken it, because the kaleidoscope was not immediately visible. His heart sank and he felt almost physically ill at the thought that it might be gone forever, leaving him trapped with his monstrously deformed new wife. Then he looked again and saw that it was there after all, lying deep among the bushes, right up against the foundation of the house. Either it had rolled there when he put it down, which seemed unlikely, or perhaps he or Samantha had kicked it accidentally while they were rescuing Toby.

Ted crouched, propped the light on the grass so that it pointed in the right direction, then reached slowly and carefully into the mesh of thorny branches and leaves. As he did so, the closest strand of rose bush dropped and slid across his hand, digging tiny furrows in the skin with its thorns. He withdrew his arm with a shout of pain and toppled backward onto the grass. The small wound stung like crazy and he pressed it to his mouth, cursing softly.

He tried again, jerking his hand back almost immediately when another branch shifted slightly. There was only the faintest of breezes, certainly not enough to stir such a sturdy plant. It was almost as if the roses sensed his purpose and were trying to prevent him from retrieving the kaleidoscope. After moving the light even closer, Ted got down on hands and knees and tried again, being very careful this time. As soon as his hand was within range of the outer perimeter of the branches, one of them dropped onto his forearm. This time it writhed like some bizarre snake, wrapped itself around his flesh, and the thorns pierced his skin. There was no question in his mind this time; the roses had moved purposefully. Ted tried to draw his arm back, and the plant squeezed even more tightly. He only freed himself by using his other hand to grasp the end of the branch and unwind it, and even then it resisted, as though he was wrestling with some malevolent animal instead of a simple shrub.

Ted stepped back, his arm burning. His fear turned to fury. . "All right then, if that's the way you want it." He left the light where it was and returned to the garage. The axe was mounted so high on the wall that he had to find something to stand on, but a moment later he was back beside the rose bushes. "I've had just about enough from you." He raised the axe over his head.

Technically speaking, he could have stopped after the first few blows. They had split the bush neatly in two and left a clear path to the kaleidoscope. But Ted's pent up emotions had finally found an outlet and he continued to hack away at the roses until his breath was short and the muscles in his arms were complaining about the unaccustomed exercise. He let the axe fall then, put his hands on his hips and took several deep breaths while regarding the wreckage of the rose bushes. Here and there, surviving branches writhed and twisted as though suffering the agonies of the damned. Maybe they were.

He picked up the kaleidoscope, tucked it under his arm, retrieved the axe and lantern and walked away.

Although he could have changed things right away, Ted acted with his usual respect for his tools, returning the axe to the wall and the flashlight to its cabinet. He started toward the connecting door to the house, then stopped. There was no way he was going to deal with Jennifer, this version of Jennifer, again. He walked back outside and around to the rear of the house. There was a small bulkhead door to the basement, rarely used, secured with a combination lock. It took him a few seconds to remember the combination, but it opened on the first try and Ted descended into the basement.

He remembered his resolve to keep a list of changes. It didn't seem as important just now, but it wouldn't hurt and it might help later on. He found the pad, drew a line under the previous entry to indicate that there had been a shift, then glanced through his previous notes. It was his handwriting, but nothing that he read sounded familiar. Samantha had been Beth's sister last time, he was sure of that. He remembered making the note. But now it said that she was Beth's daughter, and that Beth was a single mom. Carl and Heather were married, and Mary was Carl's older sister. That couldn't be right. He'd never written any of this. What was going on?

For all his faults, Ted wasn't stupid, and the answer occurred to him after only a few seconds. The list had been subject to change along with everything else within range of the kaleidoscope. The notes recorded there reflected an earlier version of this reality, not the one from which he'd just traveled. Ted felt no elation at solving the problem. Instead he felt more lost than ever. Could he preserve anything from one reality to the next, other than his unreliable memories?

He might make notes and move them beyond the range of the next change, but since marriage and other records were altered to reflect the new conditions at Bailey's Court, there was no guarantee that the notes wouldn't change also. Maybe if he carried the notes on his person? After all, he hadn't changed at all, was still wearing the same grungy jeans and drab shirt that he'd put on after showering. Or had he changed somehow? Would he even know if that was the case? Maybe the only thing that wasn't malleable was knowledge of how the kaleidoscope worked.

Ted experienced an emotion entirely new to him. Despair. He threw the notepad into the trash, moved things aimlessly around on his bench, then turned and walked back up through the bulkhead door into the night. He was outside, staring up at the sky, before he even realized that he still had the kaleidoscope in his hand. Well, if the situation was already hopelessly beyond redemption, what did he have to lose?

He walked around to the front of the house, regaining some

measure of composure. The streetlights glowed brilliantly and there was a nearly full moon. Ted paused, raised the kaleidoscope toward the nearest light, and, with some effort, turned the drum. It was beginning to resist again. The prospect of being trapped in some warped reality still troubled him, but in a sense, he was already trapped. He couldn't stop now. He had to keep moving forward.

His arms dropped and he stood silently for a minute or so. The faint breeze strengthened a bit and it felt good whispering across his face. Everything was quiet except for some traffic noises in the adjacent block and a dog barking somewhere in the distance. He turned slowly and looked around. All three garage doors were open and all three driveways were empty. There was a light on in the Hastings house and several at the Rogers. Through his own front window he could tell that the kitchen light was on, but the rest of the house seemed dark. There was no one in sight and, for a few minutes at least, he preferred it that way. It all looked perfectly ordinary. He would be happy with ordinary now. There were advantages to ordinary that had never occurred to him before.

The front door of the Hastings house opened suddenly, spilling dim light into the night. Jennifer appeared, almost falling out the door, went to one knee on the front walk before pushing back to her feet. Ted was relieved to see that she had knees and feet again. Unaware of his presence, Jennifer glanced behind her, gave a shrill scream of terror, and began to run across the lawn, but it was obvious that something was wrong with one of her legs. Her left foot was in a cast and she couldn't manage more than a hobble.

Almost immediately a second figure emerged from the house, larger, shrouded in dark clothing. It took a few seconds before Ted could identify the second party. It was Carl Rogers, wrapped in an ankle length dark coat and rain hat. Carl was carrying a familiar looking axe. He also appeared oblivious to Ted's presence, fixated on Jennifer. He started after her and Ted felt an intense sense of déjà vu. He had seen this all before somewhere. But how? And then he remembered the horror movie that he had glimpsed on the television set once or twice and realized that he was watching that very scene. And he knew what inevitably followed, would follow unless he interceded.

"No! Wait!" The words burst out of their own accord and Ted took a step toward the others.

Jennifer managed to cover half the distance between them before her bad leg betrayed her and she fell headlong. She twisted around, looking back the way she had come and saw Carl bearing down on her, the axe already rising into the air.

It didn't seem real to Ted; it was like a bad horror movie. He felt no sense of personal danger, even when the axe came down the first time. That couldn't be real blood; it was all some kind of weird special effect. The blade had caught Jennifer in the right shoulder. She'd been pushing up with both arms, trying to get to her feet, and now she fell onto her injured side, screaming. The axe went up and down again and again. Ted stopped moving and just watched, and after the fifth or sixth blow, Jennifer wasn't moving either. But Carl kept chopping and chopping as though he had to be certain that he had killed not just Jennifer but every individual part of her. If Ted had been able to accept that this was real, he would have been violently sick on the spot, but it had to be an illusion and, if it wasn't, he only had to turn the drum on the kaleidoscope and make it into one. Death didn't have to be final. He had the power to bring the dead back to life. Or did he? If he turned the drum, would Jennifer be restored, but only if someone else was sacrificed? Was there a law of conservation of attributes?

And even if he did bring her back, would the next reality be even worse?

Carl stopped finally, but he didn't drop the axe. He looked at Ted. "Hi, neighbor! How's it going?" His voice was hearty, cheerful.

There was, of course, no possible answer.

"Sorry about the mess." Carl's manner was completely relaxed, as if it was perfectly normal to slaughter and dismember a young woman on the front lawn. Maybe for him it was. Ted wondered how all of this would play with the world at large which was not, unless he was horribly mistaken, going to accept that brutal murders were perfectly okay if they happened in Bailey's Court. Maybe that's what he should do. Just get in the car – whichever one was in the garage this time – and drive out of the neighborhood to where things were normal. He could throw the kaleidoscope away, or better yet destroy it completely. He could divorce his wife or let her divorce him, if he was married now, and whoever she was, get a new job, start over, pretend all of this was just some nightmare.

"I don't suppose you approve of this." Carl was still talking, and he'd taken a step toward Ted. "But you have no idea how difficult it was living with this woman. I finally laid down the law tonight, but she kept arguing with me. I tried to explain things to her so she'd understand, but she wouldn't listen. When you come right down to it, she didn't leave me any choice." He glanced at Jennifer's body. "And I made it quick. I didn't want her to suffer." He took another step forward.

Ted was watching the axe rather than Carl's face and he took a step backward. "I'm sure she didn't suffer. I have to go into the house now."

Another step. "No, I don't think so. I know how you used to watch Jennifer all the time. You were always on her side. If I let you go inside, you're just going to call the police, aren't you?"

"No, of course not." Another step backward. "I wouldn't dream of it. What a man does within his own family is nobody else's business."

"Well, now, I agree with that, neighbor, but you have to admit that when one man looks at another man's wife, he's taking some risks."

Ted knew that he shouldn't run, shouldn't show fear, but it was as if someone else had taken control of his body. He turned and bolted toward the open garage door, wondering if he could retrieve his own axe before Carl cut him down. It never even occurred to him that there was only one axe, that the garage wall would be bare, until he rounded the corner and saw it for himself. But he was committed now and he raced inside, hearing slow footsteps behind him. Carl wasn't running, but he was coming steadily onward. The axe looked bigger every second.

The lip of the garage floor threw him off balance and he flailed with both arms, keeping his balance but losing his grip on the kaleidoscope in the process. It slipped from his hand, hit the floor, bounced, then rolled under the SUV and out of sight. Even with an axe wielding madman behind him, Ted remained fixated on the kaleidoscope. Instead of heading toward the connecting door and escaping into the house, he ran around to the front of the

SUV, dropping to one knee and groping beneath the bumper with his hand. He couldn't reach the kaleidoscope and a quick glance told him he'd need some sort of tool to fish it out of there. Or he could move the SUV, maybe, although he quickly discarded that idea. Something might go wrong and cause him to hit it with a tire, damaging it beyond hope of repair.

"Come out and play, Ted." He'd almost forgotten Carl. How could he have forgotten Carl? His neighbor's voice still sounded casual, almost chummy.

A quick look around told Ted that he was in serious trouble. Carl was standing in front of the connecting door, cutting off that escape route, the axe cradled in both arms. He looked perfectly calm and relaxed. Ted glanced around but there was nothing in sight that he could use as a weapon. His only consolation was that Carl couldn't reach him at the moment. He could keep moving so that the SUV was always between him and the axe.

As if to prove the point, Carl started toward him and Ted skipped around the side and edged toward the rear bumper. He could run out into the night, but he wasn't sure that he could stay ahead of Ted. The man was older, sure, but he kept in shape and he had longer legs.

"You're just making this all much more difficult than it needs to be." Carl raised the axe with both arms and brought it down on the windshield of the SUV. The safety glass splintered and shattered into thousands of tiny pieces. "I'm very disappointed in you, neighbor. I thought we were buddies."

Reason told Ted to stay where he was, that Carl couldn't hurt him so long as the SUV stood between them. But reason hadn't played a big part in his life this past day. Ted had a sudden, absolute conviction that he was going to die if he remained in the garage. Sooner or later, he'd trip and fall, or Ted would lull him into a moment of carelessness. The garage was just another trap inside an even greater one. All things considered, he'd rather take his chances out in the open. He knew he'd have to act now or he'd waver again. He feinted in one direction, then reversed course and ran out of the garage.

He turned to the left immediately, without checking to see if Carl was following. He almost certainly was. If Ted had had a moment, he might have considered the irony of the situation – he was running to the Rogers house seeking shelter from Carl Rogers. But presumably Carl didn't live there any longer.

The front door was unlocked. He tore it open without knocking, threw himself inside, and slammed the door behind him. He could already hear footsteps on the front walk. Carl had followed him, naturally. Frantic, Ted locked the door, which promptly began to shake in the frame. Ted recoiled, backing away. The shaking stopped and there was a short silence, followed by a loud thump as something hard hit the outside of the door. The axe?

Ted stood frozen in terror, knowing the door wouldn't hold up long under a determined attack, but the blow wasn't repeated. After a minute or two, he thought he heard footsteps moving away, but it might have been wishful thinking, or Carl might just be trying to fool him into thinking the crisis was over. There was a window from which he could have checked, but Ted was too terrified to even touch the curtains, let alone open them.

Catching his breath, Ted looked around the room. The television set was on but the sound was turned down. No one was watching it. In fact, no one was in the room, and nor had anyone come out to find out what all the noise was about. Maybe no one was home, but if so, would they have gone out without locking up? That wasn't like Carl or Mary, but then again, Carl didn't live here now and Ted had no idea where Mary might be.

Something flickering on the television looked familiar and Ted took a step in that direction. The screen showed Samantha and Heather squatting on the floor of the very same room he was standing in, furnished identically as far as he could tell. Ted assumed it was some sort of home movie made with a camcorder. The sisters were watching television and the movie playing was a perfect reproduction of Carl attacking Jennifer. The axe was still rising and falling when Ted turned the set off, shuddering with revulsion.

There was a sound behind him and he whirled around to see Beth, wearing a filmy nightgown, descending the stairs from the second floor.

"Who's there?" she called, then relaxed as Ted stepped out into the light. "Ted Croner? Is that you? What are you doing in my house at this time of the night? What's going on?" She sounded more querulous than outraged. Ted recognized her bathrobe, a ratty thing she'd had since before they were married. Before the original Beth had married, he amended.

"Someone just tried to kill me." His voice sounded strange, thin and tremulous. "And he's still out there. Where's your telephone?"

"Is that all? I thought it might be some kind of emergency. The telephone's out in the kitchen. Follow me and I'll show you." She gave no indication that she was alarmed. In fact, she seemed bored. She came the rest of the way down the stairs and headed for the kitchen with Ted in her wake. He noticed that she wore a single slipper; the other foot was bare.

Ted glanced warily at the far corner as they entered, but the cocoon was gone. The back door was illuminated by a night light and he hurried over and made sure the bolt was thrown, cursing his stupidity in not having done so earlier. Where was Carl anyway? Had he given up and gone home or was he lying in wait outside? Beth opened the door under the sink and – with some difficulty – pulled out a telephone and set it on the counter. "Here you go."

Ted dialed 911 before listening for a dial tone. There wasn't one. "No dial tone."

"Well, I'm sure I paid the bill." Beth yawned dramatically.

"Carl must have cut the lines then." He was talking to himself, not Beth, but she answered anyway.

"And who's going to pay to get that fixed? Not me, I can tell you. I paid to have the swimming pool drained when the two of you played your little game with Toby, but I'm drawing the line this time."

Ted had no idea what she was talking about so he ignored her and looked out the back window. The outside light was on but he couldn't see anything more than a few feet away. "Is your garage door locked?"

Beth shrugged. "I don't know. Probably not. I haven't bothered in ages. No one's going to come in that way."

"Why not?" He was almost afraid to ask.

"Because of the spiders. You remember what they did to poor Heather, don't you? I told her they weren't suited to be pets, but she wouldn't listen. They're cute when they're small, but then they get bigger and the novelty wears off, so who has to feed them all the time, and clean up their mess? That's the problem with young people nowadays. They never listen to their elders."

Ted made an impatient sound. "How about the windows? Are all the windows locked?" But it occurred to him that this really didn't matter. If Carl wanted to come in through one of the ground floor windows, he'd just break the glass. "Do you have any weapons? I don't suppose you have a gun in the house?" Carl had talked about hunting when he was younger, but Ted couldn't remember if he still had any firearms.

Beth, however, was laughing. "Of course not. Why would I need to have a gun when I have the spiders?" She yawned again. "Look, if you don't need me, I'm going back to bed. I was up early this morning working on the ham tarts for the cookout tomorrow. You do remember that I promised to bring dessert?"

"Yeah, sure." Ted felt a totally illogical urge to laugh. "Why not?"

"Then I'll see you in the morning. Good night." And she turned and walked back toward the stairs as though it was perfectly normal to have a neighbor hiding out in her kitchen while an axe murderer prowled in the yard. Maybe it was normal now. Ted felt nauseated. He had to get the kaleidoscope back somehow.

He went back to the front room and finally gathered enough courage to inch a curtain open so that he could look out front. The streetlamp provided more light on this side of the house, but he couldn't see any sign of Carl. That wasn't necessarily reassuring since there were lots of shadows where the light didn't fall, and Carl could very easily be lurking somewhere out of his line of sight. He let the curtain fall back and glanced up at the cuckoo clock mounted on the wall beside the door. It was just after nine, though it seemed much later. Ted paced the room for several minutes, his thoughts so chaotic that he spent more time trying to get them under control than in actually coming up with a plan. At one point he turned the television set on again and immediately saw the image of a dark figure prowling around a suburban house. He turned it back off, shivering.

Back in the kitchen, he found a clean glass in one of the cupboards and ran some water in the sink, but when he sipped at it, there was a funny taste and he poured the rest out. A quick glance into the refrigerator was even more disturbing. It appeared to be filled with glass jars of dead mice. He slammed the door shut and returned to the living room, eventually lowered himself into one of the armchairs and closed his eyes, meaning only to relax, but he caught himself drifting into a doze and stood up, terrified of what might happen if he fell asleep.

The sound of an automobile engine drew his attention and he went to the window. A familiar looking station wagon was approaching slowly. It turned into the driveway in front of him and the engine died. He heard the car door open and then close but he didn't have an unobstructed view and couldn't see who had been driving it.

Ted went to the front door, arrived just as he heard a key moving in the lock. He threw the bolt himself, opened the door with one hand, and saw Samantha standing there with a puzzled expression on her face. "Mr. Croner? What are you doing here?"

"Get inside! Move!" He grabbed her by the forearm and pulled her into the house, slamming and locking the door behind her.

Samantha, once more wearing the THINK shirt, looked puzzled and angry, but not at all frightened. "What's going on, Mr. Croner? Is something wrong with my mom? Did she try to feed the spiders all by herself again? I told her not to do that."

Ted's brain refused to process this. "No, she's fine. She went back to bed. Did you see anyone outside when you drove up? Someone hanging around the house who shouldn't have been there?"

"No, Mr. Croner. Except for you, of course." Samantha gave him a strange look and sidled past him. She went to the television, turned it on, but there was still no sound, just what appeared to be a still shot of the front of the Hastings house. Samantha peered at the vase of roses that sat atop the screen. "These need water. I'll be right back." She went out to the kitchen.

Ted stared after her disbelievingly. "Forget the damn flowers! There's a killer outside and the phones aren't working!"

He heard the sound of running water and shook his head wearily. A moment later Samantha was back, carrying a soup bowl filled with water. Some of it slopped over the edge as she walked.

"Well if he's outside and we're inside, then there's nothing to worry about, is there?' She poured most of the water into the vase, but some of its splashed down across the television screen, leaving grayish streaks. The roses perked up immediately and began winding around one another like a living caduceus. "There, that's much better."

Ted suppressed the urge to grab the girl and shake her. "I don't suppose you have a cell phone?"

Samantha was stroking the petals of the roses with a forefinger. "Nope. Sorry. Mom says they cause brain tumors so I'm not allowed."

Ted was at a loss for words. He returned to the front window, had just finished making a careful scan of the front yard when they heard a loud thump from the garage.

"That's got to be him. He's broken into your garage!"

Samantha turned to face him again. "Don't be silly. That's just the spiders. They haven't been fed yet today. Come on. Give me a hand. If I have to get Mom out of bed, she'll whine about it all day tomorrow. I can do it by myself but it's a lot safer if there are two of us." She started back toward the kitchen.

Helplessly, Ted followed in her wake. "I don't think you understand. I saw a man kill someone just a few hours ago and I think he's waiting out there in your garage right now."

"You must mean Carl from down the street, right?" Samantha swung the refrigerator door open. "He's always killing something."

Ted expected her to take out one of the jars of mice, but she was pushing them around instead. Then she reached in with both hands and pulled out what appeared to be a good sized ham. "Here, take this." She thrust the ham toward him and he automatically reached out and accepted it.

"Aren't you going to feed them the mice?"

Samantha looked scandalized. "Don't be silly. The mice are for us. Now come with me and do exactly what I say."

Ted lacked the will to resist. He followed her to the connecting door to the garage. Samantha put one hand on the doorknob and motioned for him to stand slightly to one side. "Okay. Now I'll open the door and as soon as I do, you throw the ham as far as you can."

There was a loud thump as something heavy struck the door from the other side. Ted cringed. "It's got to be Carl," he protested.

Samantha shook her head. "No, it's not. He knows better than that."

"Then what have you got locked up in there?"

She looked at him as though he was being particularly stupid. "Why spiders, of course. Now get ready."

Her grip tightened on the doorknob. Ted felt a sudden urge to turn and run away as fast as he could, but his legs wouldn't obey the commands issued by his brain. Then the door was opening and something poked around the edges. Several somethings, in fact. They were long and thin and furry and it took a moment for him to realize what they were – oversized spider legs.

"Throw it!" screamed Samantha, holding the doorknob with both hands now. Ted stared into the yawning blackness of the garage, a blackness that writhed and twisted. His blood was suddenly as cold as the dead meat in his hands and his brain functions seemed to have come to a full stop. "Throw it now or they'll get out!"

He was able to move then, lifting the ham and heaving it forward with both arms. It flew into the darkness, disappearing into the garage as the shadowy twisting and wriggling became suddenly much more agitated. A dark shape about the size of a small dog slipped through the doorway so quickly he didn't see it clearly before it ran behind a chair. Samantha immediately threw her weight forward against the door which closed, but not completely. Three of the dark, furry appendages had penetrated into the house and the door would not shut.

"Help me!" she demanded.

Ted joined her. They had to open the door and slam it quickly closed several times before the battered legs withdrew, but eventually they managed. Samantha turned the lock and then sagged back against the door, trying to catch her breath. "Wow! They must have been really hungry. I've never seen them so agitated. Why did you wait so long to throw the ham? One of them got into the house, you know. We'll have to catch it or it'll make a real mess."

Ted's voice was barely more than a croak. "They're big!"

"Well of course they are. We wouldn't keep them locked up in the garage otherwise, would we? Did you see where the little one went?"

"The LITTLE one?" Ted shook his head. "It ran behind that chair." He nodded in the appropriate direction. "It's probably still there."

"All right. You keep watch while I go for the net."

Ted watched all right; he couldn't tear his eyes away from the chair in question, though he backed up to the opposite wall and picked up a table lamp to use as a weapon. It was a spider, he realized, a spider as big as a cat. Tarantulas creeped him out even on television. This was much worse than that.

Something made a skittering sound, like chitin on hardwood floors. Ted raised the lamp above his shoulder, telling himself it was probably more frightened of him than vice versa. On the other hand, it hadn't been fed and the ham was now out in the garage with the others. What was he going to do if it came toward him?

Samantha reappeared carrying a long wooden pole with a mesh net on one end, something like a butterfly net except much heavier duty. She looked serious but unworried and Ted tried to compose himself. Samantha was only a kid and her opinion of him didn't matter, but he didn't want to shame himself. He straightened up and put the lamp down, but he didn't come any closer. "How do we do this?" he asked.

"You lure it out and I'll snag it."

Ted's mouth was dry. "How do I lure it out? Make a sound like a baked ham?"

Samantha rolled her eyes. "It's hungry. Go get a mouse from the fridge and tie some string around it. Then drag it across the floor in front of the chair. It's easy."

Ted managed to work his way around the perimeter of the room without looking too foolish. He opened one of the screwtop preserving jars in the refrigerator and removed a dead mouse. His experiences cleaning up after Roscoe had taken care of any squeamishness he might have felt. "Where would I find some string?" he called.

"Try the freezer compartment,"

There was a roll of twine all right, sitting adjacent to a stack of paperback westerns. Ted shook his head, unwound some string with considerable difficulty since it had frozen in place, and tied a loop securely around the body of the bait. He unwound much more twine than he really needed, but he had no intention of getting anywhere near the spider.

"Hurry up. I think it must have moved."

Ted joined Samantha, swinging the dead mouse on the end of its line. "Where did it go?"

Samantha crouched and peered around the room. "I think it went under the coffee table, but I didn't see where it got to after that. I'm sure it's watching us, so it should be able to see the mouse."

Ted realized he had completely forgotten about Carl during the past few minutes, but oversized spiders had priority. He took a deep breath. "Here goes then." After a couple of tentative swings back and forth, he cast the mouse across the room where it thudded against the side of an armchair and fell to the floor.

"Reel it in slowly. They're smarter than they look so it'll have to be really tempting to lure it out of cover."

The dead mouse bumped along the wooden floor, snagged on the edge of the carpet, then came free and bounced before resuming its slow, dead crawl toward them. Ted's aim had been good and it moved quite close to the presumed hiding place of the escaped spider, but nothing happened. "What now?"

"Try it again." The second time had no better result so Samantha used the end of the pole to nudge both chairs a few inches, then probed beneath them. Ted was beginning to wonder if they were mistaken about where the spider had gone when there was a sudden dark flash of motion and something ran out into the open, then leaped up onto an end table and from there to the floor behind them, skittering away into the kitchen.

"It jumps!" Ted's throat was dry.

"Of course it does. Come on. We've got it cornered now."

There was no sign of it in the kitchen and there were fewer places for it to hide. Ted peered at the top of the refrigerator and behind the microwave – both from a safe distance – but there was no sign of it. The cupboards were all closed. "It must be behind the refrigerator or the stove."

Samantha nodded. "We need something smelly to attract its attention."

Ted lifted the string so that the dead mouse dangled between them. "This won't smell much until it's defrosted."

"I can fix that." There was a knife rack mounted on the wall. Before Ted realized what she was doing, Samantha had retrieved a paring knife, slashed a line across one palm, and was dripping blood on the dead mouse. His stomach lurched and he had to look away.

"We could have used something else from the refrigerator."

"No big deal," said Samantha casually. "I do this all the time. Now throw it over there and let it lie there for a minute."

This time it landed alongside the refrigerator, splattering droplets of blood onto the linoleum floor. Long seconds passed and Ted began to think that they were wasting their time when he saw something move in the shadows. Then, very slowly, the spider emerged from behind the refrigerator.

Ted wanted to turn and run from the room, but Samantha seemed unconcerned and he refused to look craven in front of her. Or behind her in this case. He stood his ground as the oversized arachnid's entire body emerged into view, eight long furry legs, a bulbous body slightly larger than a squirrel – it was smaller than he'd thought but still obscenely gargantuan. It moved to within striking distance of the mouse, then hesitated as though suspecting a trap. Smart little bugger, thought Ted.

Samantha extended her net but kept it high overhead, trying to angle it so that not even its shadow passed near their quarry. The spider advanced slightly, nudged the dead mouse with one of its legs, and Ted felt his gorge rise. Then the net flashed down and there was a thin, high pitched cry like nothing he had ever heard before. Its frantic efforts to escape just enmeshed it more thoroughly in the net, but it kept struggling and, judging by the way Samantha struggled to control the pole, it was disproportionately strong for its size. Ted knew he should offer to help, but his body wouldn't respond and instead he dropped the coil of string and just watched.

"Open the dishwasher!"

Ted blinked, the words incomprehensible until she repeated them. Then he worked his way around the teenager as she worked a drawstring mounted along the side of the pole which drew the net tighter. There was a built in dishwasher and Ted pulled the front open, then stepped away, puzzled. "What good does this do?"

"Just hold the door ready." She lifted the squirming, writhing bundle into the air and slowly began moving it in his direction. It took all of his will power not to run from the room, but he figured out what she must be planning and forced himself to grip the door by its handle. He closed his eyes when the net came closer, sweat pouring down his face. "Close it now!" He slammed the door shut, or almost shut since it caught on the pole. Somehow Samantha managed to disengage the net, which slid off the pole as she pulled it out, and a second later he was able to engage the door completely. He could hear something moving furiously inside.

Samantha, looking greatly relieved, walked over and calmly turned on the dishwasher, choosing the ultra hot all pots and pans cycle. Ted grimaced. "Isn't that going to make a mess?"

She shrugged. "Won't be the first time."

Reaction was setting in and Ted's legs felt wobbly. He made his way back into the living room and dropped onto the couch. Samantha followed but sat down facing the television. She played with the channel control until she found a test pattern, then settled back to watch it. When Ted finally recovered enough to stand up, she was still there, apparently entranced by the unwavering image.

"Do you have a flashlight?"

Samantha never glanced away from the screen. "Sure. Look in the oven."

"Of course. Why didn't I think of that?" He returned to the kitchen, reassured himself that the back door was still secured, then opened the oven door. Inside he found a heavy duty flashlight, sitting between a bowl of fruit and a carton of cigarettes. Back in the living room, he peered out through the front window for several minutes, but could see nothing moving except the shadow of a cloud cast by the moon. Reasonably satisfied, he went to the front door and very slowly turned the lock to avoid making noise, then began to edge the door open. There was a deep scar in the wood where the axe had bitten.

Ted stepped outside and used the flashlight to examine the front yard, or as much of it as he could without stepping away from the door. The axe was visible on the grass about six feet away, but there was no sign of Carl. Had he gone for another weapon? Ted still wondered if there were any firearms in Bailey Court.

His fear told him to go back inside, close and lock the door, and wait for…for what? Morning? There was no reason to think the morning would be any better than the evening. No, he had to act now. He had to recover the kaleidoscope and use it. There was no other guaranteed escape from the madman. Ted stepped away from the house. Each subsequent step became easier because nothing happened. He reached the side of his own garage without incident, inched his way around to the front, and crouched, looking to see if a pair of telltale feet would reveal that Carl was lurking on the other side of the SUV. But there was nothing.

He ran then, straight for the switch for the overhead door. It seemed to take forever to drop into place, but when it did, Ted exhaled a breath he hadn't realized he'd been holding. He was safe, at least for the moment, but he knew that could change at any time. He found a garden rake and dropped to the floor, located the kaleidoscope with the flashlight, then probed under the vehicle and gently nudged the kaleidoscope until it rolled free. A moment later he had it in his hands.

Although he was tempted to use it immediately, his recent near disaster had made him doubly cautious. There probably was no truly safe place to stand while the world changed, but he always felt most comfortable in the basement workshop. The connecting door to the house was unlocked and he went inside, still holding the rake. If Ted was hiding there, waiting for him, at least he wouldn't be completely defenseless.

He heard the sound of running water as soon as he stepped inside, then Jennifer's voice drifted down the hall. "Ted? Is that you?"

He froze. "Yes, dear. It's me. I was just cleaning up something in the garage."

"You've been gone an awfully long time." She sounded offended. "I've decided to take a long, soothing bath, so if you have any naughty ideas, they'll just have to wait until later."

Ted felt a wave of relief. "All right, dear. Enjoy yourself."

He turned and went down the basement stairs. Roscoe was asleep on the workshop, and Ted scratched his ears for a few seconds, reassured by the small touch of familiarity. "How are you doing, Roscoe old buddy?" He set the kaleidoscope down on the bench. Despite his earlier attempt to repair it, the drum was still obviously misshapen. Ted was tempted to use it immediately regardless of the consequences, but now that he was in his element, it occurred to him that he had the time to improve on his handiwork. He searched through his tools, found a rubber mallet, vice grip pliers, and a few other items, and set to work.

No one disturbed him as he set about reversing the damage he'd done, gaining a little here and a little there, slowly restoring the drum to its original state. He rested from time to time, even napped a little before returning to his tools. It wouldn't be perfect, he knew, and he had added some scratches and scuff marks in the process despite taking exaggerated care, but when he finally set his tools aside, he was confident that it would take close examination to reveal that the drum had been damaged, and when he looked through the eye piece, the mosaic display also seemed to be fine.

He turned the drum. It took considerable effort, but he managed one full turn this time. Roscoe was still there when he was done and the basement looked unchanged. Of course, that might mean that it hadn't worked. Still holding the kaleidoscope, Ted went upstairs, wondering if he'd become firmly trapped in an endless cycle of change, disaster, desperation, and more change.

Apparently he'd been working longer than he had realized because the sun was up, well above the horizon, and dust motes played in the air in the front room. The house was quiet, but Ted went directly to the front door rather than explore. What he could see as he walked through the house looked very much like it had been originally, nothing noticeably out of place. On the other hand, he was no longer sure that he would recognize his original reality even if he chanced upon it.

Ted walked out onto the grass and glanced quickly left and right. The SUV was back in the Rogers driveway and the sports car was on the opposite side. His own garage door was open and the station wagon was parked in its usual stall, next to a veritable mountain of boxed yard sale items. The birdbath was on the Hastings lawn, which he was pretty sure was wrong, but it was upright and there were no other obvious anomalies. Now that he was outside, he could hear voices from the rear of the house.

Judging by the height of the sun, it was probable that the neighbors had begun to gather for the ritual feast. Ted wasn't sure he wanted to face them as a group without knowing how the world had changed this time. In fact, he wasn't sure he even wanted to encounter them individually.

Putting things off wouldn't help. He started to walk around the corner of the garage, then realized he was still holding the kaleidoscope. That wouldn't do at all. He turned and walked inside. He could hide it here among the yard sale items and come back for it later, or sooner if things were bad. He glanced around, decided that one of the overhead cabinets would be better, but when he opened the door, the interior was jammed full of paint cans, varnish, rags, and paint brushes. They were the right items but this was the wrong cabinet. Ted took a step back, set the kaleidoscope down on the hood of the station wagon, and began rearranging things to make room.

Samantha Rogers walked into the garage. Ted caught his breath, but was relieved to see that she looked perfectly normal. "Hi there, Mr. Croner. Your wife sent me to look for you. The ham's almost done and she says you have to carve it because you always make the slices so neat they look like they were made in a machine."

"Okay, I'll be there in just a minute. I have to take care of something here first."

"What are you looking for?"

"Just a tool I need."

Samantha walked past him and picked up the kaleidoscope. "What's this?"

Ted felt a shiver pass through his body. "Put that down please." He took a step toward her and reached for the kaleidoscope. Samantha skipped back warily. "I just want to look at it. I'll be careful."

Before he could say or do anything else, Samantha had raised the kaleidoscope to her eye and tried to turn the drum. Ted froze and his heart missed a beat. There was no sensation of change and Samantha lowered her arms, frowning. "It's stuck. I can't get it to turn."

Relief washed through him. "It's broken. I'm going to try to fix it later. It's an antique, worth a lot of money." He held out his hand.

Samantha ignored him. "Maybe it'll turn the other way."
She twisted the drum again and, to Ted's horror, it moved.

Samantha raised the kaleidoscope to her eyes again and
aimed it toward the street. She tried to turn it a second time, but
now the drum wouldn't move in either direction. She dropped her
arms, frustrated, and leaned back against the SUV. She was alone
in the garage, but not for long.

Her sister Heather joined her, wearing rose patterned
slacks. Her boyfriend, Arnold, was close behind. "There you are.
We've been looking all over for you. We're almost ready to eat."

"I was just trying to find Mr. Croner. I thought he was
probably playing with his yard sale junk again." She gestured
eloquently at the collapsing stack of boxes. "He was here a minute
ago but he sneaked off when I wasn't looking."

"Don't be ridiculous. He's out in the back yard, where
you're supposed to be." Heather noticed the kaleidoscope for the
first time. "What's that?"

"This? Nothing. It's broken." She turned and tossed it
underhanded into one of the cartons stacked in the other garage
stall. "Let's go."

Everyone else was already there. Ted Croner was sitting at
the picnic table, his arm in a sling, looking pale and a bit
distracted. His tee-shirt said THINK. Carl Rogers stood at the
grill, watching fat drip from the roasting meat, pretending that he
was overseeing the process. Mary and Jennifer were also seated at
the table, talking a mile a minute while they fiddled with the bowls
of garden salad, potato chips, and other side dishes. Samantha
glanced past them to the pen at the rear of the Croner property. A
nicely crafted doghouse stood in one corner, with the name TOBY
painted over the door.

Beth came out through the back door, carrying a large
platter of roasted vegetables, potatoes, carrots, cauliflower, and
green beans. "I see we're all present and accounted for." She set
the platter down on the table directly in front of Ted, who blinked
but showed no other reaction, then turned to Carl. "How's the
main course coming?"

"It's just about ready. Who's carving?"

"Well, since the master chef is still feeling a bit under the weather, I suppose we'll have to make do with a pinch hitter. I guess we'll have you do the honors this time, Carl. Unless you'd like to do it, Arnold?"

Arnold shook his head nervously. "Not me, Mrs. Croner. If I carve it would look like I did it with an axe."

Carl smiled. "I'm afraid I won't be able to manage those perfectly even slices that we're used to."

Beth laughed. "I'm sure it'll taste just as good as it does when Ted carves."

Samantha felt that something was not quite right, but she couldn't put her finger on it. Beth was a little more animated than usual, and her father more subdued, and she wondered why her mother had borrowed Jennifer's raspberry patterned blouse, but there was nothing actually alarming about any of this. She told herself she was being silly and walked over to the pen.

"Can we give Toby something, Mrs. Croner? He looks like he's starving."

"Toby always acts like he's starving, Samantha, but yes he can have the trimmings as a special treat."

Mary shifted over on her seat. "Come on girls. Time to sit down. Toby can wait a little while."

Samantha glanced down at the pet pig. "Just be patient, Toby. I'll bring you a treat as soon as I can." Then she turned and went to join the others.

Carl, meanwhile, had begun slicing hot meat and piling it up on an oval platter. When he'd finished half of the roast, he put the knife down and carried the main course over to the table. Beth hastily pushed things to one side to make room. "I hope everyone is hungry because we have lots to eat. I'd particularly like to thank Ted for his contribution, because even though he's still in a lot of pain, we have him to thank for the roast." She glanced around. "I think it'll be easier if we pass the plates to Carl and he serves."

Carl stood at one end of the table with a serving fork in one hand. "All right, there's plenty to go around. Just let me know if you prefer thigh or calf."

Everyone at the table raised their plates. Everyone that is except for Ted, who just looked wistful. He shifted uncomfortably and felt a twinge of pain in his left foot, which was very strange since his left leg was missing from the middle of the thigh down.

Ted had put a lot of himself into this meal.